BAD MOJO

A ZORA BANKS NOVEL

BY SHANE BERRYHILL

GORDIAN KNOT BOOKS

ACKNOWLEDGEMENTS

It takes a village to complete a novel. Thus, more than a few acknowledgements are in order.

First and foremost, to my beloved wife and best friend, Lesley Robinson Berryhill, for all her love, support, and help on the home front. Her contribution to the making of this book is immeasurable.

To David Wilson, David Dodd, and the entire Crossroad Press team, I send thanks for your friendship and loyalty through thick and thin—and, of course, for your willingness to give *Bad Mojo* the home it deserves. You guys are absolute saints.

To the fine people of the Southeastern United States, for your inspiration and support. This book may outrage some of you. But believe it or not, this is my love letter to you, my kith and kin.

Finally, thanks to you, Dear Reader, for choosing to spend your valuable time and hard-earned money on my work. May good mojo be ever upon you and yours.

Shane Berryhill
Chattanooga, TN
July 2014

ONE

If there is one thing I've always hated about the Nooga, it's all the goddamn vipers.

Most folks call them vampires thanks to Stoker and his book. Well, Stoker wrote at least one other book on the subject. And while over in Transylvania, bloodsuckers might flitter around on little black bat wings, here in the South, they tend to be a lot more mean and low down and so do a lot of slithering about as a consequence. Zora says it's on account of how God cursed them in the Garden of Eden when the world was new. "Thou shalt grovel on your belly and eat dust all the days of your life," the Bible says where the serpent, aka viper, is concerned. Or at least some shit like that.

But don't the good book also say man came from dust and to dust he returns? Ask me, it sounds like God was serving up dinner that day, and it was regular folk, not the vipers, who were cursed.

All the more reason to hate the bloodsucking sonofabitches. And hate them with good reason, I do. So you can understand why the sight of a low-rent count and his bride standing outside my bar has my hackles up. Through the barred, Plexiglas door, it's obvious that the count is a southern-fried Anne Rice novel reject—long and pale with sharp, predatory features. The business end of his sandy mullet is greased to quill-like perfection. The stringy party-in-back dangles unkempt over the upturned collar of his dark brown duster. And where the hell did he find a lacy ruffle shirt in camo green?

I got to admit, he knows how to pick a bride though. Despite her botched blonde dye job and overabundance of pink pleather—*or because of it*—she's a looker and carries a ridiculous amount of curve in all the right places. Like Dolly Parton in her heyday.

Despite my mingling anger and lust where she's concerned, I chuckle as I imagine the bride in her former life, sitting in a trailer on a plastic-covered couch as she eats Bonbons and watches Billy Ray Circus sing about his aching, broken heart. Doubtless she takes Billy Ray in via a new TV sitting atop of an older, broken-down model. Hell, she probably thought it was the greatest damn thing ever when ol' Count Billy Bob came a'knocking back in 1991. Then again, he could've turned her yesterday. This is the South after all, and 1991 is still alive and well in the hearts and minds of many of its inhabitants. Hell, 1971.

I should know. I'm a bit of a caveman myself. But then, the snakeskin cowboy boots, faded blue jeans, and *tre* cool T-shirts I wear never go out of style. Zora teases me that I think fashion begins and ends with the Dukes of Hazzard. She has a point, but so what? Her spirit guides may be Matthew, Mark, Luke, and John, but mine are Waylon Jennings, Bon Scott, and Ronnie Van Zant.

The vipers eye the threshold warily for a moment. Then the door opens of its own accord, and the two of them glide inside, their feet barely touching the ground.

The vipers' cold, dead eyes take stock of the neon signs and sports memorabilia hanging on the bar's unpainted, sheetrock walls. But it ain't Peyton Manning's college jersey or the autographed picture of Bear Bryant they've come for.

The two of them split up. Count Billy Bob saddles up to a high-top while his bride slinks over to flirt with two drunken college boys shooting pool in the corner. The latter are of the well-muscled, squared-jawed variety. Student athletes from UTC. Wrestlers, maybe. Football linemen more likely. Mere snacks for the bride and her count.

I grit my teeth, wishing I could tell these two undead parasites they aren't welcome here and send them slithering back to whatever hole they came out of. But as the bar is actually Earlene's and I just bunk in a storage room in the back, it's not my place to say so. Not Earlene's either as this is her place of business rather than her residence. Catch twenty-two. Admitted on the basis of a technicality. The laws of homestead mojo do not apply.

How fucking convenient for them.

I hear Zora's voice inside my head, scolding me for failing to lay down the trick she prepared for me weeks ago to prevent just such an invasion. Like a lot of things in my life, I meant to get around to it but simply never did. The truth is, I was a little nervous about the thing. Zora assured me so long as I kept the mojo hand she made for me on my person, I could come and go as I pleased. But when you're like me and "that time of the month" rolls around, mojo hand or not, I'm not sure even a trick from Zora would prove so discriminating. And the last thing I want to deal with during that time is being barred from the one place where I can lay my head in peace.

Oh well. At least I have another full month to think about it. Provided things don't turn to shit here with the count and his bride, that is.

I gaze at Earlene where she stands behind the bar. I see her short, spiked hair rise and fall as her head nods atop her bull's neck. Her beefy hand creeps downward, disappearing behind the bar to grasp the sawed-off I know she keeps there. The load it carries ain't simple buckshot. I know what you're thinking, but it ain't silver either. Silver's all well and good for killing a variety of spooks, vipers included, but it's a damn sight pricey. Zora and me have found that ammo blessed by a true man of the cloth or a hoodoo like herself works just as well on your average Homo occultum. And while vipers might be nastier than your average spook, if you hit them in a vital area like the heart or brain, they fall just as easily as any wereperson, changeling, or ghoul—or normal human for that matter. It's a little secret I've let Earlene in on, and she preps accordingly, thank goodness. As I don't have my piece on me, I'm definitely going to need her for backup.

I feel a warm, wet tongue lick my ear and remember I'm not alone. This evening's sweet thing, a shapely post-teen with daddy issues and enough tats to make Queequeg jealous, is in the booth beside me, her hand massaging me through my faded, overstretched jeans. I'd like to say it's my animal magnetism that's got her so riled at this particular moment, but the truth of the matter is Count Billy Bob probably has his thrall mojo cranked to full blast. I know the bride does. My cock is an iron bar in my pants, and I can't take my eyes off her. Sweet thing notices the latter and removes herself from our table in a huff.

She joins a couple of country boys sitting a few tables over. They're dressed in plaid button-ups and green John Deere caps, their bills creased to a knife's edge. She drapes her thin, heavily inked arms across their shoulders and whispers into their ears, watching me out of the corner of her eye all the while, hoping I'll come over in a jealous rage and make a stink. I won't, hon'. And neither will daddy, no matter how many tattoos you get.

Anyway, it's for the best. She's saved me from having to make excuses regarding what I'm about to do. What that is, exactly, I ain't figured out yet, so I take another sip of beer from the amber bottle in my hand and mull it over. I glance over at Count Billy Bob. His thrall mojo has done its trick. A chubby, big-haired waitress with a short apron strung across her much-too-small Daisy Dukes is beside him, giggling as he whispers in her ear.

George Strait begins playing from the antique juke in the corner. *This is where the cowboy rides away.*

Oh, if only.

But this is my bar, goddamnit. You expect this kind of shit at the Stone Lion or Lamar's, but this. Is *my*. Bar.

I turn to see the bride by the pool table constituting the meat of a linemen sandwich, the three of them grinding slowly to George's woeful twang.

This has gone far enough. Plan or not, if I don't step in, it won't be long before the linemen and the waitress become dinner for Billy Bob and his bride. I adjust my erection so it doesn't appear to be exploding out of my jeans and stand up. I glance at Earlene from the corner of my eye, then stride up to the dancing trio.

"Hey, darling," I say, my southern accent dropping the g off the end of the word so that it swaggers into air, dripping with cowboy sexuality. "Mind if I cut in?"

The bride and her would-be victims fail to notice me. They're too busy gazing longingly into one another's eyes as they continue swaying to the music. I clear my throat and repeat my question, this time louder. The linemen remain oblivious to my presence, but this time, the bride looks up and smiles. Her thrall mojo seizes me full on, and the fire already burning between my legs becomes an all-consuming inferno. I must have her here and now.

So stupid of me to have looked her in the eye. I figured on Zora's mojo keeping my head on straight for me, but apparently, this bride is more powerful than I thought. Or maybe it's just been too long since I got laid. Either way, it's too late now. My hands move of their own accord to unbutton my jeans. I get them halfway down my pelvis before spotting the red flannel bag hanging against the ugly scar running along my bare right hip. The bag dangles from a leather strap no bigger than a shoelace tied about my waist.

I freeze. The bag is important. It's something ... something ...

I cup the bag in the palm of my hand, and the viper's enchantment disappears. Its vanishing feels like what it's like for a junkie to quit cold turkey, go through days of withdrawals, then reach full-blown sobriety weeks later but all compressed into the space of mere seconds.

Zora's mojo hand has saved me after all.

God I love that woman.

The bride spots the mojo hand, and her face immediately changes. Not her expression, her actual face. Her flesh becomes so white, it's transparent, exposing blue and purple veins that crawl like wriggling snakes. Her nose collapses in upon itself, exposing twin nostrils that could've been made by slashes of a knife. Her eyes enlarge, the capillaries in the sclera flooding with blood and expanding even as the pupils contract into serpentine-thin slits. She opens her mouth and hisses as her canines lengthen into fangs. The bone-chilling sound of a snake's rattle splits the air, the hollow, bony plates that have risen along her spine shaking faster than the eye can follow.

The sound fades as quickly as it began. She's done warning me. Time for blood. "Boys, this man is bothering me." The bride pronounces bothering like bah-then. Her drawl places her as being a Georgia girl in her former life. Savannah would be my guess. Plenty of spooks running around down there. Even more than here in the Nooga.

I finish buttoning my jeans as the linemen surge forward. There's murder in their eyes. They'd follow me to the ends of the Earth now, not stopping until I was as cold and lifeless as their mistress. Such is a viper's power over most mortals.

The smaller of the two meatheads is still twice as big as me. But I've handled bigger. The larger one, we'll call him Lenny, swings wildly with his tree trunk of a right arm. If the blow were to connect, I have no doubt it'd be enough to crack my skull and drive shards of it into my brain, making short work of yours truly.

So I make sure it doesn't connect.

I drop to a knee, ducking beneath Lenny's ham-sized fist as I punch him square in the testicles with everything I have. To say the strike produces the desired effect would be an understatement. Lenny shrieks, his yell as high as any preteen at a Justin Bieber concert. He crumples to the floor, his hands cradling his genitals. But awareness has returned to his eyes. You might say I did him a favor ...

Nah. Who am I kidding?

Before I can get back on my feet, Lenny's slightly less big pal, Squeaky, brings his fist crashing down on my jaw. I hear something crack like a tree branch under the strain of too much snow, and the taste of copper fills my mouth. Blinking UFOs flit in front of my eyes. The room goes molten, and I start to melt right along with it. But then good, old-fashioned rage takes over, and the room crystallizes into the same bright red as my neck. I spin and clothesline the back of Squeaky's knees, sweeping him off his feet. There is another crack as the back of his head smacks against the threadbare carpet-over-concrete floor. His eyes roll in his head for a second. When they settle, he stares up at the tile ceiling like a newborn baby. He'll have one hell of a headache, but like his pal Lenny, he's back among the living.

For now.

I'm going to have to do something quick about the real problem at hand to keep it that way.

"Get out of the way, Ash," Earlene shouts. "I can't get a clear shot at her."

Speaking of the bride, I feel a clawed hand dig itself into my calf just as the floor drops out from under me. My guts enter my chest as I fly free through space. I crash against the rack of pool cues lining the wall across from the bar. Wood splinters, and I rebound to land on top of the green felt of the pool table, feeling the agony of all the broken vertebrae I'm sure now run the length of my spine.

A piano drops onto my chest, squeezing the wind from my lungs. Gasping for air, I raise my head and see the bride, her mouth open impossibly wide. Her forked tongue reaches toward me from between her fangs like a tentacle. I flail my arms and legs in a desperate attempt to unseat her. I know my actions are useless. The least of the vipers is still as strong as a bull.

The bride throws back her head, readying to bite, when my right hand brushes something rough.

And sharp.

The splintered end of a pool cue.

It ain't silver or a consecrated bullet, but it's made of wood and will work just as well where a viper is concerned. My hand clamps around the broken cue just as the bride's head plunges toward my neck. Moving with adrenaline-fueled speed and strength, I drive the makeshift stake through the left side of the bride's rib cage and on into her heart. She gives a howl I'll take to my grave and flops off the table to bounce around the room, black blood spurting in fountains from around the pool cue to blanket the bar and its screaming, horrified patrons. Finally, her tap runs dry, and she drops to the floor, her unlife gone.

The juke goes silent, but the screams continue.

Before I can move, the piano is on top me again, this time in the form of a pale, serpent-eyed Count Billy Bob. I feel as much as hear the rattle sounding down his spine. It reverberates through his body into my own, filling me with fear.

He pops his fangs, and I sag beneath him, knowing I don't have any more broken pool cues to bail me out. Then a spray of blood and gore covers my face, and Count Billy Bob's fangs are gone. Also gone are his eyes, nose, lips, ears, and just about everything else above his neck.

The screams fade into whimpers, allowing me to hear the clack of Earlene pumping her sawed-off followed by the sound of an empty shotgun shell clattering onto the floor. What's left of Count Billy Bob sloughs off of me to pile in a bloody heap at the foot of the pool table.

I exhale in relief. "About goddamn time."

"Shut your cocksucker, Ash, and get to cleaning this shit up," Earlene bellows. "Room and board may be free, but all the beer you've been drinking sure as hell ain't."

All heart, that Earlene.

TWO

Despite the existence of spooks being more or less public knowledge, I've found most humans are more than happy to pretend this type of shit simply doesn't happen in their neck of the woods. Denial is one hell of a coping mechanism, after all. So while everyone was in agreement about keeping the slaying of the vipers quiet, the ordeal prevents me from having time to get properly shit-faced. When at last I get to bed in the wee hours of the morning after scrubbing the place clean of viper bits, the monster comes to me in my dreams. He does most nights since I began wearing Zora's mojo hand on my hip. Especially when the moon begins to wax full. Trade-off, I guess. When you never let your demon out to play, he's always rattling his cage door so to speak. This night, he comes to me whispering dark promises of shadows and moons. Of hunts and kills. Of blood and madness.

I start awake from my nightmares around eleven to be greeted by an extraordinary amount of pain caused by the thousands of knives sticking into my jaw, back, and right calf. I roll out of bed, my cot popping and creaking with the action almost as much as my naked body, and stumble to the doo-doo-brown mini-fridge sitting in the corner of my makeshift bedroom. I reach inside the fridge and take out a Budweiser tallboy.

I pop the tab and say, "Hair of the dog that bitcha," and give an ironic snort before downing half of it in a single large swig. Just like I do every morning.

I shuffle to the bathroom, kicking dog-eared paperbacks and an empty beer can or four out of my path. I gaze at the mirror and wince as I examine the swollen, purple lump my jaw has become. Similar black-and-blue lumps run the length of my chest and abdomen, crossing my ribs on their way to my tattooed back. Even with the mojo hand on my hip, I will heal faster than a normal man. But in the meantime, I'm still going to hurt like hell.

I take a piss and then leave the bathroom to slip on a less-than-fresh pair of blue jeans I take from one of several mounds of clothes carpeting the cold, gray concrete floor. I don't bother with underwear. I rarely do. It's not a sex thing. Okay, maybe it is a little. But the fact is, most of the briefs I own are simply too dry-rotted and full of holes to be of any use.

Hi diddly dee. A bachelor's life for me.

I take a bottle of aspirin and a pack of smokes from the worn, black leather saddlebags lying beneath my cot. The saddlebags hold just about everything I own in life.

The cot *creaks* beneath me as I take a seat. I wash the aspirin down with a swig of Bud and then light up. Earlene doesn't like me smoking back here, but right now, I couldn't give a rat's ass. I take a drag off the cigarette, and the fog in my head starts to clear a little. My gaze drifts along with the cigarette smoke over the ten-by-ten room, taking in the sheetrock walls and piles of books and dirty clothes.

I toast the room's one decoration, a tattered poster of singer-songwriter Kasey Lansdale, and sip beer.

I think about Sarah, Little Anna, and everything else my curse has cost me. It's only at the familiar approach of my tears that I stand up and kill the Bud. I toss the empty can at the garbage pail, a white, moldy toadstool sitting open-mouthed next to the outdated CD-radio. The beer can misses. Of course. Basketball and life were never my games.

I take another beer from the fridge and head up front, navigating through the grease-caked fryers of the kitchen and then the empty stools and high-tops of the darkened barroom on my way to the door. I walk outside, and the light of the bright autumn day nearly blinds me. I curse at myself for having forgotten my sunglasses. It may be September, but here in the Nooga, the temperature will be in the seventies by noon.

I sit on the sidewalk running along the bar's exterior and light another cigarette, thankful it's Sunday and Earlene's place is closed for business. I sniff the crisp fall air and stare across the road at the Pizza Hut, liquor store, and Dollar General nestled at the foot of the forested ridge separating this part of town from Redbank proper.

"Christ Almighty. How'd I ever end up here?"

Redbank, often called "Foot-washing Redbank" by locals possessing a sense of humor, is a small town just northeast of and butt up against the greater city of Chattanooga. Redbank is known for having a church on every block and a traffic camera on every corner. The majority of folks who live here get up and go to work or school every day, never guessing they're living their good, God-fearing lives right on Hell's doorstep.

Well, that's unfair. It's not just Hell these folks skirt. According to Zora, it's Heaven too and a whole mess of places in between. Some better. *Some worse.*

I've heard at least a dozen names used to refer to the byways connecting these places. But the only one of them that matters down here in the South is the one Zora uses—the Crossroads. And the type of critters who dwell in the Crossroads are some royally fubarred pieces of creation. I should know. It's one of their kind who caught hold of me and made me into a Homo occultum—a spook—one of the damned.

One day, I'm going to find that sonofabitch and tear out his beating, black heart with my fucking teeth—the very same ones he gave me.

My cell phone buzzes inside my pants. The call goes to voicemail before I can fish the damned contraption out of my front pocket. I go into my voicemail and discover it's completely full. The majority of messages are from sweet thing and her predecessors. Those get deleted.

The final two saved messages are doozies.

The first is from Zora just as I knew it would be. She invites me to church and then to Sunday dinner afterward. Church, I won't make (I never do). Sunday dinner, I wouldn't miss (I never do).

I delete Zora's message and move on to the last one. My

eyebrows raise in surprise when I hear the sound of Mayor—uh, pardon me—*Senator* Bob Jones' nasal, pseudo-southern accent come out of my cellular's speaker. "Ashley," he begins. I hate it when people call me by my full name. And yes, like thousands of other southern ladies of her day, my mom was a fan of *Gone with the Wind.* Want to make something of it?

"This is your old friend, Bob Jones," the message continues. "It's been a while. But then, that's the thing about guys like us. We can go without talking for years then pick up again right where we left off." Jones persists in making with the folksy small talk the way all politicians do before finally getting around to his point. "Listen, Ashley, there's a matter I would like to discuss with you—one that requires your special brand of attention. I'll be in town tomorrow, Monday. The usual place at two? It will be good to catch up with you, pal. See you then."

The presumptuous bastard. No "if you can," or "call me back." Just, "see you then." Never mind the fact we both know without a doubt that I'll be there. The senator's money is good. *Damn good.* But it's the principle of the matter. He could at least pretend not to know that I know he knows I need the cash.

With Zora having little use for him, Jones relied heavily on me during his days as mayor of Chattanooga to take care of problems falling outside the normal realm of politics as usual. Problems he couldn't fix with the authority his title lent him or the money his construction company brought by the truckload. Problems that invariably had to do with the Crossroads and its associated persons getting out of hand within Chattanooga city limits as often happens.

After leaving office, Jones moved on to bigger and better things and wound up getting himself elected as a junior senator for the state of Tennessee.

Republican, of course.

I haven't heard from him since and can't imagine what he'd want with the likes of little ol' me at this late date. Surely by now, he's found a bigger swinging dick to handle any affairs the Crossroads might bring him at the state level?

I finish my beer and smoke and head back inside to shower. Thirty minutes later, I'm clean and dressed in fresh jeans and a

Fox-brand dirt-bike T-shirt purposely one size too small so as to accentuate the goods. What can I say? I got it. I flaunt it.

I go back out into the barroom and look at myself in one of the mirrors hanging on the walls. This one frames the bruises lining my whiskered, angular jaw, close-cropped noggin, and baby blues in Nascar racing stripes and forward-slanting number threes. Looking at myself, I decide to nix my usual attire of too-tight T-shirt in favor of one of the few Western-style button-ups I own. It's Sunday after all. Best to showcase my raw animal magnetism another day.

Dressed, I grab my saddlebags, black leather jacket, and brain bucket and head outside, this time exiting through the steel door leading from my room to the small, gravel lot out back. I take the cover off my bike—a 1993 Harley Davidson Fatboy with hellfire flames on the tank and sterling chrome everywhere else—and toss it into the bed of my other vehicle, an '89 Ford F-150 jacked to the hilt and caked in sunbaked mud.

I love my truck, but the bike is the last remaining beautiful thing I have—the only lady who has never left me or let me down.

I secure the saddlebags to the Harley then extract a pair of fingerless leather gloves and a set of tinted barnstormer goggles. The heavy scent of leather invades my nose as I suit up and throw my leg over the bike. I pop the kickstand, key the ignition, and then press the starter button. The Harley roars to life and then settles into an almost soothing chant of *potato-potato-potato*. I creep out of the lot, gravel crunching beneath my tires as I go. I gun the throttle as I hit the open road, feeling as free as a man damned to Hell can.

THREE

I cruise over the Ogiati Bridge, the wind whipping in my face, the roar of my Harley in my ears. The Ogiati is the largest of four bridges linking the Nooga's north shore to downtown. But that's neither here nor there where spooks like me are concerned. It's the river running beneath the bridges that holds our rapt attention. If a creek gives land-based spooks pause, the mighty Tennessee River stops them dead in their tracks (no pun intended).

Oh, they can cross the running water if they're able to find some trick strong enough to do for them what Zora's mojo hand does for me. But that kind of power is rare among spooks. At least in these parts. So, for all but the oldest and most powerful spooks, an attempt at crossing the river would mean the almost certain dissolution of their corporeal form.

Being on the river isn't the best idea for normal folk either. More and more boats—and sometimes even entire barrages—disappear ever year, those unlucky enough to be aboard right along with them. The humans chalk it up to bad weather or negligence or both. But they don't know about the massive things that dwell in the flooded tunnels beneath the river bottom, things that were already ancient before the first Cherokee or Creek ever set foot here. I still hear horror stories about their surfacing during the Great Flood of 1867.

Anyway, as a result of the river being a supernatural barrier, distinct clans of spooks have cropped up along its opposite shores, and none of them much care for one another. That's bad for peace and quiet. But, hey. Peace and quiet don't pay the bills.

As I continue over the Ogiati, I notice with surprise that the air actually smells sweet. Then I remember that it's the weekend, and the manufacturing plants lining the river's northwestern shore are closed. As a result, the mingled stench of raw sewage and dead fish that usually hangs over the city is absent. The fall weather is probably helping in that regard too. The crisp autumn air and blue sky combined with the green mountains to the west would almost make you believe things are just as untouched as the days when Chief John Ross would sit on the riverbank, casting his line. But come down here in the middle of summer, and believe you me, your nose will tell you a different story.

I toe the bike into a higher gear. Downtown swells on my left, the piers, fountains, and stone amphitheater of the newly refurbished riverfront inflating before me like a balloon right along with the bowl of BellSouth Stadium, the triangular glass roofs of the Nooga's tourist-trap aquarium and the modest business buildings lying beyond.

Nooga, you've come a long way, baby.

The city got its start as a hotspot for river commerce then went full boom town with the introduction of the railroad in the mid-1800s. But it was brought to its knees when General Grant stopped off for an opening act on the way to his headliner in Atlanta.

Maybe the War Between the States is why so many of my kind have settled here? Blood and death are like a siren's song for us spooks. The ground here is so soaked with them that we are still being drawn to Chattanooga more than a century later. Regardless, the Nooga and its people, both alive and undead, recovered from the war to become such an industry magnet that, at one point, the smoke spouting from the factories caused the city to have the most polluted air in the nation. Recent years and administrations have done a lot to change things for the better. My *pal* Jones is foremost among the latter admittedly (hey, credit where credit's due).

I bitch and moan, but the truth is I can't think of another place I'd rather live. I'm like Goldilocks, I guess, and the Nooga is just right.

I leave the Ogiati by way of the exit ramp leading downtown

and make a right onto Market. From here, it's a straight shot to Zora's house in Alton Park.

The construction of Zora's neighborhood was an early component of the city's ongoing efforts at the revitalization of its south side. Around the turn of the millennium, numerous projects in this impoverished area were demolished to make way for new, affordable housing complete with incentives for potential residents.

In other words, black people live there.

I'm not being racist (Arguably, being a Homo occultum makes me the ultimate oppressed race.), just stating the facts. I'd give an arm and a leg to have a house in Alton Park. It's a hell of a lot nicer than that shit hole I frequent in the back of Earlene's bar. And I'd be a lot closer to Zora and Sonny.

But go just around the corner, and you'll still find *Roho* and *Pooky* slinging rock and turning tricks. City Hall can change the Nooga's scenery, but downtown and much of its outskirts remain the same as they ever were. You can't wipe away decades of crime and degradation simply by planting flowers after all.

And that's not even taking into consideration Papa Lim and his crew or some of the nastier things that live on the Nooga's south and east sides—things that crept over to the States below the decks of slave ships or that were created by the inhuman suffering the city's African-American population has had to endure.

Thank God for Zora and Chattanooga Creek. Though it doesn't quite have the stopping power of the Tennessee River, the creek serves as a deterrent for the more rambunctious spooks. They hate that shit and can't cross it without enduring substantial pain. Regardless, Zora's just being on the south side tends to keep an acceptable level of peace over there.

But a new generation of spooks is coming in Papa Lim's territory in the east, one that has its eyes and ears turned to its Homo occultum brethren in Memphis and Atlanta. If they start getting any big ideas, Zora and the creek or not, Chattanooga is fucked. Royally so.

I let thoughts of things I can't control recede from my mind as the glass, concrete, and steel of the buildings downtown give way to the trendy restaurants and boutiques of Warehouse Row. Five miles farther south, the scenery changes to include industrial parks and trucking companies surrounded by high, metal fencing capped with barbed wire. At last, I come to the gas stations, churches, and liquor stores of Alton Park. All of these buildings have black iron bars spanning the length of their windows and groups of African-Americans congregated out front. Those outside the churches are elderly and clothed in big hats, dresses, and Sunday-go-to-worship-meeting suits and ties. The teens and twenty-somethings in front of the gas stations and liquor stores are dressed in oversize T-shirts and baggy pants worn low on the hips so as to create the perfect balance between utilitarian function and fashionable sag.

All stop and stare as I cruise past.

I turn left off Market and enter the tree-surrounded oasis that is Zora's neighborhood. I navigate through two-story, prefab homes of red brick and earth-tone siding. The more upscale homes have small, white columns supporting porch roofs or simple awnings. All have well-manicured lawns free of clutter.

I reach the nice, cookie-cutter home belonging to Zora, and her daughter Sonny races out the front door, barely giving me enough time to shut off the Harley's engine.

"Ashley," she yells, her arms open wide. She's still dressed in the dark-green, lace-trimmed dress I'm sure she wore to church.

I know I said I normally don't like people calling me by my full first name. But when Sonny or her mother do, I've got to admit, it sounds pretty damn good. It's the kind of thing a guy could get used to hearing every day of his life.

Any guy but me that is. Such is no longer in the cards for yours truly, end of story.

Sonny reaches me and squeals with delight as I scoop up her long, scrawny, ten-year-old body and deposit it in front of me on the Harley. "Watch your leg," I say, warning her away from the bike's exhaust. I wrap my arms around her and plant a big wet one on her cheek before plopping my brain bucket onto her head.

Sonny pushes my helmet up on her head so she can better

examine the bruises on my face. "Your face is all purple, Uncle Ash."

"You should see the other guy."

"Did you bring me a present?"

I feign shock. "Did I bring you a present?"

"Yeah," she yells.

"Sure I did, hon'." I reach into my jacket pocket. "It's right here."

I yank my hand from my pocket and hold it up so that Sonny can plainly see it has transformed itself into the tickle claw. She recognizes the claw for what it is and screams, but it's too late. The tickle claw has already begun its work eliciting big laughs and shrill squeals from any little girls unlucky enough to be within its reach.

"Sonny."

I twist atop the bike and rip off my googles. Zora stands on her front porch, tall, slim, and gorgeous in her royal blue Sunday dress. The dress opens beneath the delicate hollow of her throat, exposing the cinnamon skin above the modest swell of her breasts. A zebra-striped headband dyed to match the dress holds her stylish neo-afro in check, pushing it back from her aquiline face and the hoop earrings dangling below her slight ears. But Zora's most striking feature is the deep purple haze of her eyes.

Zora's Aunt Jackie says her niece's eyes sparkle with the twilight of the Crossroads. I've never ventured far into the In Between, but what little I've seen of the place has made me inclined to agree with her.

Zora is, and always has been, one of the most striking women I've ever laid eyes on. The only imperfection in her otherwise flawless features is a thin, jagged scar running down from her left cheek to the corner of her mouth. I've considered on a number of occasions how it's very much like a tiny version of the one I carry on my hip. The wound is something she brought home with her from New Orleans. Like a lot of things with Zora, the subject of how it got there is a sore one, and I quit bringing it up a long time ago.

Regardless, Zora's mixed heritage has made her a creature of exotic beauty, and therefore an object of jealousy and ridicule among many both black and white. What the fuck these people's problem is, I can't figure. It's as though coming face-to-face with true beauty shakes the pillars of the ugly little worlds they've built for themselves, so they try their best to chase it away so they can pretend it never existed.

Damn fools if you ask me.

"Sonny," Zora continues, "you quit horsing around with Ashley and get in here and finish your dinner, you hear?"

"But—"

"No buts. Get on in the house, now."

Sonny sags in defeat. "Yes, Mama." She starts to climb down off the bike, and I hug her to me so I can whisper in her ear. "If you're good, after dinner, I'll see if I can't talk your mama into letting us take a trip to Toys 'R' Us. 'Kay?"

Sonny turns and looks at me, her eyes becoming twin hard-boiled eggs in their sockets, the pearl white of their sclera contrasting heavily against her obsidian-hued skin. While Sonny is as beautiful as her mother, it's a different kind of beauty. I once asked Zora if Sonny takes after her father. But, like with her scar and much of her time in New Orleans in general, Zora quickly let me know the topic wasn't open for discussion.

Sonny slips off the bike and trots into the house, Zora giving her daughter a loving swat on the bottom as she disappears inside.

"Hey, darling," I call with all the Matthew McConaughey drawl I can muster.

Zora is unimpressed. "You're late, Ashley. Food's getting cold."

I take off my gloves and stuff them into my jacket pocket. "Takes time for me to look this good, Zora." I roll off the bike and unzip my jacket. I unclasp my saddle bags from the bike and toss them over my shoulder. Then I swagger up the walk, knowing I look sexy as hell doing it despite the bumps and bruises lining my jaw. I climb the porch steps and prop an arm up against a column so that my face is mere inches from Zora's. I catch scents of red clay and honeysuckle beneath that of her cocoa-butter lotion and jasmine perfume. "Unlike you, who it just comes natural to."

Zora crosses her ex-athlete's arms—thin arms, hard with wiry muscle, yet somehow still feminine in every respect—and looks me over. "One of your lady friends finally kick the hell out of you, Ashley? Good for her."

"She was jealous of my feelings for you, Zora." I slip my arms around Zora's slim waist. "Marry me," I say, surprised at how much I mean it—at allowing myself to even have such feelings after the things I've done. But when it comes to Zora, I just can't help myself. "Marry me, and the three of us will run away somewhere out West."

"Shush your mouth, Ashley."

"I'll take a job as a ranch hand until I can buy some land and raise my own cattle."

Air presses its way through Zora's lips in a perturbed hiss. "Uh huh. And what are Sonny and I supposed to do in the meantime? Churn your butter and darn your socks?"

"Oh, I do so love a good sock darning."

Zora playfully pushes me away. "Ashley, this isn't the Ponderosa. You aren't Little Joe. And I sure as hell am not Hop Sing. Get your skinny white ass to the table with Sonny and the rest."

"You could never be Hop Sing, Zora-bird." I lean in and kiss Zora's cheek before making my way inside. Zora follows, closing the door behind us. I suffer no ill effects from the bounty of protective mojo Zora has prayed into existence, her commanding of my person to come inside reinforcing her open invitation where I'm concerned.

The golden, picture-covered walls of the small foyer spill into those of her living-room-slash-dining area. They're interrupted twice. Once by the hallway leading to the bedrooms and the code-violating cellar I helped dig out, then again on either side of the chocolate accent wall housing her hearth and flat screen TV.

My mouth begins to water in preamble as I catch a whiff of the home-cooked meal awaiting me.

I hang my jacket and saddle bags on the coat rack standing in the corner and leave the foyer for the living room. The place is warm and inviting and makes me think this is what it'd be like on the inside of a giant Reese's peanut butter cup.

Sonny and Aunt Jackie—*and Woodrow*—sit at an oak table positioned in front of the sliding glass doors separating the dining area from the back porch. Heaps of fried chicken, glistening collard greens, creamy macaroni, gravy-drenched mashed potatoes, and other soul food goodies are piled high atop their plates.

I fucking love Zora's cooking.

Like Zora and Sonny, Aunt Jackie—*and Woodrow*—are still clad in their Sunday best. Jackie's ensemble is a lacy peach dress. Its matching hat rests on Zora's bed, I'm sure. Like most of her clothes, it looks voluminous on her wiry, fifty-something frame.

"Ashley," Aunt Jackie mumbles through gritted teeth. She's never made a secret of the fact that she doesn't much care for me. I tolerate her scorn because I know it doesn't originate so much from her dislike of me as from her love and concern for her nieces. And I can't much say I blame her. I'm a sorry sack of shit if ever there was one, and theoretically speaking, I wouldn't want my own loved ones hanging out with me either. But Aunt Jackie knows Zora, and especially Sonny, adore me, so we keep an uneasy truce in front of them.

"Ashley," Woodrow beams, his baritone voice full of smarm. "I was just telling Jackie and everyone else about—"

"Ash."

"Pardon?"

I level my gaze. "Call me Ash, *Woodie*."

Woodrow takes the folded silk handkerchief from the breast pocket of his gray, thousand-dollar suit jacket and wipes away the sweat I've caused to pop out on his glossy, bald brown head. He may be stupid, but his instincts are good. On some primal level, he knows better than to test the likes of me.

Knowing exactly when to bark and when to heel has made him a small-scale success on the local business scene. His chain of shops specializing in pawned jewelry and God knows what other under-the-table goings-on has made him one of the Nooga's more affluent African-Americans. He's blinged out with his product, as usual. Gaudy trinkets of gold and platinum ring his fingers and neck, matching the studs in his ears and the caps on his teeth. My guess is it's all compensation for a small penis and an even smaller soul.

It goes without saying I can't stand Woodrow or the fact that he's the latest in a long string of highfalutin posers who can claim the privilege of having held Zora's affections for a time. What she sees in him and his ilk I just can't figure. Zora's the smartest person I know, yet like so many good women, her taste in men is for shit. I mean, Aunt Jackie loves Woodrow if that tells you anything.

Then again, I may just be fooling myself. I've always assumed Zora does well with her bookshop and the work she and me do on the side. I mean, she bought this house while supporting Sonny, Aunt Jackie, and herself all on her own. But I've never talked brass tacks with her. I mean, we're in a recession despite what Senator Jones and his pals would have us believe. Could be that a little extra financial security the Woodrows of the world offer—the kind that could get Sonny into private school and college later on—might seem pretty damn attractive to her.

But in the final analysis, I just don't buy it. Of all people, Zora would know a marriage based on money is no kind of marriage at all. So, try as they might, Woodrow and his fancy, punk-ass predecessors fail to scare me where the subject of Zora is concerned.

It's Elijah who's my real competition.

He always has been, the bastard.

Woodrow regains his composure, and his expensive fake smile returns to his face. "Um, ah, yes, well, Ash, I was just telling the ladies about the time I met President Obama."

"Do tell."

Zora bumps me, *hard*, as she walks by, stopping me before I can get good and started in on Woodrow. She takes a seat at the table beside he who I know full well to be her future ex-boyfriend. Woodrow cups her long, lithe hands in both of his short, stubby ones and gives her a conspiring wink as he continues his story.

"Well, in truth, he was merely Senator Obama then."

"I was at a convention in Illinois for prominent minority businessmen and—"

Much to my delight, the yowl of a cat outside the dining area's sliding glass doors interrupts Woodrow.

"Kittie," Sonny shouts. She hops down from her seat and sprints the short distance to the glass doors. That's when the supernaturally enhanced alarm bells inside my head start going ape-shit. Zora yells a warning before I can open my mouth, a step ahead of me as always.

"Sonya, no."

"Come in, Kittie." Sonny throws open the glass door and a large, black cat bounds past her to vault onto the dinner table. This is upsetting enough. But what really has Aunt Jackie screaming for Jesus and Woodrow cursing as he leaps up from the table is the intelligent, human face spanning the width of the feline's onyx-shaped head.

The cat-thing turns and regards me with accusing, brown eyes—eyes resting in a smooth, chocolate oval of flesh where there should be fur. The creature hisses, and this time, I'm the one who yells for his maker.

FOUR

This ain't what I was expecting when I came to Sunday dinner at Zora's. I was supposed to enjoy her and Sonny's company, endure that of Aunt Jackie and Woodrow, and stuff my face with greasy fried chicken until finally settling down on one of Zora's leather couches to watch whatever football game was on the flat screen and drift listlessly off into dreamland.

A fat black cat with the face of a woman was definitely not supposed to jump up on the dinner table and hiss at me.

Un. Fucking. Cool.

The angry expression on the cat-thing's human face changes into one of agony, and its hiss becomes a feline yowl near indistinguishable from the high-pitched wail of a woman. The skin beneath its fur begins to bubble and writhe as though the creature was sitting inside a microwave turned on high.

I hear the front door slam and realize Zora's gentleman caller is no longer with us. Told you Woodrow was a future ex.

"Christ Almighty," I say, more pissed off now than scared. Luckily for the cat-thing, my Glock isn't within reach.

Sonny presses her slender, ten-year-old frame against her mother. "Mommy."

"Jacqueline," Zora commands, "get Sonny into the cellar right now." Somehow among all the commotion and noise, she's managed to remain calm and in control. As usual. I swear, the woman has enough steel to put a Sherman tank to shame.

Aunt Jackie rises from her chair and takes Sonny by the shoulders, gently pulling her away from Zora. She ushers the young girl across the living room into the hall. They disappear through the door leading to Zora's bedroom to use the hidden trapdoor leading to the cellar.

The sound of shattering glass turns my attention back to Zora's dinner table. A transformation has begun there—one of a domestic house cat into a full-grown woman. I reach out, intending to grab the shape-shifting spook and sling it back out through the sliding glass doors.

Zora speaks my name in warning, and I draw back to let things play out as they will. I watch as the cat-thing's right forepaw inflates and contracts, growing slowly one moment then quickly shrinking in again the next as it tries to decide whether to become hand or remain paw. I hear the thing's bones shift and resettle with a sound like Jiffy Pop on a hot stove as the creature balloons in mass to something more human than feline in shape. It overturns plates of food and glasses of sweet tea in the process. Its fur falls away, leaving dark skin lathered with ectoplasm.

On and on the transformation goes, the cat-woman issuing blood-curdling screams and cries throughout. This metamorphosis from animal to human ain't like anything in the monster movies. There's no proportional, symmetrical change here. No ballet of the macabre in motion. This is a raw, uncontrolled mess, as unpredictable and painful as life itself. When at last the show is over and the remains of Zora's dinner rest on the floor around the table, I almost expect to see an umbilical running from the plump, naked young woman the cat has become.

The woman who was a cat reaches for Zora, mewling cat sounds still issuing from her throat. She faints, and Zora rushes forward to her before she can smack the table, uncaring that the slimy film of ectoplasm now blanketing the woman's brown body will smear itself irrevocably into her Sunday dress.

"Ashley," Zora says, turning my name into a command, "she's going into shock. Help me get her off the table."

Damnation.

I begin unbuttoning my Western shirt. Zora might not care if the woman's after-trans gets all over her clothes, but then her wardrobe is a hell of a lot more extensive than mine.

"Now, Ashley."

Double damn.

I surge forward and take hold of the woman, cringing as I feel the gunk covering her soak into my shirt. Twenty dollars on sale at Target, and you better believe she's going to pay me back every red, goddamn scent.

I slip the young woman's flabby right arm across my shoulders as I slip my left across her wide back and secure a grip inside the fleshy well of her armpit. I catch a whiff of her and almost gag.

"That slimy shit she's covered in smells like ass."

Zora ignores me and my redundant, juvenile vocabulary as I take the reeking woman from her arms. The spook's limp lower body slides off the table like wet mud, and the sudden, full weight of her causes me to stumble.

"Get her to the couch," Zora orders.

I obey and stretch the greasy, naked woman out on Zora's brown leather sofa. It'll ruin the piece of furniture. But I don't care. I'm simply happy to be free of the extra load. I look down at my poor shirt and curse as I wipe the foul-smelling gunk from the palms of my hands down my sides. Oh well, it could've been worse. I could've been wearing one of my much-coveted T-shirts. Now that would've been a damn shame.

"Watch her."

Not bothering to wait for my reply, Zora races out of the dining area and through her bedroom door. I hear the cellar trapdoor open and close in quick succession. Zora returns moments later, carrying a blanket and a small glass jar with a tiny, gnarled root in one hand and two leather-bound books in the other. The books' covers—one red, one black—are worn with age and use, more use than could be had in a single lifetime or even two. I know the first volume is her great-great-grandmother's Holy Bible. The other is a hoodoo grimoire known as the Sixth and Seventh Books of Moses. Such books are some of the most powerful weapons in a conjure person's arsenal, and I've seen Zora use either and both to great effect.

But don't let me give you the wrong idea. I call 'em weapons, but they ain't wizard wands or nothing. Real mojo doesn't tend to be like Harry Potter or some shit. You don't shout bastardized Latin and make lightning bolts come hurling out your ass. Well, maybe Elijah could, but he's a freak of nature.

What I'm trying to say is, most folks can't use hoodoo in direct attack. Or even in quick defense for that matter. Real mojo takes time, energy, and prayer. All with the right ingredients and circumstances to be in place. At least that's what I gather from Zora, and I've picked up a thing or two about hoodoo in the years I've known her. But that ain't to say you can't use mojo to blow some shit up given a little preparation. I've already told you a conjure person can bless a bullet into being just as terminal for a spook as a human. But Zora has plenty of other surprises stockpiled downstairs and at her book shop too. My favorites are her mojo hand-grenades. Get it?

Okay, go ahead. Roll your eyes. Zora did the same when I coined the phrase.

Zora throws the blanket over the woman. Next, she removes the tiny root from the jar and forces the woman to eat it. Then she opens the books and begins reading them aloud simultaneously, mixing and mashing their words into a whispered prayer, somehow making it sound as though this is exactly how their passages were always intended to be recited.

After a time, the woman's eyes flutter open, and awareness fills them. Her right hand strikes out like a snake and snatches Zora's arm. I surge forward, but Zora holds up a hand, warning me off.

"I need …" the woman pants, all remnant of the cat's cry now absent from her voice.

Zora gently removes the woman's hand and wipes away the slime from her forehead. I've seen her stroke Sonny's forehead in the same tender fashion a thousand times over. In this moment, Zora is so beautiful it hurts me to look at her. There's a naked female in the room, but I would never know it. I only have eyes for the curve of Zora's perfect forehead. The gleam of her immaculate smile. The strong yet feminine outline of her jaw. Even her scar is alluring. It's the tether binding the otherwise heavenly creature she is to Earth so that mere mortals like myself may gaze upon her. But as marvelous as Zora's physical attributes are, it's the brilliance of her soul—the same brilliance possessed by my late wife and daughter—that brings the tears I quickly wipe from my eyes. Sometimes, these things hit you all sudden-like, you know?

"Sssh," Zora says, her voice soothing. "It's all right, Honey. You're safe here among friends now. No need to be afraid.

"I need—" the woman rises up on an elbow, and the blanket falls away to expose a thick, dark-nippled breast caked with gunk. "I need your help."

"Of course, sugar. I'll do whatever I can for you. Just tell me what's going on."

"I … I can't. Not in front of him." She spits the last word out of mouth as though it were a rotten fish head.

"Ashley's my partner, dear. Whatever you have to say—"

The woman's arm once again clutches at Zora's, though this time, the gesture is plaintive. "Please. I need your help, and I will tell you. But not in front of the likes of him."

"But I—"

"Please, ma'am, you got to swear. Don't say nothing to him. I got nowhere else to turn."

"Okay, I swear it." And the damage is done, just like that. For those who traffic in Zora's and my circles—namely spooks and hoodoos—to swear an oath is about the strongest mojo there is. To go back on a swear is to break off a piece of your own soul, or unsoul as the case may be. Either way, it's bad fucking news for the oath-breaker.

"Now wait a damn minute," I shout, pissed to high heaven.

"You need to leave, Ashley," Zora says. "I'll call you when I can."

"You've got to be fucking kidding me, Zora. You don't know this spook from Eve, and yet you're kicking me out? She's the one who needs to get the fuck out."

"Ashley," Zora chides. One day, I'm going to have to tell her to stop treating me like I'm a fucking child. But then I guess I'd have to stop acting like one.

"But I'm your partner," I plead. "You and me, Zora. Brains and brawn. Lightning and thunder. I can't walk out of here now and leave you and Sonny alone in this—*with her.*"

"I can handle this, Ashley. You know I can. Please. Trust in me now as I have always trusted in you."

Damn her. How am I supposed to argue with that? The truth is I can't. But that doesn't stop me from letting Zora know how pissed off I am about having to tuck my tail and go home.

"Fine. But when you see Sonny, you explain to her it's your fault I didn't take her to Toys 'R' Us." Pathetic, but it's all I got. Almost. I storm out of the living room into the foyer, the scar on my hip hot beneath Zora's mojo hand. I snatch up my jacket and saddlebags and leave the house, slamming the door closed behind me. I hear glass shatter on the door's other side and nod in satisfaction, knowing I've caused some of the pictures hanging in the foyer to fall onto the hardwood. But my moment of triumph is short-lived.

Reality sets in, and my entire body sags as I wish more than anything I could take back the last forty seconds. Oh well. Zora is used to it by now. Yet, for whatever reason, she keeps taking her favorite stray dog back in. Some flowers, new picture frames, and a lot of groveling should have me back in her good graces soon enough.

Hopefully.

One day, I'm going to screw up so bad that she'll send me packing for good. And on that day, I don't know what I'll do because without her and Sonny in my life, the sorry thing just ain't worth living.

FIVE

Autumn moans with pleasure as I massage the furry eye-spots of her half-furled butterfly wings. I whisper obsceni-ties into her ear, and her already labored breathing quickens to a familiar staccato rhythm. Seeing she's ready, I increase the speed of my caresses and the depth of my thrusts. She screams, her wings snapping to attention as her sex clamps tight around my own. The last of my restraint dissolves, and I join her in climax. My molten mind leaves my rigid body, riding out on the sound of my roar. My hips continue to pound Autumn's backside, moving of their own accord so that Zora's mojo hand bounces against me like a speed bag. Then it all ends in a cre-scendo that leaves me empty and weak.

I withdraw from Autumn and collapse onto the burnt-orange carpet of her seventies-festooned double-wide. We never made it to the bed.

Autumn drops beside me and drapes a slender, freckled arm over my chest and fleshy leg the color of sweet milk across my thighs. I look at her lovely, pale face framed by her fire-kissed curls and see my own reflected back at me in the large jade mirrors of her eyes. They're the most beautiful and exotic I've ever seen. They make me wish I could fall in love with her. But when I reach for that feeling as it might apply to Autumn, it simply isn't there. Just as well. I don't know if her kind, a woodland nymph, is capable of love as defined in human terms.

Autumn chuckles. "Hello to you too, Ash. Long time, no see."

Autumn and me have a long-standing, if unspoken, arrangement. And being as angry and frustrated as I was after leaving Zora's, it wasn't a desire for conversation that brought me knocking on her door. In fact, I didn't bother with words at all when I arrived. I simply let my body do the talking. As always, Autumn proved one hell of a listener.

"You loved it, and you know it."

Autumn's smile broadens. She lazily traces her long, razor-sharp nails down the length of the wiry muscles lining my chest and abdomen. "No doubt. I'm just saying, sometimes, it would be nice if you would call first. I could've had company, you know?"

I cock my eyebrows. "Another *friend*?"

Autumn huffs and rolls the sparkling jewels that are her eyes. "Please, Ash. Even feigned jealousy is unattractive coming from—"

I silence her with a kiss. Ever hungry, Autumn nibbles her way down my chin, my neck, and my chest, leaving lipstick and gooseflesh in her wake. I bury my face into her curls. They smell of candied apples and crisp, fall breezes.

She slides the rest of the way on top of me and sits upright to straddle my pelvis. The sight of her creamy, fire-dappled curves works its mojo, engorging me. Autumn's wings spread wide in anticipation. The fading sun shines through their delicate membranes, bathing me in countless shades of orange and red.

"Round two, cowboy?"

I grasp the fleshy triangle of her hips and raise her into the air, her body light as feather-down in my hands. She gasps then coos as I lower her onto me.

Hours later, when we are both satiated and sound asleep, it's not Autumn's face I see in my dreams but Zora's. She's young, her dark hair cropped short like she wore it in high school—cropped short in the style of a boy, though on Zora, there is nothing boyish about it. Somehow, I know that here in the dream, I'm just as young. Just as naïve.

We sit alone on a mountainside overlook carpeted with deep-green grass made gray by the evening twilight. Marion County stretches across the countryside below, the light of its businesses shutting off for the retreating day as those of its homes switch on for the coming night.

That's when I realized what I'm experiencing is more memory than dream. I'm reliving the night of befores. The night before Zora would leave for New Orleans. The night before Elijah would be transferred to a federal penitentiary. The night before I'd walk into an army recruiter's office and set in motion the course of events sealing my fate and that of my future wife and daughter.

I study the sadness in Zora's statuesque profile, realizing even then—even now—on some deep level that I'm in the night of befores and that the afters to follow will irrevocably sour the good life I have thus far known.

"Don't go," my younger dream-self whispers. "Stay. Stay and—"

Zora places a hand on my chest, and I grow silent as the intoxicating sensation of her touch courses through me. She leans into me and nuzzles her face against my neck.

"Hold me."

It's Elijah she's really whispering to, not me. I know this. Knew it then. But I don't care no matter the when. I take her in my arms and close my eyes as I kiss her, the electric fire of unrequited love passing between our lips and tasting almost as sweet as the real thing.

When I open my eyes and draw away, I see that it's not Zora I've kissed but Sarah. She's covered in her own blood and dying yet still has the strength to voice a scream only a mad person would be capable of.

I start awake and sit up in bed, the scar on my hip white-hot with pain beneath the mojo hand.

"You all right?" Autumn half sits up in bed (we finally made it there), the sheet slipping from the abundant swell of her breasts. They are as alluring as ever, but right now, I'm too frazzled to care. I search the bedroom for Sarah's bloodied ghost, my gaze moving from the dated wooden paneling on the wall to the puke-green curtains covering the room's only window before at last coming to rest on the old-fashioned wind-up clock ticking away on her nightstand. The time reads two o'clock in the afternoon. But that can't be right if it's still—?

"Shit. It's Monday. Ain't it?"

Autumn yawns, nodding as she gives her body and wings a good stretch. Her auburn curls are still perfect despite having slept on them. Her morning breath smells like the sun-kissed frost of a dawning fall day. We should all be so lucky.

I get out of bed and shimmy into my blue jeans one plus-leg at a time, knocking over the wine bottles we emptied on our way in here from the living room. "I'm late for a meeting."

"Aaaaw," Autumn beseeches. "Don't go, Ash." Her echoing my dream-self's words sends a cold shiver down my spine. But then she smiles, and the sensation vanishes. "I could call a girlfriend and have her come join us. You know Summer? The Nereid from Suck Creek? Blonde hair. Golden skin. And legs from here to Sunday. They don't come any tastier." A flirtatious wink. "Besides me, that is."

I grin as I slip my jacket over my bare shoulders. Autumn can have the ruined shirt. "Tempting. But business calls. Maybe next time." I bend down and give Autumn a parting kiss. She tries to turn it into something more, but I gently push her away. "You'll be the death of me, girl."

She snorts in laughter. "There's a long line in front of me gunning for that privilege, Ash."

True enough.

"I'll call you."

"Right."

"I will next time. Promise."

"Pardon me if I don't hold my breath."

"Oh ye of little faith."

Autumn takes a pillow from the bed and tosses it half-heartedly in my direction. "Get your fine ass on out of here."

I blow Autumn a goodbye kiss and exit the bedroom, my snakeskin boots in hand. Seconds later, I'm outside the trailer staring at the miles of surrounding forest that's Autumn's true home. The double-wide is primarily for my benefit and that of the other spooks and normals I know she brings here. She is a nymph, after all. Despite her pretense, a Crossroads Faye, even a lowlier one like Autumn, typically has little concern for human ideals like monogamy and faithfulness. But then neither do I these days. I guess that's why we get along so well.

I take my smokes from my jacket and light up. I give a few good puffs then sit down on the stone steps leading from the trailer's front door so I can pull my boots on. Shit-kickers in place, I step up to the Harley and shed my jacket onto the bike's black leather seat. I produce a clean but wrinkled white V-neck from my saddlebags and slip it over me. Senator Jones won't be happy when I show up an hour late reeking of smoke, alcohol, and sex, but fuck him.

Cigarette finished, jacket and brain bucket in place, I ignite the Harley's engine and tear ass down the dirt road leading from the double-wide, leaving a cloud of yellow dust in my wake.

SIX

Exactly one hour later, I take the MLK exit off Highway 27 and enter Metro Chattanooga. A quick left onto Chestnut Street, and I'm at the River City Club. The RCC is an unassuming two-story building of red brick located on the corner of Seventh and Chestnut between the Nations Bank building, the city's First Presbyterian Church, and the infamous copper-windowed Blue Cross Blue Shield high-rise. If you didn't know any better, you'd mistake RCC for a small business complex or even the Fellowship hall of the nearby church. There is certainly nothing about the building's exterior that alludes to the power broking that goes on inside.

River City Club has served as the backdrop for future making and breaking in the Nooga for over a century. It's here that the real business meetings of the city's human elite are held. Fortunes are won and lost over drinks and *hor d'oeuvres* on a daily basis. *I'm sorry, Rick. It's just not working out. Now, would you please flag our waiter on your way out?*

Zora won't come near the place. As a two-headed doctor, I guess she's able to sense all the greed and covetousness the place must have soaked up over the decades.

Me, I've never felt the first malignant flicker here other than what would be obvious to any outsider. But then, I'm a covetous bastard myself. Especially when it comes to other men's wives.

I park my bike at a meter on the far side of the street and walk across, being sure to put some swagger in my step for the benefit of any sweet thing who might be about to come around the corner, bumps and bruises or not.

The effort is wasted on two fat, balding men coming back

from a late lunch. Blue Cross employee badges hang beneath
their double chins on bands of clear plastic.

Win some. Lose some.

I walk up the beige concrete steps rising to meet the ol'
R-double-C and enter through the first of two sets of oak double
doors leading inside. I'm greeted by a small foyer decorated with
striped, lime-on-forest-green wallpaper and cedar wainscoting.
Another set of double doors stands on the foyer's far side, these
glass-paneled in a checkerboard fashion. I proceed through and
enter the lobby, the cherry hardwood creaking beneath my feet
as I go. The green-peppermint wallpaper continues on inside,
the cedar wainscoting beneath it expanding to also circle the
room. Dark leather chairs and couches sit sandwiched between
oak end tables adorned with brass lamps and ashtrays. Painted
portraits of the club's Victorian era founders ring the walls, the
hard gazes of their extremely serious, oil-based visages sizing
me up and finding me wanting.

Fuck you and the jackasses you rode in on.

The wooden-paneled ceiling above opens into a large
rotunda that showcases the sparse bookshelves of the study
upstairs. The décor screams the kind of masculine you would
expect out of a business club that only opened its doors to
females a little over a decade ago. The only thing missing is a
giant, stone hearth directly on the room's other side—the kind
a proper gentlemen's club would have for its members to throw
firecracker powder into before beginning some ancient tale full
of mystery and warning.

Money talks and bullshit walks, the imaginary voice I've
anthropomorphized for River City Club says. I nod reluctantly
in agreement.

"Ashley."

I grit my teeth, trying to stay calm as I look over at the guest
bar adjoining the lobby at its left front corner. Senator Jones is
there, a dark-blue Armani and obligatory red-state tie hanging
on his short, fifty-something frame. He smiles at me, the bar's
sparse light gathering in the whites of his expensive dental
veneers. Rather than rise in greeting from the dark, wooden
table he occupies, Jones merely makes a slight *come here* motion

with his right hand before resuming his conversation with the gentleman seated beside him.

Like any good dog for hire, I obey.

The lobby's masculine theme stretches into the bar. The aftermath of countless cigars hangs in the air. Dark wood and bar stools covered in leather abound. The latter are blood-red in color so as to play off the green-striped walls. Three flat screens hang above the actual bar, tuned to MSNBC, ESPN, and FOX News respectively. A middle-aged African-American dressed in black with a gold name tag reading *Vernon* stands beneath the televisions. He's keeping himself busy by cleaning already spotless beer glasses as he pretends not to overhear Jones' conversation with the other man. Save for the four of us, the bar—and seemingly the club itself—is empty.

I approach Jones' table. Only then does he rise and offer his hand in greeting. "Ashley, glad you could make it," he beams, seemingly oblivious to my tardiness and less-than-refined appearance. Or at least ignoring them in light of his apparent need for my services. What little money I have is on the latter.

My mouth forms into a mocking grin. "Anytime for an old paycheck like yourself, Senator." I take his hand in mine, noting its baby-soft palm and commercially manicured nails. If the senator ever had to pick up a hammer in the early days of his construction company, you wouldn't know it now.

He gives a laugh at my joke at his expense, one far more boisterous than it deserves, then gestures to his conversation partner.

"Allow me to introduce Congressman Jack Walker."

Congressman Walker is dressed in a gray suit and mustard-yellow tie. He is almost as tall as me and stands a full head taller than Jones. His dark hair is cut in the same Baptist preacher-style as the senator's own gray mane. They even share the same vastly receded hairline. But only in his late forties, Walker is tan, fit, and trim. He is exactly the kind of guy you would expect to still see throwing a football around in the backyard with his kids on a sunny Sunday afternoon. A regular Republican poster boy.

"Jack Walker. I don't believe I've had the pleasure." Walker gives me his best baby-kisser smile.

"Ash Owens," I say. "Actually you have, Congressman. Though there's no reason you'd remember it. I sat a few seats over from you and your family at a UT game once. I was sorry to hear about your daughter."

Five years ago, Jocelyn Walker, the congressman's then-sixteen-year-old daughter, was a blonde-haired, blue-eyed beauty with her whole life in front of her. That changed in an instant when she lost control of her vehicle and drove off the two-lane W-Road leading down the side of Signal Mountain. The W-Road is so named because of the continuous series of sharp Vs that constitute its many twists and turns. It's a tough route for an experienced driver, but for a young person with a fresh license, it is your clichéd recipe for disaster. Jocelyn was not the road's first victim, and she certainly won't be its last.

Personally, I steer clear of that particular deathtrap. Pun intended.

Walker's smile leaves his eyes. "Yes, thank you. Jocelyn's loss is still strong in my and my family's hearts. Especially that of her brother, Christian. But we take comfort in knowing all things work toward the glory of the Lord and that one day, we will all be reunited with Jocelyn in Heaven."

Jones gives a concerned smile and places his small hands on our shoulders. "Yes, well, Ashley, Jocelyn's unfortunate passing has to do with the reason I've asked you here today." The senator gestures to the chairs around the table. "Please, sit."

Vernon appears at my elbow, a smile even more practiced than that of the politicians on his face. "May I get you gentlemen something from the bar?"

Jones starts to speak, but I interrupt. Walker's furrowed brow lets me know my rudeness is not lost on him.

"Whiskey, friend. On the senator's tab."

"Certainly, sir. In house, we have Johnny Walker—"

I wink at the senator. "Blue label will do just fine."

Vernon nods, his smile unwavering. "And for you, Senator?"

"I'll have a glass of Merlot, please," Jones says.

"Congressman Walker?"

"I don't indulge in alcohol myself," Walker says, a

condescending tone in his voice. "But how about a Diet Coke?"

"Very good, sir." Vernon dismisses himself then returns moments later with our order. I pick up my glass, my mouth already watering at the sight of the amber liquor housed inside, and start to drink.

Walker gently places his hand on my arm. "Gentlemen, before we begin, might we say a prayer in opening?"

I cock an eyebrow in Jones's direction. He gives a slight nod and closes his eyes before clasping his hands together in front of him. Walker repeats the gesture then waits for me to do the same. And waits. And waits.

"I see you're reluctant to pray, Mr. Owens," Walker says. "Do you not believe in the Lord our God?"

"Oh, I believe all right, Congressman. It's just that the good Lord and me don't have much use for each other these days."

Walker turns to Jones, his displeasure obvious. "I thought you said he was someone we could trust."

Jones smiles and shakes his head. "He is, Jack. Let's not get our feathers ruffled here."

I toss back half my glass. "Yes, Congressman. Let's not."

"Ashley is just a little, well, rough around the edges," Jones continues, "You know, the noble, blue-collar type who says what he feels and feels what he says."

I take out my cigarettes and light up. "If you two gentlemen are done talking about me as though I weren't sitting right fucking here, I'd like to quit wasting time and get down to business." I look around the bar. My gaze finds the portraits hanging in the lobby. "Money talks and bullshit walks, after all."

Walker rises from his chair, fuming, ready to punch my lights out.

Go for it, Congressman. See what happens.

"This is a joke, Bob. I don't know what you see in this … this reprobate, but I've had enough of him. I say we take this up with someone who knows how to act with a little more—"

Smoke leaves my lips in a voluminous cloud. "Mr. Walker, if Senator Jones has brought you to me, it's because you are up to your nose hairs in the kind of things-go-bump-in-the-night shit that only this *reprobate* knows how to handle. There is no one else, Congressman. The sooner you quit putting on airs and come to terms with that, the sooner I can get to digging your puckered, right-wing ass out of the mire. Hear me?"

Walker turns to Jones, a questioning scowl on his face. Jones nods reluctantly. Walker oozes back into his seat, and my butt cheeks unclench. Tough talk or not, I need the money these two douche bags represent. It would've been a damn shame if my lip had sent them walking out the door in a huff.

I ease back into my chair and take another drag. "Good. Now, gentlemen, tell me, what seems to be the problem?"

Jones sighs and pyramids his hands over the table. "Well, Ashley, I was just telling Jack here how, when it comes to dealing with … *out of the ordinary situations,* there is no one better, or more discreet, than yourself."

Smoke jets from my nostrils in twin streams. "And I take it that an out of the ordinary situation is exactly what we have here?"

"True enough."

I nod.

"Earlier, you mentioned the passing of the congressman's daughter, Jocelyn," Jones continues. "I'm afraid Mrs. Walker hasn't taken the loss quite as well as Jack let on."

"Over the last five years, my wife has become a drunkard and a dope fiend," Walker states matter-of-factly.

Jones quickly interjects. "Suzanne has been to some of the finest doctors and rehabilitation centers in the country. Despite all that Jack and his family have tried to do for her, nothing seems to help. So far, it's been kept out of the press. But recently, there's been a new, more volatile development."

"Being bored with her previous forms of intoxication," Walker continues despite the senator's best efforts, "my wife has discovered a new way to foul her body and dull her mind. One created and distributed by your people, I believe."

"If by 'my people,' Congressman, you mean spooks, then I assume you're talking about bad mojo?"

"You know of the drug?" Jones asks.

Walker's contemptuous scowl returns. "Of course he does."

The congressman is right. I do know of bad mojo. All too well. I was strung out on it when Zora found me and cleaned me up. True bad mojo comes from the Crossroads. It's a mix of any number of things from firefly shine to the tears of a Faye gone sane. It's more potent than cocaine and more addictive than heroine and has been a plague on spooks—and humans able to fit the bill—since before night was divided by day.

I take another drag. "Sounds to me like you need a hoodoo, gentlemen. I solve the kind of problems that can be strong-armed into resolution."

"It's not rehabilitation we're seeking, Ashley," Jones says. "Mrs. Walker disappeared two weeks ago."

I shrug. "So call the police."

"I'm afraid it's not that simple."

The politicians exchange glances from the corners of their eyes. Walker reaches inside his jacket and produces an eight-by-twelve manila envelope.

"This came in the mail three days ago." He tosses the envelope in my direction.

I take the envelope and open it to find a picture of Suzanne Walker inside. In the photograph, the congressman's wife lies in a small, darkened room, half-naked on a bed with an antique iron frame and torn, yellowed sheets. She stares up at the ceiling, her eyes blank and unaware, the lovely curves I remember from that day in the stands replaced by hard angles covered with track marks. Her formerly striking blonde hair is now brown with grease and sweat. But the most telltale sign that the congressman's wife is tripping on bad mojo is the ghastly, luminescent shade of green lining her lips.

I start to tell the two politicians to quit wasting my time and simply start checking any number of flea-bag hotels in the area when the photograph reveals to me the reason these men have brought their problem to my attention. A cracked mirror hangs above the bed in the picture's background. Within the mirror is the reflection of a flashing, disposable camera—one that floats unsuspended in the air.

But the camera is not really floating. The photographer's image simply couldn't be captured in the mirror or on film.

"Those ain't track mark on her arms and legs at all," I say. "Fucking vipers."

"He's quick," Walker says to Jones. "I'll give him that at least."

"You should've told me it was vipers to begin with, Jones. I'd almost do the job for free."

"You agree to help then?" Walker asks.

"Don't get ahead of yourself, Congressman. I said, 'almost.' The truth is, I'm a hell of a lot more expensive now than when I used to run errands for the senator."

Walker nods. "Money is not a problem."

Then and there, I decide if the congressman keeps talking that way, I may have to start liking him after all.

"Then neither is my finding your wife's kidnappers."

The two politicians exchange glances.

"We do not believe she has been kidnapped," Jones says. "Based on her behavior of late, we think Mrs. Walker has taken up with these so-called vipers of her own accord."

I nod. "It's blackmail then."

"Precisely," Jones says. "We think whoever Suzanne is staying with is intent upon using this and other such material to extort the congressman."

I cock an eyebrow. "Other such material? You mean there are more *compromising* pictures?"

Jones shrugs. "Not exactly."

Walker swallows hard, unable to meet our eyes. "You see, Mr. Owens, my wife kept a journal. A very detailed one. And it appears to have gone missing right along with her."

Now we're getting to the nitty gritty. This shithead could give a fuck about his wife. He's just afraid of what her words might do to him and his career.

I think about Sara and for the thousandth time how fucked up it is I have to live without her while dirtbags like Congressman Walker here go around taking their own wives for granted.

But, uncharacteristically, I manage to keep my cool. At least outwardly.

"Skeletons in your closet. I get it. We all have them."

Walker gives a nervous chuckle. "Yes, true, but it's especially inconvenient to have them in my case."

"Surely, you've heard that Congressman Walker is running for governor?" Jones interjects.

"Sorry. I don't much keep up with politics these days. One lying windbag is as good as the next. No offense."

Jones sighs. "But you can see the potential public relations nightmare that would be created if news of Mrs. Walker's current state got out?"

"Or if my wife's journal were to fall into the hands of the unfaithful," Walker interjects.

"I needn't tell you, Ashley," Jones continues, "that this is to be kept out of the public eye at all costs."

I grin and give the two politicians a wink. "Not to worry, boys. My lips are clamped tighter than a virgin's legs on prom night."

SEVEN

Fucking vipers.

These days, the world thinks they're some kind of sex symbol—pretty, melodramatic teenagers who sparkle in the daylight. It's an image vipers have worked hard to cultivate in the minds of humans over the past century and one that is a far cry from the real thing.

After I'd hooked up with Zora, I came upon this viper one time in the backcountry down around Scottsboro, Alabama. I found him on a dirt road leaned up against the sky-blue Taurus of the family he had just murdered—a young couple with a little girl and a newborn baby boy, every one of them drained to the last drop. The viper was naked and covered in the mingled remains of their blood, the scaly, white flesh of his belly distended like that of a fat tick above his rail-thin legs. He was too full to even move off the road.

I took my time with that one. And when morning finally came, I made sure that sonofabitch *sparkled* right on into ashes, one piece at a time.

The monster did not utter so much as a peep that month. Not even during the full moon.

Vipers like to believe they're at the top of the food chain, but the truth is, they're nothing but spook trash. Anyone tries to tell you different, they're a fucking moron. Tell them Ash Owens said so.

There is only one thing I can think of that is worse than a viper, but so long as I keep Zora's mojo hand on my hip, it ain't a worry.

So, all that to say, if a couple of douchebag politicians want to pay me a lot of money to get all Van Helsing up in this bitch, who am I to argue?

Well, they're actually paying me to find the wife of the oh-so-righteous Congressman Walker. But it appears Mrs. Walker is strung out on bad mojo in some kind of viper-run drug-house, so same difference.

The viper drug-house business means Jubal is involved. And if I'm going to get to Jubal, then I have to go through his attorney lackey, Ralph Whitaker. And the one place I can count on Whitaker showing up at some point in the evening is the Stone Lion.

The Stone Lion is my favorite bar in the Nooga proper and a literal manifestation of the Crossroads on Earth. As such, it is sacred ground. Spooks and humans alike rub elbows there, neither having to fear anything from the other. There are other bars in the Nooga where this happens, places like Lamar's and Alan Gold's, but none of them hold the promise of security offered by the Stone Lion. But then, none of those places have Aslan sitting on their doorstep acting as a silent, ever-watching sentry.

No, I don't suppose the feline I'm referring to is the real Aslan. In fact, it's not even a real lion but merely the concrete statue that gives the Stone Lion its namesake. But there is some kind of ancient mojo going on with it that not even Zora can explain. The thing gives me the willies. But in a good way, you know? It's like having a guard dog around who you know could tear everyone to shreds, yourself included, but won't so long as you all play nice. The lion statue is just one of many mysteries the bar holds and far from its greatest.

Knowing where I have to go, I leave the River City Club and head to Earlene's to grab a shower and some shuteye before switching vehicles. When I clock in later tonight, I'll be on company time. And company time calls for the company car. Jobs tend to take me places where a ding or a scratch would be the least threatening thing that could happen to the Harley, so the girl stays home.

I reach Earlene's and throw my saddlebags over my shoulder before heading inside. I enter through the back. When I open the door to my room, I'm unsurprised but somehow still a little disappointed to see that the Cleaning Faye has failed to stop by during my absence.

Oh fucking well.

I take my cell phone out of my pocket, hoping to find a message or missed call from Zora.

No dice.

But considering how I made my last exit from her abode, my chances of that having occurred were worse than those of the Cleaning Faye making an appearance.

I tighten my grip on the phone and stare at it, knowing I should be the one to make the call and apologize. Unfortunately, the prideful asshole inside me decides it's still a little too early. I stuff my phone back into my pants, strip naked, and hit the grimy, standing-room-only shower inside the closet that is my bathroom. Afterward, I lie down on my cot, damp and soggy but relaxed.

Sleep comes, dreams of blood, fangs, and terror along with it.

Afterward—once I'm up and dressed in a leather jacket, jeans, and a threadbare T-shirt I bought at a Shooter Jennings concert—I walk outside and open the truck's driver-side door, having to reach up to do so. The familiar odors of metal, grease, and cigarettes long-smoked wash over me.

Time to go to work.

I toss my saddle bags into the cab and hop in behind them. And I do mean hop. The Ford's knobby, oversized tires hold its mud-encrusted chassis a couple feet off the ground.

The truck's interior is just as fancy as its body. Instead of vinyl, a tattered patchwork of fabric scavenged from various old quilts covers the bench seat, most of it held together by duct tape. A clutter of empty cigarette packs serves as the only carpet for the steel gray floorboard. A few tattered issues of *Playboy* constitute its only matting. Of all my truck's adornments, I'm especially proud of the small, chrome skull riding atop the vehicle's gear shift. It's the height of redneck-spook detailing. Zora said as much between guffaws when she gave it to me a few Christmases back.

I take a moment to massage the mojo hand hanging from the rearview mirror (also a gift from Zora). Then I step on the clutch and stick the key into the ignition. The engine coughs then sputters. I pump the gas pedal with my other foot until, at last, the filth-drenched behemoth shudders to life. I shift into neutral and hold my foot on the brake as I roll down my windows and light up. Adequately cancer-sticked, I open the glove box and sift through the mass of scratched, caseless CDs housed inside (it broke my heart when I had to upgrade from eight-track) until I find something to score this particular ride. My search is rewarded when I come across an early album by Southern Culture on the Skids. I slip it into the truck's CD player, a gadget already as outdated as the rest of the vehicle, and press play. The familiar rockabilly riffs of "Camel Walk" begin bopping out of the vehicle's severely inadequate speakers, taxing the bass and treble to their limit.

I think about what I could be getting myself into, and somewhere deep down inside me, the monster stirs. Just a flinch. And only for a moment.

But that's okay. Considering I'm about to be up to my eyeballs in viper-related shit, I think I'm going to need to be a little bit of a monster to stay alive long enough to get paid.

EIGHT

It's only seven in the evening, but night has fallen by the time I reach the Stone Lion. The dark here in the Nooga grows with each passing day, each sunset coming just a little earlier and each sunrise a little later. Winter and its chill will be here soon.

The Stone Lion stands on the hilltop at the corner of High Street and Fourth. It's flanked by a parking lot, brick apartment buildings, Veterans Bridge, and the corrugated steel building serving as the local World War II museum. The bar is a modest, two-story building of gray stone. A double-decker porch— green and floorless at its bottom, graffiti-riddled at its top— extends from the building's first floor entrance to the sidewalk, corralling patrons and boxes of empty beer bottles beneath the neon signs hanging in the windows of the bar proper. Beyond the porch, the bar's namesake stands guard beside a set of stone steps leading to a mid-level landing, the latter nicely concealed by vines and other shrubbery from any passersby who might not approve of all the pot smoking and other shenanigans that tend to go on there.

From there, the steps take an upward turn to the black iron tables, stools, and free-standing heaters that adorn the porch's graffiti-laden upper deck. A pair of sun-bleached Chuck Taylors hang by their strings from the power lines running level with the porch top, capping it all off.

I park the truck along the curb opposite the bar and cross the street, not giving a second thought about having to leave my Glock in the cab. I'm used to the fact by now.

Years ago, back when I was young, dumb, and full of cum (*so much has changed, hardy-har*), I made a bet with Earlene I could smuggle a loaded weapon into the Stone Lion.

I got halfway across the street before the worst nausea I have known before or since struck me. I took another step, and I dropped to my knees just as my dinner exploded out of mouth and nostrils.

At that moment, I happened to look up, and I swear to you, that fucking lion statue was staring me directly in the eye. The sensation was somehow familiar and left me cold in my soul. But money was on the line, so vomit dripping off my face, I actually tried to crawl forward with the gun still on me.

Big mistake.

My bladder and bowels emptied into my pants in a warm, rank gush. Yeah. Gross. Tell me about it. Long story short, blood had begun to run from my every orifice before I finally cried uncle and turned around to face Earlene's gloating, butch ass. Needless to say, it was the first and last time I ever tried such a dumbass maneuver.

Now, I look back on the affair and, instead of being sore over it, it gives me peace of mind to know that anyone dumb enough to try that kind of stupid shit will get the same.

I reach the Stone Lion's porch and nod to the three hippie burnouts standing out front. The rag-tag men are dressed in threadbare baja hoodies, faded jeans, and sandals. They range in age from forty-something to twenty-something, but the skin of the youngest is as leathery and wrinkled as the oldest. Their hair is tied into long, stringy braids that run the lengths of their backs.

They nod in return. To this crew, my bruises are a welcome sight rather than a turn-off. The youngest of them cocks an eyebrow. "Buying?"

"Mojo?"

"Nah, man. No primo. Poppers. MJ."

"I'll think on it."

"Cool."

I open the bar's steel-framed, Plexiglas door, a thing yellowed by decades of spilled beer, cigarette smoke, and the faded stickers of rock bands who've been around since dinosaurs roamed the Earth, and go inside.

You know the phrase, "hole-in-the-wall"? The Stone Lion coined it. Crammed into a space no bigger than your bedroom are two wooden high-tops and a bar stocked with the best selection of brews both foreign and domestic in the tri-state area. A large air duct and a simple wooden hitching post separate this area from a split-level platform accommodating a Golden Tee arcade game and the most eclectic juke in the city. Beyond this lies a beer-crate-littered hallway leading to two bathrooms awash with flies and two-day-old shit.

Take all this, slather over a century's worth of filth and graffiti on top of it from floor to ceiling, add in folks from all walks of life and unlife, and you have my favorite bar in Chattanooga—my home away from home.

"Ash," James calls from behind the bar, having to raise his voice a bit to compete with the punk rock music echoing out of the CD juke. "Long time, no see. The usual?" He pushes a stray dread behind his ear and nods. James is the "day bartender" here at the Stone Lion although the term "day bartender" is pretty much irrelevant when you don't open your doors until two o'clock in the afternoon. His cognizant manner and the fact that he doesn't stink from here to high heaven lets me know he's fed recently. It's only the slight gray tinge of his otherwise brown skin that gives him away as a zombie, or one of the unliving as his breed of spooks prefer to be called.

"PBR still cold and cheap?"

"Fucking A."

"Pabst it is."

I could have ordered any number of microbrews. Like I said, the Stone Lion carries the finest selection of beers this side of Appalachia. But until I've pocketed all the congressman's money, I prefer to err on the side of frugality. And the truth is, I'm a simple man with simple tastes. That's part of the reason I dig the Stone Lion so much. They don't even serve liquor here. Little extras like liquor license fees tend to complicate things and cause overhead. And if the Stone Lion does anything, it keeps a low overhead.

I roll up to the bar and take a brown-bagged tallboy from James' hand.

"Thank you, sir. You're a gentlemen and a scholar."

I throw back the beer, and its familiar, aluminum-laced tang washes down my throat.

"How you been keeping yourself, Ash?" James asks.

"'Bout the same as always."

"That bad, huh?"

"This pretty face tells no lies. Seen Whitaker around?"

"Not tonight, but he's bound to show up sooner or later."

"What I figure."

"Want me to holler if I do?"

"S'alright. I'd rather say 'hi' on my own if you know what I mean?"

James nods.

I turn to my right. Big Worm is there, hunched over in front of the video poker machine, the massive, pinkish segments of his lower body falling out from beneath the bottom of his sole item of clothing—a brown suede jacket that I'm sure was cool in the eighties but just sad and dated now—to coil around his barstool and leave a puddle of slime beneath him.

"Hey, Ash," he says to me excitedly, never taking his eyes off the game. "You ever seen a score this high?"

I take a pull off the tallboy. "No, Worm. Never." I don't bother to look.

A smile spreads across the vein-work of his pink, fleshy face, creating deep dimples on either side of the coarse, insectoid hairs rimming his mouth like a goatee. "Damn right you haven't."

I'm lighting up when I feel a small hand come to rest on my shoulder. "Where the hell have you been?" a woman's voice says into my ear. Except she says it like, "Vhere zee hell hast du been?"

My eyes roll of their own accord as I pocket my lighter and take a drag off my cigarette.

"Hello, Helga."

Helga is as ugly as her name. She looks like a refugee from the concentration camps of her native country's infamous past. She's gaunt to the point of emaciation. Her teeth are yellow and jut every which way, and her hair looks like it hasn't been washed in a decade. All this I could forgive—have forgiven, in fact. What I can't forgive is her annoying fucking mouth.

I made the mistake of being less than an asshole to her once. What I got for my trouble was a night trapped in a corner here at the Lion listening to her yap about how she comes from a long line of Norn ancestry that still holds prominence in Germany's Black Forest.

I've seen Faye folk. Know them, pureblood and mixed. And I'm here to tell you, the closest Helga and her antecessors ever got to being one of the Faye was her great, great granddaddy cornholing some medieval goblin hag around back of the pig sty.

"Why haven't you returned my calls?"

"Sorry, darling. My cell's been on the fritz."

As if on cue, the damnable contraption rings in my pocket.

"Uh, excuse me. I gotta take this."

Helga looks at me, her brow furrowing above her eyes. The track on the juke changes to "London Calling" by the Clash, and I make my exit.

"Owens here."

A recorded voice begins telling me my account with Verizon has a balance due. Before it has a chance to say by how much, I snap the Captain Kirk gizmo closed.

"So your phone is on the fritz, huh?"

Helga is at my elbow once again, talking into my ear. But I'm not having it.

"Excuse me, *fraulein*."

I make tracks once again, a difficult thing to do in a bar the size of your rich friend's bathroom, and gently slide in among the group of giggling, young coeds gathered around the twin high-tops, leaving Helga with no way to follow. Dino is in their midst, telling the same stale jokes he's regaled the ladies with since the eighties. Nineteen eighties, eighteen eighties, seventeen eighties, take your pick. Dino has been hanging out at the Stone Lion since it was a little more than a frontier trading post. Seemingly in his early thirties, Dino is short and stocky with close-cropped, salt-pepper hair and beard. He's dressed in jeans, a heavy wool sweater, and a pair of coke-bottle-end bifocals that make his eyes appear gigantic in their lenses. A large, brown bottle of Sammy Smith's Winter Stout sits in his left hand. A lit cigarette dangles from his right.

Dino is not the stereotypical chick magnet. He doesn't flaunt money or dress in nice clothes. Hell, he's not even handsome. But whether it's some kind of immortal mojo or just proof positive that if you're loud and brash enough, people will trip over themselves in an effort to see what all the noise is about, he never hurts for female company.

He's got almost as much game as yours truly.

Almost.

"I just want to know—" Dino stands and slides his barstool back with his foot.

"Has anyone seen your belt?" I finish for him, a satisfied smirk on my face.

Dino scowls at me as his jeans drop to his ankles, revealing the trademark tighty-whiteys and pale, hairy legs that always punctuate his joke.

The girls look at Dino and then at one another, unsure if they should be laughing or if my ruining of Dino's gag was part of still yet another rub.

The corners of Dino's frown wriggle and then twist upward into a grin. He laughs, and his entourage follows suit, relief flooding over them.

"Fucker," Dino says, a smile on his face. "Get your sorry arse over here and talk to me, Owens."

Dino shoos a couple of his ladies out of my way, even making one get up from her barstool so that I will have a place to sit. I place my hand on her shoulder and ease her back into her seat.

"That's all right, hon'." I laid an elbow onto the hitching post separating the high-tops from the Golden Tee machine. "I can talk to your boy just fine from right here."

I ground out the remains of my cigarette on the hitching post and take another from my pack. Dino tosses me his lighter. I snatch it from the air and do what follows.

"What the fuck happened to your face?"

"Knitting accident." I pitch Dino's lighter back to him and inhale. "Seen Whitaker around?"

"Now why the fuck would you want to see that viper lickspittle?"

I shrug. "Ain't so much a case of want, Dino."

"Ah. On a job, then?"

"Maybe."

"Well, if it is, and if you want to keep any hope of getting paid, you better duck."

"Pardon?"

Something crashes into the back of my head with the force of a Mack truck, and I go sprawling into Dino's crowd of girls. My subconscious registers their frantic scattering, slowing the action down to molasses-drip speed so that I'm able take in every jiggle and bounce as they bolt for the door. I'm even able to see each subtle twitch and flex of Dino's fingers as he wraps his fist around his beer and yanks it from the table, preventing me from landing on top of it and crushing it into a hundred amber shards as I crash into the high-top and bounce off onto the bar's filthy, concrete floor.

Johnny Cash's "Ring of Fire" begins playing on the juke. I'm hefted into the air and brought face to tusked face with the biggest, meanest half-blood troll I've ever seen. His gray-green Cro-Magnon brow furrows above his beady yellow eyes. He's dressed in a leather biker vest and faded blue jeans stretched to their limit. Black tattoos run the length of his bare, tree trunk arms, muscle-knotted chest, and fat, round belly.

"Hello, Baby Shit," I say. "You're not still sore over the thing with Aprhilis, are you?"

He roars, and I almost gag as the putrid stench of his breath washes over me. In this moment, I am extremely sorry the Stone Lion's ban on weapons doesn't extend to fists—particularly those of angry mountain troll hybrids whose comely Faye wives I've slept with.

NINE

Okay, so I'm a womanizing asshole. We've established that. But what makes this particular instance in my long history of cuckoldry especially bad is the fact that the five hundred pounds of pissed off troll-man about to reduce me to a greasy spot on the bar is actually one of my best friends in the world.

Baby Shit—*Ronnie*—and me go way back. Hell, I was with Ronnie when he got his nickname. It was after a particularly rough dust-up with a gang of were-kiyotes. When we'd cleared out the last mutt in the den, Ronnie marked the occasion by commenting, "We beat those fuckers from here to baby shit."

The nonsense expression became a name, and the name stuck.

For his part, Ronnie didn't mind. He took to it with a sort of noble pride, even. The nickname was a reminder of our victory, after all. And Ronnie has a great sense of humor. I mean, otherwise, how could anyone be crazy enough to nickname a creature who can reduce your bones to powder after baby poo?

But the thing about Ronnie—standup guy that he is—is, well, he has a beautiful Faye wife. I mean, Aprhilis is the kind of drop-dead gorgeous that only comes out of the high courts. The kind that, well, would cause best friends to kill each other over. Not that I'd ever consider doing such where Ronnie is concerned. I might be an asshole, but I'm not a murderer.

At least, not when I can help it. *Usually.*

Ronnie's only mistake was thinking still better of me and trusting me alone with Aprhilis one too many times. So if you think about it, in a way, what happened is kind of his fault. After all, it's *me* we're talking about here.

So said the asshole. Yeah, yeah. You're right. *Fuck me.*

"Baby Shit," I say, my feet dangling a foot off the ground, "I swear to God. It didn't mean anything. It was just sex."

My poor choice of words sends me flying into the glass-windowed coolers behind the bar. They shatter along with countless bottles of booze. I land on the floor in a heap of broken glass, metal racks, and beer foam, reeking of alcohol. The bar disappears before my eyes as Ronnie rips it up with one massive, clawed hand and hurls it.

That same hand and its twin somehow manage to wrap the thick sausages masquerading as their fingers around my comparatively small throat. Ronnie hauls me up to my knees and begins to squeeze.

"Baby Shit," I gasp, "Ronnie. Please—"

He cuts me off. "How could you fucking do this to me, Ash?" His voice is the sound of woeful thunder. "We were brothers."

"You know me, Baby Shit," I wheeze. "I'm an asshole. I can't help it."

"Bullshit." Ronnie's fingers tighten around my windpipe, leaving me less than a trickle of air. Black roses bloom before my eyes. I picture my face turning an unhealthy shade of Smurf blue.

"It was just the once," I rasp. "And you were gone, off hunting in the Crossroads with your troll brethren. Aprhilis wanted to make you jealous. So you'd stay home. She fucking loves you, man."

This is a bit of an exaggeration. Ronnie was gone, and Aprhilis does love him to death. She told me so each night for several weeks while I was doing any number of deliciously nasty things to her. But she wasn't necessarily trying to make her husband jealous. That only came about when Ronnie returned from his hunting trip a few days early and caught us making the much-lauded beast with two backs. Like I said, Faye are fickle that way.

But thanks to Aprhilis' intervention, I was able to get the hell out of Dodge that night without Ronnie doing any serious damage to me. But that was then, and this is now, as they say.

"What did you say?" Ronnie bellows.

Sensing an opening, I use every ounce of strength at my disposal to push wind through the needle eye now serving as my esophagus. "I said. She. Fucking. Loves you."

Miracle of miracles, I feel Ronnie's grip on my throat loosen the slightest bit.

"She does?"

Okay. Now we're talking. New ballgame, folks. "Of course she does," I muster. "You're Ronotu the destroyer, son of Zogroth, the saint killer. You crushed half a dozen were-coyote skulls with one blow. You take a piss, and folks call it a monsoon. You take a dump, and Heaven and Earth tremble. Who wouldn't fucking love you?"

Tears begin to leak from Ronnie's eyes.

"You were my brother, Ash."

"I am your brother, you big fucking cuss. But I told you, I'm an asshole. And we assholes tend to fuck up first and ask for forgiveness later."

"So?"

"So I'm asking you. Brother to brother. Forgive me. *Please.*"

An anguished scowl crosses Ronnie's tear-stained face, and his hands close tight again upon my throat. But just when I'm sure I've played the wrong hand, he releases my neck and scoops me up into a bear hug that's as equally suffocating.

"Don't you ever fuck me over like that again, you stupid bastard."

I massage my throat and then pat the twin cannon balls that are Ronnie's shoulders. "I love you too, Baby Shit."

It is held tight in Ronnie's arms that I peer through the yellow funk of the Stone Lion's Plexiglas door and spot James outside, talking to Whitaker. Whitaker is tall and lean with a hawkish face and a head full of long, dark hair. He's dressed in a brown Western suit, Bolo tie, and cowboy boots made of eel skin.

James ends their conversation by pointing at the bar and shrugging nonchalantly before moving on to another customer, oblivious to the fact he's just placed my mark on the alert. Whitaker's gaze cuts through the cloudy Plexiglas, and our eyes lock. He quickly decides he doesn't like what he sees and hightails it out of sight.

I struggle and try to free myself from Ronnie's grasp, but by the time he lets me loose and I make it outside into the street, Whitaker is nowhere to be seen.

TEN

Istand in the street outside the Stone Lion, smelling of spilled beer and blood and cursing under my breath as I consider what my next move should be. Under normal circumstances, those circumstances being where I haven't acted like a dick and pissed off the one woman I care about more than anything in the world, I would go to Zora and ask for her help. I'm sure she'd be able to whip up some kind of hoodoo-homing device and locate Whitaker lickety-split. But as I've yet to apologize for having shown my ass at dinner yesterday, calling her up just because I need something wouldn't be the best thing to do at this juncture in terms of our relationship.

Waiting for Whitaker at his home, or even at his office tomorrow, are also out of the question. Now that he knows I'm looking for him, he'll go to ground with the very vipers I'm trying to locate. Tell every goddamn one of them to avoid me and the Stone Lion at all costs.

Fucking James. I know he was just trying to help, but *man* did he shit all over my plans. Not that it's his fault. I should've been more careful. Regardless, Whitaker's trail is now colder than a well digger's ass, and I've no way of picking it up again.

That's not true, the monster says inside my head. *There is more than one way to skin a cat. Or in this case, a human. And you and I know all about skinning people, don't we Ash?*

"Fuck you," I mutter under my breath.

Cold laughter echoes up from some dark abyss inside me.

"You all right, Ash?"

I turn around and see all seven-plus feet of Baby Shit towering over me, a concerned look on his gruesome, tusked face. He hands me one of the two brown-bagged PBR cans he's carrying.

"I didn't squeeze you too hard, did I?"

I pop the can's top, bring it to my lips, and take a huge swallow.

"Nah, Baby Shit. I'll live. And it wasn't nothing I didn't deserve."

I wipe the leftover foam from my lips.

"Just missed somebody I needed to talk to. Now I've to go looking for them. That's all."

He nods, the action causing the huge, corded muscles he carries in place of a neck to roll like ocean waves. He downs his beer in a single gulp and crushes the empty can into a paper-thin disc between a gargantuan thumb and forefinger.

"Anything I can help you with?"

The last time Baby Shit helped me with anything, an entire city block was laid waste. I love the big guy, but in terms of the job, he's like working with a walking, talking powder keg—he's to be used only as a last resort and even then as sparingly as possible. And as my benefactors are calling for discretion in this matter, it's not one for Baby Shit's involvement.

Not that what I'm contemplating at the moment is much better.

I clap Baby Shit on his enormous shoulder. "Nah, man. It's all good. But thanks for the offer."

"No prob, Ash." Baby Shit turns toward the bar. "You change your mind, you know where to find me."

Baby Shit begins walking away. I almost tell him to give my love to Aprhilis. Thankfully, I snag hold of my tongue before it has a chance to wag and land me back in a mess of hurt.

First time for everything, I suppose.

Baby Shit opens the Stone Lion's door, and loud rock music erupts into the open night. He enters the bar, and the door closes behind him, leaving me in quiet and darkness.

"Sheeit." I kill the tallboy and toss the can.

I cross the rest of the street and open the driver-side door of my pickup. The cab light blinks on, and my reflection appears in the driver-side window as a series of bright, orange ridges and dark, shadowed valleys. These twist and swirl in the glass, becoming something monstrous and vile.

Cold sweat pops out on my forehead. I look down and see that my hands are trembling. The world spins around me. I place my hand on the cab's bench seat to steady myself.

"What the hell am I doing?" I ask the empty night.

"Exactly what you have to."

Exactly what you want to.

Tittering laughter echoes inside my mind.

I shake it off.

"You'll be all right," I tell myself. "It's weeks before the full moon."

Without further hesitation, I reach down and unbutton my pants, revealing the brown leather cord securing Zora's mojo hand to my pelvis. I twist it around on my body so that its tie is positioned directly below my belly button. I claw at the tie until it gives up its ghost. I tear the cord, mojo hand and all, from my waist and stuff it inside my jacket pocket so that several layers of fabric now separate me from Zora's trick.

Everything comes alive with a new, terrible brilliance, and I double over, feeling like a newborn breaking free of its constrictive womb. The colors of the world dim into a gray monochrome, but objects take on a new crispness of definition. I'm able to see every single pore and hair lining the backs of my hands in vivid detail. I grab my knees to steady myself and become astonished to realize I'm able to feel each individual thread of my jeans beneath my fingertips. I also realize the muffled music and conversation of the Stone Lion is now reaching my ears in clear, stereo surround sound. If I left the mojo hand off my hip, by month's end, I'd not only be able to hear the heartbeats of those inside the bar but distinguish between them.

But what truly overwhelms me here and now are the smells. There are so many. Pavement. Exhaust. Rubber. Metal. Plastic. Gas. Oil. Concrete. Glass. Steel. Water. Grass. Trees. Dirt. Bugs. Squirrels. Smoke. Beer. Piss. Flatulence. Bad breath. Soap. Shampoo. Lotion. Toothpaste. After shave. Perfume. Filth. Sickness. Death. Decay.

Flesh.

Blood.

Blood.

Blood.

And hundreds more, each of them fighting for my attention. But none of them are what I seek.

Momentarily forgetting myself, I drop onto all fours and sniff the ground, searching for the scent of my prey. After a moment, my nose finds it. Ralph Whitaker's aftermath wafts up to me from the concrete—a mixture of sweat, too much Drakkar cologne, boot leather, and blood.

Always blood.

I scamper forward, coming up on my hind legs, feeling invincible. Feeling like a thousand bucks. Feeling like I own the night and every goddamn thing in it.

I follow Whitaker's scent to an empty parking space and then latch onto that of the car he drove away in. My nose has no problem placing it as a 2007 BMW Z4. One in bad need of an oil change, by the smell of it.

Whitaker's mine now.

Before I realize what I'm doing, I throw back my head and roar. And why not? After all, the night is young, and I'm a monster on the prowl in the heart of the city.

ELEVEN

I leap into my truck and turn the engine over. I give it a few revs and then throw some AC/DC into the dashboard stereo. "Highway to Hell" begins reverberating out of the truck's speakers. I roll down the window and light up as I crank the volume. I make quick work of the cigarette and flip the leftover butt out into the street. I stick my head out the window and allow the scent of fine German engineering low on oil to fill my nostrils.

My quarry has headed south on Georgia.

You can run, Whitaker, but you can't hide.

I shove the truck into gear and stomp the accelerator, burning rubber as I do a Uey in the middle of the street. An oncoming Honda swerves to miss me. Its driver lays on his horn, and I do the same as I scream at him to fuck off.

"Buy American, you shithead."

I consider chasing after him for a moment but decide I'm after bigger prey—namely one Mister Ralph Whitaker, Esquire.

Not being able to walk around in sunlight severely limits vipers in accomplishing the kind of simple, everyday tasks most normal folks take for granted—the kind that tend to only be achievable during hours when the sun's shining—like mailing postage, applying for loans, getting a driver's license, or any number of mundane things.

Long story short, vipers need someone who doesn't burst into flames at the first sign of UV to wheel and deal on their behalf. Such is why they tend to enlist human familiars and why those of Whitaker's profession are preferred. After all, who better to serve as your legal representative than an attorney?

Now, my boy Whitaker is Jubal's number one familiar, the Renfield to his Dracula. Whitaker was a slimy SOB before he hooked up with Jubal. The only thing that changed afterward is he got a lot slimier and a lot richer. Story is Whitaker came into contact with Jubal when he put out the feelers looking for someone to off his wife, a lady who apparently was giving him an especially large amount of grief at the time. Here in the Nooga, word of that kind of thing inevitably reaches the circles spooks inhabit. As a rule, we Homo occultus all try to play nice if for no other reason than the sake of our continued survival here in this modern age. But the truth of the matter is, we're all still monsters at heart, present company being no exception. So, if you need killing done, we're the monsters to call.

But back to Whitaker.

Jubal finally caught wind of his plans, learned he was about the most crooked attorney this side of North Georgia, and saw he could gain leverage over him because of it.

Come to find out, no leverage was needed. Whitaker was more than happy to come on board with the vipers. Seemed, deep down, he'd been waiting his entire life for an opportunity to run with the things that make normal people fear the dark.

I was surprised when I first heard this story although I don't really know why. There's a lot of folks like Whitaker out there—human beings who carry a monster's soul. And they're all the more worse for it. At least we spooks can't help what we are.

Anyway, as Jubal's foremost lackey, it's likely Whitaker's the only one who will know exactly where Jubal has set up shop on this particular night. A viper can never be too careful after all. Bed down in one place too long, and meddling sonofabitches like Zora and myself are likely to catch you napping in the daytime and wreak tee-total hell up in your shit.

That said, Jubal's no fool. He moves his operation two or three times a month. Sometimes that much in a week if he's being extra careful. Never the same place twice. It made working with him a real pain in the ass, let me tell you.

Oh, yeah. Forgot to mention that little detail, didn't I?

Yeah, I used to run and gun some for Jubal before Zora came along and straightened me out. Not to get into the details, but I acted as a liaison of sorts between the vipers and another outfit that's just as bad if not worse. The arrangement worked out well for all parties at the time. Especially the vipers. Along with their never-ending stream of attorney lackeys, the vipers love having other creatures of the night on their side who can walk abroad during the day.

The gig was the easiest money I ever made. Cars. Clothes. Power. The vipers have the lion's share in this city, and back then, so did I.

As to how it all came crashing to an end, well, let's just say the entire affair is the main reason I now hold such love in my heart for the Nosferatu and leave it at that.

I turn right off Georgia onto MLK before heading south onto Market, my head hanging out the window like that of a dog on a joyride, so I have no trouble following the scent of Whitaker's beamer. I pass between the Cigna and TVA high-rises, and the track on the CD changes to "Back in Black."

Don't I know it.

It's about here that I notice the same pair of headlights has been trailing behind me for several city blocks, always staying just a few cars back. Maybe I'm just being paranoid, but old habits die hard. I crane my head, trying to pick up the scent of the car and maybe even the driver.

No dice. They're downwind.

The defunct brick train station now serving as the Chattanooga Choo-Choo Hotel appears on my left, the gaudy neon sign on its roof blazing away, and I decide to test my theory. I pass the Choo-Choo and make a quick left turn onto Fourteenth so that I'm sandwiched between the hotel and its neighboring bar, the Terminal. The Terminal is a narrow, triangular building of brick, mortar, and wood. Ironically, it was the actual station hotel back in the Choo-Choo's heyday. Between then and now, it's served as a speakeasy, a casino, and even a brothel. Zora claims there's enough haunts running around in either building to make the hotel in ol' Stevie King's *The Shining* look like Disneyland's Haunted Mansion. None of them have ever harmed me, so I live and let dead. But then, I've never set foot beyond the place's foyer, so I'm hardly what you'd call an expert on the subject of the Terminal.

I pull into the small lot located behind the bar and park so that I face Market. I cut the engine, and the stereo silences.

Then I wait.

Two cars drive by. A blue Chrysler and a green Taurus. A third comes to a rolling stop at the intersection—a white Ford van with tinted windows in the front and none whatsoever in the back. It's the kind of vehicle a plumber or electrician might drive except this one is free of any logo advertising its business.

Because you're not a plumber, electrician, or any such thing, are you, my friend?

I grit my teeth. This is my tail. No doubt. And he's no rook. Granted, I made him, but then I know a thing or two myself. And his choice of vehicle and the fact that he was smart enough to hang back while tailing me lets me know he isn't some pissed off ex-girlfriend or a spook gangbanger I'm dealing with.

If I'm about to go up against a pro, it's best I should do it with a clear head. It's likely he's not alone.

I look down at the slight bulge the mojo hand creates in my jacket pocket. It stares back at me as Zora's chastising voice echoes inside my mind.

What the hell did you do, Ash? You get that shit back on your skinny white ass right now, you hear?

"I had to take it off, Zora." Talking back to the voices in my head is becoming a habit with me. "It was the only way."

Bull. Shit.

"Well what the hell was I supposed to do?"

You could've called me. You could've called, and I would've helped you.

"Yeah, and I never would've heard the end of it."

That may be, but at least you wouldn't have done some dumb shit like this. Anyhow, it's over for now. You got bigger problems need dealing with. Now put that mojo hand back on you right this minute.

The mojo hand and me continue our staring contest.

Ashley Owens.

The minivan turns down Fourteenth, and I sigh.

Slowly, reluctantly, I reach into my jacket and grasp hold of the mojo hand's leather cord. As I do, a suffocating electric current ebbs up from the hand into my arm.

Not having time to properly fasten Zora's trick to my pelvis, I stuff it into my right pants pocket so that it will at least lie near my scar. As quick as I do, an entire cocoon of mojo spins itself over my body, constricting me, dulling my senses, cooling my desire to rip and tear. The monster inside me roars, enraged. But then the cocoon contracts, and the beast is silenced as it's squashed smaller and smaller. At last, it's little more than a pinpoint somewhere deep in the recesses of my soul. My mind clears of the thoughts of blood and death I didn't realize were circling there, and I exhale in relief.

It's been so long since I let the monster free, even for a second, that it's easy to forget how intoxicating and dangerous it can be. For a moment, I'm saddened by the fact that I'll carry the monster on my back for the rest of my life. Then I *remember* and realize it's less than I deserve and better than the alternative.

I take my Glock out of my saddle bags, cock it, and then stuff it into the back of my pants where my jacket will conceal the handle. Locked and loaded, I climb out of the truck and walk up the sidewalk, heading for the entrance to the Terminal. The minivan creeps by. The van's tinted windows prevent me from getting a look at the driver and, at this distance, the mojo hand stops me from catching his scent.

Sometimes it's just easier being a monster.

I push through the Terminal's glass double doors and make a beeline to the tall windows lining Fourteenth. The minivan passes the lot and moves farther down the street before parking at the curb where anyone sitting in the cab could keep a close eye on the bar and any vehicles leaving and entering its parking lot.

Just as I expected it would.

"Fuuuuuck me."

"Excuse me, sir. May I help you?"

I turn and see a tall twenty-something male in a black button-up and trousers I take for the host giving me a faux smile. Behind him, more young people dressed in black wait on happy young couples seated at high-tops and booths made of lacquered birch. There's not a seedy character in the entire joint, much less any spook, and the usual cloud of smoke that hangs over such an establishment is noticeably absent.

In other words, it ain't my kind of joint at all.

"Yeah, kid. This shithole have a bathroom?"

He sees the bruises, old and new, on my face, inhales my current cologne of stale beer and cigarettes, and retreats an involuntary backward step.

"D-d-do you need to go to the hospital?"

"No insurance. Now, bathroom...?"

"Y-y-yes, sir. Just down the hallway there. But I'm afraid—"

"Which side does it face?"

"Pardon?"

"The bathroom. Which side of the fucking street is it on?"

"Ah, south. Sixteenth."

"It got a window?"

"Sir—?"

"Do you not speak English, kid? I asked if the bathroom has a window."

"Yes, but—"

I shoulder past the kid through the bar. Heads turn at my approach to gawk. I snarl at them and move into the hallway where the kid claims the bathroom resides. I open a door made of still more birch marked "Men" and step inside to discover the he wasn't lying. Several windows big enough to climb through line the top of the bathroom's southern wall. I walk over and hop up onto the sink. Moments later, I'm shimmying the last of my body outside onto a small green that extends to Sixteenth Street.

The view around me is a ghost town of empty streets and hulled out business buildings. I drop to the grass and stay low, moving stealthily as I circle around the Terminal's parking lot and then on up the street to where my would-be tail is parked. I take out my piece and move in from behind, taking it slow and easy, making sure I don't give myself away in a rearview mirror.

I reach the driver-side door and spring up as I aim my gun where the driver's temple would be on the other side of the tinted window.

"Get out of the—"

The wind changes, bringing me the smells of body wash and deodorant that I can tell are supposed to be unscented but aren't. Not to my nose. Not when I've only just put the mojo hand back on.

Before I can turn to see who's behind me, my body is slammed into the van's metal door hard enough to knock the wind from my lungs. My gun leaves my hand and skids off down the street. The next thing I know, I'm down on the ground eating pavement. It's damn near a relief when blackness at last comes and swallows me.

TWELVE

In my dream, I'm within the high clay walls circling the Hatra ruins in Iraq. Evening has blessedly fallen. The harsh desert sun has disappeared behind the crumbling sandstone temples, columns, and arches constituting the ancient city's remains, the sky left blood red in its wake. Kowalski is with me. We're dressed in desert BDUs and K-pots. Our M4s are balanced across the fronts of our Alice packs. We stand over a dig, smoking Kowalski's last two Lucky Strikes, guard detail for the Prof and his wife.

She's a looker, the Prof's wife. Her golden hair and skin are the only saving graces of this otherwise bullshit assignment. Kowalski and me have been innocently flirting with her all day, competing for her attentions and, although I'd never dream of cheating on Sarah, it's done my ego good to be the one who's come out on top.

For his part, the Prof has failed to notice, or he simply doesn't care. He's quite a bit older than the three of us (my guess is wifey was once his GA), and I get the impression that if it doesn't concern sticking his nose into two-thousand-year-old latrines covered in sand and dirt, he could give a shit. No pun intended.

Never one to give up without a fight, Kowalski has gone into his version of the Aristocrats joke, trying to outdo the comedians on the DVD that Butler's wife sent over and make Mrs. Prof laugh while impressing her with just how disgusting he can be.

Of course, it backfires, and when I embarrass Kowalski by calling him out on his lack of social skills, Mrs. Prof laughs hysterically. It causes her whole face to light up and makes me think of the way Sarah's does the same when she gets the giggles, and my heart begins to ache for her and Little Anna.

Without warning, the earth beneath the Prof and his wife gives way, and her laughs become screams. I spit out my cigarette and leap down just in time to snag her arm and keep her from plummeting into the dark hole that has swallowed her husband.

Kowalski has grabbed hold of my boots, anchoring the three of us as best he can in the loose sand pouring into the hole where the dig used to lie.

I try to assure Mrs. Prof I've got her, but she continues screaming. It's a high, shrill sound. Like the cry of a bobcat in heat.

But the screams of her husband echoing up from the darkness below are louder still.

Until they aren't.

His cries cease, and I peer into the shadows. There's something about the abyss that feels *wrong*. Like it isn't a cluster of shadows I'm staring at but a living, breathing thing. An animal. A predator.

A nightmare.

I see a pair of eyes like glowing embers divide the pitch, and someone else starts screaming. I've seen horrible things since being stationed here. Dead men. Women. Even children. Shot up or mangled beyond recognition by IEDs. But these two disembodied eyes hovering in the dark are the most terrible, frightening thing I've ever encountered. With a single look, they tell me the universe doesn't work as I've been raised to believe— that God isn't real, or if he is, like the Prof, he simply doesn't give a shit about the living.

It's at this moment I realize the other person screaming is me.

A flicker of movement, and the eyes vanish. Mrs. Prof jerks in my grip like a fishing lure with a huge river cat at its end, and a geyser of blood erupts from the blackness surrounding her to soak us. Then she's yanked down into the darkness. Kowalski and me don't even have time to think about letting go, so we're pulled down right along with her.

I jerk awake. The action causes me an infinitesimal amount of pain. Insult is added to injury when I realize I'm still lying on the sidewalk in the middle of the night. The view down here shows me a rusted green dumpster and a brick building with a pallet-strewn loading dock on this side of the street, and I realize I'm still across from the Terminal, out behind the Chattanooga Choo-Choo's main kitchen. The stench of rotten meat wafting out of the dumpster overpowers even my own funk of soured beer and smoke.

"What the fuck do you want to do with him?" A voice says above me. Except what he really says is, "What da fuck you wan' do wit' 'im?"

"What the fuck you think I want to do with him?" the other voice answers. "I want to fucking have his balls for breakfast."

The stink I smell ain't coming from the dumpster but my newfound friends. This realization brings another: I'm in deep shit.

My two oglers, Stink and Stank, are zombies. A couple of Papa Lim's bunch I'd guess. Hungry ones by the sound and smell of things.

When zombies go without food for any real length of time, the conjuration holding them together begins to break down, and their dead bodies resume the deterioration process. They get slower and slower, both in mind and body, until they at last become the drooling shamblers you know from Romero's films.

But they also get fucking strong. So much so that if they're actually able to get their hands on you, you can forget it, human or spook.

"You eat him, you break the truce. Papa Lim be mad."

"Fuck Papa Lim's old ass. I's hungry."

Stink and Stank sound and smell like they're on a three-day fast, somewhere just this side of stupid and Herculean.

I notice the absence of my Glock and curse as I recall the memory of it clattering off down the street. I scan the area of road where it went tumbling, but my search comes up null and void. Consecrated or not, one bullet to the head would've been enough to put these sonofbitches down. But, as usual, my luck's for shit.

"He do look pretty tasty."

"Yeah, he do."

"You want the legs?"

"Nah. All you. I's a breast man, myself."

That's all I need to hear. I try to jump up and run, but the pain this seemingly simple motion incites causes my legs to betray me. They buckle under, and I collapse back to the sidewalk.

Hands that feel like rot over steel seize the back of my neck.

"Uh uh. Where you think you going, white boy?"

I'm hauled to my feet and spun around so that I look the two zombies in the face. True to Papa Lim's form, they were mere boys when they died, neither one of them a day over eighteen. Their once brown skin is now a yellowish-gray. Their lips have begun to dry and shrivel, peeling back from their mouths, leaving gold- and platinum-capped rictuses in their stead. Diamond studs rest in each of their shriveled ears. They're dressed in the athletic jerseys of Atlanta's pro ball teams. One for the Falcons and one for the Hawks. The bulging outline of a pistol is visible beneath each. Not that Stink and Stank need to use them at the moment. Stupid as they appear, they've probably forgotten the guns are even there. That could prove very lucky for me.

"I don't suppose you boys'd let me go if I was to agree to treat you to a dinner of steak tar-tar?"

"Haha," Stank laughs. "He funny."

Stink draws me in close.

"He dinner what he is."

Stink is missing his left eye. The empty socket is crusted with yellow puss and black, dried blood. The horrid smell emanating from it rivals even his B.O. It activates my gag reflex. If Stink here goes a few more days without sustenance, his empty socket is going to make the happiest of homes for any nest of wriggling maggots in the market for such.

"That's what I thought."

Moving with a quickness, I lift up the front of Stink's shirt and snatch the Beretta resting in the waist of his sagging, baggy jeans. Before he can move, I've put two in his head.

Bang. Bang. He dead. Again.

Stink drops. Freed, my legs wobble but hold. Stank looms large in my field of vision, much closer than I originally thought. I pop one off. It goes wide to grazes his temple and take off the remains of his left ear.

Christ, Ash. How could you miss at this range?

Stank keeps coming. He seizes my arm with one hand and the gun with the other and tries to wrench it away from me. The gun. Not the arm, thankfully.

I fire three more shots into his torso before he succeeds, but I might as well have been shooting peas from a straw for all the good it does. Like I said, it takes a headshot to down a zombie. The brain has to be destroyed. Unlike most spooks, a heart-shot's no good for reasons I will not go into at this particular time.

Stank wads the gun into a ball of scrap metal before dropping it onto the sidewalk. I go for the gun tucked into his own pants, make it, and stick its barrel directly between his orange-tinged eyes.

"Say good night, fucker."

Click.

Click. Click. Click.

Empty. Goddamnit. This fucker was stupid even before he was dead.

Stank takes me in an inescapable lover's embrace and opens wide the gold-plated rictus serving as his mouth, readying to take a chunk out of me. I squirm like the trapped rabbit that I am as he ever so slowly brings his face toward my own. Then light explodes all around us, and I decide to go back to sleep for a while.

THIRTEEN

I wake up to see the sky above me has shrunken to an uneven manhole surrounded by a black void, and I realize I'm not awake at all but merely continuing the nightmare I began before my interlude with Papa Lim's boys. There's a weight on my legs, and I kick and scramble until it sloughs away. I fumble frantically with the flashlight hooked to the shoulder strap of my Alice pack until I manage to switch it on. It shines on Kowalski. Or at what's left of him. His torso ends just below his rib cage in a series of shredded cloth and entrails dark with blood.

I sense movement somewhere out in the void, and cold spiders of panic scurry up my spine and seize hold of my heart. I bring up my rifle and swing my body around, trying to catch a glimpse of whatever's out there so I can put a bullet in it. But all my light falls on are stone walls covered in hieroglyphs far older than the Aramaic covering the ruins above.

A low, guttural sound of something that is neither man nor animal echoes from behind me, and I spin and shoot, too afraid to waste time taking aim. Three quick bursts. I'm scared, but I'm trained. It keeps me from wasting any more bullets than I do.

The sound of my fire reverberates throughout the chamber I'm in for several seconds after I've stopped shooting. Then all is quiet once again save for the noise of my staccato breathing.

Deep, inhuman laughter sounds, this time from my left flank, and I open fire. A blur of motion streaks across my field of vision as my rifle is ripped from my arms. Something hits me with enough force to drive the wind from my lungs and send me flying backward through the air. I pinwheel in open space before coming to land, my face kind enough to break the fall for the rest of my body. There's a crunch of glass, and my light flickers then sputters out.

Gasping for air, the taste of snot and copper in my mouth, I roll onto my back and fumble in the darkness for the small, collapsible spade I carry in my pack. I find it along with one of the glow sticks I carry. I snap them both into place and scramble to my feet. The spade and the arm holding it glow a ghastly green in the glow stick's light.

All else is darkness and silence.

I know what comes next. At least, I think I do. I've lived it a thousand times over in my memories and dreams. But this time, things change. The monster's glowing eyes appear in the dark beyond my periphery, just like always. But instead of surging forward as it rushes to attack, they remain hovering in place.

I can now hear the monster's heavy breathing above my own. The noise is like that of a dragon slumbering in its cave or of one relaxed and content to wait a while longer for its prey to deliver itself into its terrible, fanged jaws.

"We could've avoided this," the monster in the darkness says. Its words are equal parts voice and growl. "We've could've torn the mitutu apart with our bare hands. But you had to put the witch's talisman back on, didn't you?" Apparently, my encounter with Papa Lim's boys is mingling with the reality of the dream.

"F-f-f-fuck you," I stutter, my voice trembling with fear. "I should have let the zombies have us."

The shadowed monster repeats my stuttered words then bellows laughter. My fear starts to give way to anger.

"I'll fucking kill you. Kill us both. If it's the last thing I—"

More hellish laughter erupts from the void, causing my newfound courage to retreat like a whipped dog.

"Please, Ashley." The hackles on the back of my neck rise with the monster's mention of my name. "We both know your threats are empty. If you were still too much of a coward to take our life after what we did to your precious Sarah and Little Ann, then you're certainly not going to end us now, my boy."

Tears swell in my eyes. My bottom lip begins to quiver. He's right, goddamn him. I'm a coward. I murdered my own wife and child, and I still didn't have the guts to kill myself. To kill us. No matter how many times I put a hoodoo-anointed gun to my head, I couldn't do it. God damn me to hell, I couldn't do it.

A pause. Then a deep inhalation of breath. Like a cyclone in reverse.

"Now, now, Ashley. That's all in the past. Your inability to kill us just proves what we already know—that you were Telal even before we were one-in-same. That, from the day of your birth, some secret part of you knew us to be your destiny."

I shake my head. Sobs choke my voice. "No—no—"

"It is the witch who has filled your head with ideas to the contrary," the monster interjects. "It is she who has caused you to fight us every step of the way. Why not rid yourself of her talisman and revel in all that we are, here and now, just as before? The world of man was ours to rape and devour as we pleased once. It could be again."

The monster's voice changes, becoming almost purr-like.

"I know the secret truth that dwells in your heart, Ashley Owens. You desire that of which I speak. As much as I. *Even more so.*"

"Never," I whimper. "Never again."

The monster's eyes blink out, and tittering laughter sounds all around me.

When it addresses me again, the words reach me as if spoken from across a gulf, as if the beast had retreated far beyond the shadows concealing it to some distant planet.

At least for now.

"Never say never, my boy."

My eyes pop open to stare into the white-purplish glow of the tubular, phosphorescent lights overhead. The smell of damp fauna and earth fills my nostrils. It's an aroma not unlike that of Zora's cellar.

There's the sensation of my head, back, and legs resting upon a hard, flat surface. I look down and realize I'm dead. I must be. My hands are crossed over my chest, a bouquet of less-than-fresh lilies resting where they meet. That's when Sandy speaks.

"Hello, Ash. Glad to see you back in the land of the living."

I crane my head back to see an inverted version of Sandy straddling his ten-speed as he tightens the three remaining strings of the acoustic guitar he holds. He's dressed in a rumpled, straw cowboy hat with a rolled, neon-colored bandana serving as its band. A black suit-vest is all that covers the dark skin of his wiry, fatless torso. A pair of black jeans and cowboy boots completes his ensemble. Dozens of flower bouquets stand on the other modest work benches encircling him, making him look like an African-American garden deity.

And perhaps he is these days.

He smiles, his eyes squinting with the gesture. His age could be anywhere from sixteen to sixty.

"How you feeling, Ash?"

As quick as he asks it, I realize I'm feeling pretty damn good. Far better than a man who's had his ass handed to him three times in the past two days has a right to. I feel the bulge of Zora's mojo hand on my pelvis and realize it's back in place.

I move the flowers off my chest and try to sit up, expecting the world to spin. I succeed, and the world does move. But only a little.

"Not bad, Sandy." I say. "I suspect that's your doing?"

I lower my legs over the edge of the bench I'm on, moving slowly.

"I patched you up best I could," he says. "But you can only polish a turd so much." He cackles.

"Haha. Very funny. You responsible for the light show behind the Choo-Choo, too?"

He nods and strums an out-of-tune riff on the guitar in answer.

"That zombie won't be bothering you or anyone else again no time soon, Ash."

I grunt as I slide off the table, my legs still a little wobbly beneath me. I look out the room's sole window, a rectangle of glass set into unfinished brick, and see that it's still night outside.

"Why the hell were you hanging out around back of the Choo-Choo?"

"It's only a few blocks over. Besides, I was told to look for you there."

"Told? By who?"

"God."

Sandy says this as though he were merely reading the time off his watch. That's not surprising. He's been known to utter crazier things since he lost his mind.

That's what happens to folks when they spend too much time in the Crossroads. Human beings aren't meant to dwell in the In Between on a regular basis. It infects them with the Faye madness. This tends to happen a lot with conjure folk.

Just like anything else, conjuration can become an addiction. Often, the more a hoodoo studies his or her craft, the quicker they want to get to the next level, taking every shortcut they can along the way.

You've probably heard rumors of Hollywood actors having to check into mental wards for a time after they've delved so deep into a character that they've lost themselves. Or maybe a famous artist flaking further and further out as he or she strives to create his or her masterpiece. The principle with conjure folk having extended stays in the Crossroads is the same.

A two-headed doctor knows he or she can learn a hell of a lot more a hell of lot faster in the Crossroads, the source of all true mojo, than fumbling their way through hoodoo here in the land of shopping malls and carbon dioxide. But as is always the way with such things, a conjuration addict doesn't know when to say when. Or if they do, they simply choose not to, stupidly believing they must suffer for their mojo.

Sandy is one such soul.

Before Zora, he was the most powerful conjure person in the Nooga. But the overtime he's logged in the Crossroads has reduced him to a mental case forced to live in the back of a flower shop (Don't you dare start to make comparisons), making less than minimum wage and whatever spare change he can squeeze out of the guilt-ridden boyfriends who frequent the bars around town where Sandy takes the shop's useless, wilted flowers.

And he's not an island unto himself.

I can think of a dozen hoodoos here in the Nooga alone who are now homeless and friendless, powerful as the day is long but with too few wits left about them to make any real use of their mojo for good or ill, their purpose entirely defeated by the very steps they took to achieve it.

I reach into my jacket, but my hand comes out empty. I begin patting myself down.

Sandy seemingly produces my pack of Basics out of thin air and holds them aloft. Knowing him, the thin air bit probably isn't a far piece from the truth.

"Looking for these?"

I walk over to Sandy and take the pack from his hand.

"Thanks, Sandy."

I pull a cigarette out of the pack and then continue rummaging around for the lighter I keep stashed there only to come up empty handed.

Figures.

"I don't suppose...?"

The insane, two-headed doctor gives me a smirk.

"A light? Not in here with the flowers, Ash."

I shrug.

"Fair enough."

I reach back into my jacket and produce the photo of Congressman Walker's wife. I show it to Sandy.

Sandy shakes his head. "Bad, bad mojo."

"You seen this woman around anywhere, Sandy?"

"Sure, Ash."

My heartbeat doubles with excitement. I'm going to break this thing in record time.

"Where, Sandy? Where've you seen her?"

He scoffs and rolls his eyes as if I'm the biggest idiot in the world.

"Well, right there in your hand, dummy. What you want with a tiny woman slight enough to fit on a sheet of paper, anyway?"

A thin stream of air presses its way through my lips.

"Right."

He laughs and resumes the tightening of his guitar strings, leaning his head in close as if he were listening to the world's most intriguing secret instead of an out-of-tune guitar.

"I don't suppose you happen to have my gun, do you?"

"Uh uh." Then he's lost again in the guitar strings. I take this as my cue to leave and head for the door.

I pull up just short and turn around.

"Tell me something, Sandy—"

"Yeah?" He doesn't bother to look up from the guitar.

"Did God really tell you look for me outside the Choo-Choo tonight?"

Sandy shrugs. "Him or the devil one, Ash. It's hard for me to tell them apart these days."

"Amen, Sandy. A-fucking-men."

FOURTEEN

I turn and exit Sandy's living quarters through the painted steel door leading into the alleyway behind the shop, beat-up, unarmed, and sans any leads.

I check the time on my cell phone. Two-thirty in the a.m.

"Great fucking night's work so far, Ash."

I lift my gaze from the graffiti-covered brick walls surrounding me and peer up into the night sky. I still can't see the moon, but I can hear it whispering to me from across the gulf of space in a voice like white noise. As the moon waxes full, mojo hand or not, the sound of its call will become a roar in my ears, shouting at me to bite and claw and rip and tear.

I shiver and walk out of the alley onto the street, wishing like hell I had a lighter as I step through puddles of days-old water and trash. To take my mind off my need for nicotine, I review the night's events in my head. Three things stick out.

One: Whitaker bolting.

That can be easily explained, admittedly. A dirt-bag attorney like Whitaker has few friends, so if he caught wind of a spook with my rep looking for him, he'd be sure to rabbit first and ask questions later. That's why I asked James not to mention I had a hard-on for the guy and why Whitaker got the fuck out of Dodge when he did.

That, or he already knows I've got the vipers' number where the congressman's wife is concerned and went running to Jubal to tell him. I don't see how he'd know, but I can't discount the possibility.

If they do have Suzanne Walker and Whitaker caught wind I was looking for him, it wouldn't be hard for him to put two and two together and figure out that the congressman's old buddy and my long-time associate, Senator Jones, put me on the trail of the lady in question. Either way, Whitaker, and by now the vipers, will be watching for me, and that could make my locating the congressman's wife very difficult.

And then there's numbers two and three. Two: Who the fuck laid into me tonight outside the Choo-Choo, and three: Why the hell did they leave me alive?

I know it's not some pissed off chick although there're several spookettes and even a Faye lass or two I'm acquainted with who could've easily pulled off such, though trolling white vans with tinted windows aren't exactly their modus operandi.

Not to mention they probably would've just killed me outright.

Also, I might be broke, but a mugger would've at least taken my jacket. Or, at least, I like to think so. This bad boy is styling-profiling if I do say so myself. But I woke up in the middle of the zombie party with all limbs and possessions intact. And if it'd been one of Papa Lim's boys who'd put me down for the count, that certainly wouldn't have been the case.

It makes no sense whatsoever.

I flip open my cell phone and stare at it. This would be a good fucking time to call Zora if there ever was one. She could loan me a consecrated weapon, maybe lay down a trick to pick up Whitaker's trail if not that of the congressman's wife herself.

But I can't make the call.

Not now. Not like this.

My southern pride won't allow it.

My Papaw was a man who grew up parentless and on his own during the Depression and then fought overseas in W-W-Two. He hails from "the greatest generation," and when he wasn't drunk off his ass, whipping the shit out of my dad, he was teaching him the Owens family values, foremost of which is a page from Charlie Daniels' book, *Don't ask nobody for nothing if you can't get it on your own.*

My father was a good learner both in regard to Papaw's life rules and his use of the rod. Dad passed these teachings on to me with great vigor and, for good or ill, I've taken them to heart.

So, however much I may need to, I'm not about to go begging on Zora's doorstep without the other issues standing between us having resolved and such time having passed so that we both can be sure I haven't made amends simply to call in a favor. Especially considering our history and how I've a track record of fucking up and leaving her to clean up the mess.

No sir.

Besides, in my experience, these types of things tend to have a way of working themselves out.

I decide to head back to the Terminal, get my truck, and regroup. Preferably over a six-pack of tallboys that will see me to sunrise.

I've hit Market Street and am well on my way there when a familiar black Humvee with deeply tinted windows comes rolling up on my left to pace me.

Have I mentioned I fucking hate vipers?

I keep walking, not bothering to look over, feeling naked and scared as hell without my Glock but trying not to show it.

One of Hummer's power windows slides down, and the muffled heavy metal music that had been playing from inside the vehicle momentarily becomes a din in my ears before vanishing altogether.

"Well, well. If it ain't Ash-my-shit-don't-stink-Owens."

I recognize the voice. It belongs to Silas, an old partner of mine from my days running with the vipers. He's a real shit-kicker of a monster whose idea of a good time is to get fucked up on bad mojo and then use hospital nurseries as all-you-can-eat buffets.

That fact that I used to call him *friend* makes me sick with myself.

"What has you out and about at this ungodly hour, Ash? Looking for Whitaker maybe?"

Still walking. Still not looking.

"That's my fucking business."

Silas laughs, his voice hoarse with over a century of booze, cigarettes, and blood.

"Same old Ash."

"Not by a long shot."

"That's not what I hear."

"I could give shit what you hear, Silas."

Still walking. Hummer still keeping pace. Silas still failing to take the hint.

"We had a couple of prospects come in from Savannah the other night looking to join the Nooga brood."

"Oh yeah?"

"Yeah. One a man. Tall. Skinny. Mullet. Not much to look at if you know what I mean. His bride was a looker though. Blonde. Nicest ass you ever laid eyes on. Good tits too. But country as hell."

"You'd know."

He ignores me.

"Thing is, they never showed."

We keep rolling and jawing.

"Sounds like a couple of smart motherfuckers to me."

"Maybe. But I'm a smart guy myself, Ash. And I got to thinking..."

"You thinking, Silas? That's a shock."

"Haha. Very fucking funny."

"Anyway, I start asking myself questions like, who in the Nooga might wish to do harm to my visiting brother and sister? Or moreover, who would have the testicular fortitude coupled with the lack of good sense to make an honest go of it?"

"That's good detective work, Silas. If I ever decide I need a dickhead for a partner, I'll be sure and give you a call."

"And you know what, Ash?"

Still no rise out of him. I'd say Silas is getting smarter with age, but then I know better.

"Not a fucking clue, Silas."

"It was one damn short list I came up with. And you and that nigger witch you run with where at the very top of it."

Silas apparently knows better where I am concerned too.

I stop dead in my tracks. The Hummer follows suit.

I slowly turn my head to face Silas. He has a beefy, tattooed arm hanging out the Humvee's open window. It, coupled with his bald head, expensive Ray Bans, small hoop earrings, and road-warrior goatee make him look like the guy who ate your local MMA fighting club.

But right now, I could give a good goddamn.

"What the fuck did you just call my friend?"

"I called her a fucking no good nig—" Silas begins, but I have already pulled the cell phone from my pocket and slung it at his face. Quick as ever, he knocks it away with his arm, but that's okay. It was only a diversionary tactic, allowing me time to run up and plant my fist right between his eyes. The blow connects, and pricey or not, his Ray Bans shatter right along with his nose. But my small victory is short-lived.

Silas vipers out, his transformation immediately correcting whatever damage was caused by my punch. He seizes me by the throat and hisses at me through tusk-sized fangs as three southern-fried, leather-clad viper clichés spill out of the truck into the street.

They promptly proceed to stomp the living shit out of me. So much for Sandy's healing mojo. Silas quickly joins in the fun, hammering me with blows that could smash through concrete. At least he's precise. He makes sure not to pound any major organs or break any bones, which tells me Whitaker must have taken his concerns with me on up the bloodsucker ladder, and Silas merely has orders to play fetch.

"We're burning darkness," a woman's voice calls from the Hummer. "Search him for weapons, then get him into the vehicle." Her accent is nondescript and lacks either the nasal twang or drawl inherent in the speech of most Southerners. A Yankee then. Or maybe a Midwesterner.

Whoever she is, Silas fails to follow her instructions or even acknowledge he heard her in the first place. He's too busy mashing my face into hamburger. Oh, the ladies he'll be disappointing.

"Goddamnit, Silas. Now."

Silas growls but lowers his fists in obedience.

I spit blood and grin with whatever teeth I have left.

"That's a good boy," I say. "Now roll over and play dead."

Silas roars as his fist swells to massive proportions before my eyes. His blow shuts me up. Black roses bloom in the air. But, unlucky as always, I fail to pass out and spare myself the agony now searing through my body like a live wire.

Even my bruises have bruises.

They pat me down and find the photograph of Suzanne Walker in my jacket.

Silas tears the picture out of his underling's hand.

"New whore, Ash? Looks a bit peeked even for you."

"Your mother was busy this week."

Smack. Pow. Boom.

They toss me into the Hummer like so much dirty laundry. They bind my arms and throw a cloth hood over my head before speeding off for whatever shithole they're wiping their viper asses in this week.

And here I thought I'd lost my chance to see Jubal tonight.

Told you things have a way of working themselves out.

FIFTEEN

Too tired and beat to hell to shoot off my mouth at Silas and his vipers, I take the opportunity to doze during what might just be my last ride to anywhere ever. I'm tied up, after all. Not to mention effectively blindfolded by the dark hood covering my head. There's not shit I can do about my predicament at the moment.

Hell, I can't even smoke.

And a little rest will go a long way if and when an opportunity to better my situation presents itself.

But hey, that's just me. Ever the optimist.

Besides, they say the stupid can sleep through anything. Blaring heavy metal included. And if the lengths I go to get my brains mashed in don't prove I'm a moron, then I don't know what the hell does.

Now, I know what you're thinking. Blindfolded or not, why I don't stay awake and use my other senses to track the Hummer's movements?

Well, I'll tell you.

This ain't the movies, and I sure as shit ain't Sherlock Holmes. I can't find my way around town simply by smell and sound. At least not with my senses dulled by Zora's mojo hand. And I ain't about to let the monster free again anytime soon no matter the situation. When I do, I'm like a ticking time-bomb who may start with some deserving sonofabitches when I go off, but it's a crapshoot as to when and where the killing would stop. I was damn lucky nothing bad happened the first time I removed the mojo hand to go after Whitaker.

So I sleep.

And Suzanne Walker comes to me in my dreams.

When she does, rather than the strung-out mojo addict, she's the former beauty queen I saw that day in the stands at Neyland Stadium—a blonde bombshell who, even in her late thirties, could still stop traffic with a look and break hearts with a smile.

She's dressed in a silk gown of pure white that billows in the breeze and sparkles in the sun. She's a creature of ethereal majesty, and I ache for her with every ounce of my body. She opens her arms, and I go to her and take her in my own. Our mouths lock, and she tastes like the sweetest sin you've ever known—a sin so delicious and wrong it's heaven turned inside-out.

We melt into the warm, green grass at our feet and then into each other. She climbs atop me and begins to ride. Waves of heat and pleasure begin radiating outward through our bodies from where they join, and I realize our mutual bliss is fast approaching. Suzanne gets there first. She yells with pleasure as she clamps her knees tight around my hips. I quickly find my own release and join her in shouting. But my satisfied yell becomes a scream of terror as Congressman Walker appears behind his wife, wielding a butcher knife. He yanks her head back, exposing her throat so that he can make short work of it with his blade. The sun dances along the knife's razor edge just as happily as it did upon Suzanne's gown, indifferent. The monster inside me finds the latter effect as beautiful as the former. More so. But then her blood comes, and everything turns dark and red and horrible.

"Shut him the fuck up."

At first, I'm surprised to hear Silas' voice and the din of heavy metal music in my dream.

But then a ringed fist connects with my jaw, and the taste of fresh blood fills my mouth, eclipsing that of the old, dried variety already lining my gums. I spit it out into the dark cloth of the hood covering my face. The vipers don't know it, but they've actually done me a favor in knocking me awake. Even here, surrounded by vipers in a Humvee likely taking me to my death, is better than staying one second longer in that nightmare.

"Stop your screaming, you fucking pussy."

This voice is younger. Higher sounding. I kick in its

direction to see if I can make it sound higher still. My boot heel connects with something brittle that snaps upon impact and, sure enough, the voice goes up another several octaves. But my success comes at the usual cost of pounding fists and feet.

What I'd give to have my Glock back.

"For fuck's sake," Silas yells. "Can't you shit-birds keep one little were-spook under control? We're almost there."

It's actually a relief when the Hummer and its music stops a few moments later, and the knees and claws pressing me into the floorboard lift away. I'm yanked up and tossed unceremoniously out of the Hummer onto the street. The wind leaves my lungs as I hit, and I spend the next few moments battling to get it back. I succeed just as one of the vipers lifts me upright so that my toes barely touch the ground.

"Smells like shit and Old Spice out here," I bark. "Don't know which is worse, but either way, I'm guessing you're my escort, Silas."

This wins me a perfunctory blow to my solar plexus that relieves me of my newly acquired wind and doubles me over.

"Had enough yet?" Silas growls.

I try to say something clever in response but only manage a few rasping gasps. It's answer enough for Silas. He gives me a shove, and I stumble forward, barely keeping my feet. I think about going limp but decide playing at dead weight would only gain me further unnecessary punishment. I *want* to talk to Jubal after all. And Silas is too unimaginative to do anything but follow what I'm guessing are his orders and take me to him.

Hooded or not, I decide at this point it may indeed do me some good to use my other senses and glean what I can from my surroundings. You never know. Silas definitely ain't the sharpest tool in the barn. He's bound to fuck up and give something away sooner or later.

Still, I'd feel a hell of a lot better about the entire affair if I knew Zora was lurking somewhere close by.

How many times have the two of us been through such a scrape together? Me getting my ass into deep shit and her to come running with the hoodoo just in the nick of time to bail it out? I was never worried then. Not once did I doubt my partner. She was the hoodoo of hoodoos, and we were the team of goddamn teams, say amen.

But now I've fucked that up just like I do everything else. And not for the first time, no less. But this go-around, here alone and unarmed in the heart of what I'm guessing is going to turn out to be viper central, I'm not so sure there's going to be a chance for me to make it right later on.

Or even a chance for a later on.

I'm jerked to a halt just as I hear the sound of a door with hinges in bad need of WD40 being opened. I'm ushered ahead, and my forehead smacks against the door jamb, sending Silas and his lackeys into delighted guffaws. By contrast, the group's sole female gives an impatient hiss. I'm doubting it's out of any compassion for me. But I'm beginning to get the feeling she carries about as much truck for Silas and his boys as I do.

I'm shoved through the door and on down a flight of metal stairs. The soundtrack of viper laughter scores my fall. My descent is blessedly short, but landing still hurts like hell. But I suffer no broken bones or sprung ankles. All things considered, I make out all right.

"We don't have time for this nonsense," the woman barks.

I'm able to tell that the floor beneath me is comprised of concrete. It's colder down here. Darker too. Very little light shines through the fabric of my hood, and what does is only for the benefit of the vipers' trusted familiars, I'm sure. Vipers have excellent night vision, after all. And judging from the echoes produced by my plummet, I'm guessing we've gone down into an industrial-sized basement or maybe a sublevel parking garage. Either would be the type of place Jubal might be inclined to temporarily set up shop. Such locations would have all the necessary prerequisites. Namely, thick, windowless walls to keep out intruders and, more importantly, sunlight.

Lying on the floor, I begin to hear the echoes of scampering feet and claws clicking against concrete coming toward me from every direction. Not at all liking the sound of it, I sit bolt upright and scramble to get to a place where I can kick my still free legs out at whatever's coming, the pain of my landing forgotten. Before I can even think about doing so, something large crashes into me and knocks me back down.

The stink of shit, damp fur, and rotting meat fills my nostrils as more of whatever has attacked me presses in from all sides, sniffing me with large, wet noses. Tasting me with licking, scaly tongues. I scream and kick like a mad man but hit nothing. My flailing brings more laughter from Silas and his crew.

The woman's voice cuts through the dark, eclipsing all others.

"Back!"

Light explodes into the air, searing away the dark. A din of inhuman screeching fills the air. For a moment, through the hood's fabric, I'm able to see a mass of black, feral shapes writhing in agony all around me.

The screeching fades, and a voice more animal than human calls out. "Please, mistress. Forgive us."

"Jesus, woman," Silas shouts, furious. "Watch it with that shit. You could've fucking killed us."

The woman answers, her voice dripping with sarcasm.

"Oh what a terrible loss that would be."

The light extinguishes, its vanishing punctuated by the sound of hundreds of clawed, retreating feet. Whatever attacked me may be leaving, but right now, I'm more scared than ever. That's because I've only just now realized how bad of a fix I'm truly in.

The female. She's not a viper at all.

Jubal has a conjure woman.

SIXTEEN

This is bad. *So fucking bad.*

I rack my brain trying to figure out how Jubal managed to smuggle a conjure woman into the Nooga without Zora and me finding out about it, but fail to come up with an answer. We've befriended the right people. Scared and paid off all the rest. This little nugget of intel should've been brought to our attention posthaste.

Regardless, the fact of the matter is the scales of power in this city just underwent some major rebalancing that is absolutely *not* in the Nooga's best interest, much less Zora's and my own.

Lord help us all.

Two of Silas' goons take hold of my bound arms and haul me to my feet. I don't resist. I'm too thrown for a loop by the new developments to even think about doing such. If I was worried before, I'm scared shitless now. Jubal with a conjure woman on his side? This is one new and extremely fubarred situation.

I've heard of unsavory conjure folk before of course. There's Papa Lim right here in the Nooga. But he's a voodoo bokor, not a true priest of the Loa, and the exact opposite of a true two-headed doctor. At any rate, he and Zora share an uneasy truce.

By contrast, Jubal and his ilk believe that truces are made to be broken. If this conjure lady adopts their mindset, there's going to be hell to pay. In fact, with a hoodoo in his arsenal, I'm surprised Jubal hasn't made a move on Zora and myself already.

But then maybe there's a reason for that. Maybe I'm making a bigger deal out of this woman than she is? From what I could tell with the hood covering my face, her trick was little more than a simple fireworks show. More shock and awe than true conjuration.

Zora can do that kind of shit in her sleep.

Maybe this lady is just some two-bit sorceress? A *sensitive* one or two rungs above mere psychic on the mojo ladder who Zora would be able to make short work of in a battle of conjuration?

I hope to God so.

Otherwise, things are about to get a lot more nasty here in the Nooga.

Man, I need a cigarette.

Having little choice, I allow myself to be led around by Silas and his goons. They push and pull me haphazardly through whatever structure we've entered, moving down one staircase after the next. The air grows still cooler around us with each descent. We walk along straight for a while on a brittle surface I'm guessing is either crawling with cockroaches or littered with glass. The constant crunching beneath our feet could be caused by either. The echoes in this place are numerous and weird and make it hard to tell.

The crunching ceases, and for a time, the air grows moist and fills my nostrils with the damp stench of mold and raw sewage as the steady drip-drip of water sounds all around us. Here, our footfalls become splashes as though we were moving through a series of puddles.

Several twists and turns later, the dripping and splashing peters out to give way to the white-noise hum of electric machinery that we never quite seem to reach.

At this point, I begin to think I realize more or less where we are. But the knowledge does me no good. In fact, it robs me of what little resolve I have left.

We walk in imperfect silence for what seems like an eternity but in reality is probably under half an hour, our boot heels clanging against metal grates and thudding against concrete as we wander left, right, to and fro, our trek taking us ever downward as the air around us grows stale, thin, and ... *smoky?*

At last, we come to a halt. I hear low moans and distant screams echo over the pop and crackle of fire. The fear already in my gut blossoms, spreading into my chest, arms, and legs, freezing me up.

"On your knees." In the second before Silas' boot kicks the back of my legs, I register that it takes longer than previously normal for his voice to bounce back and realize we must have entered a chamber of sorts. But then his boot connects, and my knees slam down into rubble atop hard floor. All I can think about is how bad it fucking hurts and how I'm going to kill Silas for it if it's the last thing I do.

"I hear you're looking for one of my boys, Ash."

If Silas' voice is gravelly, then Jubal's is like a rockslide. It's not quite on par with the telepathy Zora has told me the truly ancient vipers use to communicate—the kind she claims tears through your brain like a Teflon bullet through Kevlar—but it's still the stuff of pure intimidation and has caused the last act of many a brave soul to be that of pissing themselves.

I've heard Jubal speak many times before, so I'm relatively desensitized. Still, even these simplest of words from his mouth manage to raise the hackles on the back of neck. I swallow my fear as best I'm able and speak. I do a pretty good job. Bullshitting is one of my greatest talents, after all.

"Hello to you too, Jubal. Mind having your dog take this fucking thing off my head? It's not like I don't know we're in Old City."

The Nooga doesn't have an underground subway or the like. But what it does have is an entire fucking city beneath the city.

This is not as crazy as it sounds. Remember that big flood I told you about? The one that occurred in 1867 and wreaked so much havoc downtown? With the Tennessee Valley Authority still decades in the future, the Great Flood left the local townsfolk in quite a bind. Their entire livelihoods—businesses they'd built from scratch through years of blood, sweat, and tears—were ever at the mercy of the flood plain. It was build up or die.

So they built, simply stacking shops and businesses on top of those already in existence and filling in around them with dirt and rock.

Over the years, Tennessee's fault line and the natural forces of erosion have their taken toll on the earth covering this forgotten city, reopening passages and byways once buried and now long-forgotten by the humans treading on the concealing layer of ground above.

As a result, an expansive network of subterranean chambers and tunnels now lies beneath the city, stretching up from buried railroad warehouses and cobblestone streets through time and stone to brush against the modern day Nooga.

Over the years, this underground network has become home to countless savage tribes of spooks—those who have now or always shunned any semblance of order, preferring rather to dwell entirely in chaos and darkness.

In other words, it's Hell on Earth and had been thought to be utterly uninhabitable by anyone remotely sane.

At least until now.

It appears Jubal's conjure woman has changed the game. She must be someone with some serious mojo after all. At least that's what I figure. What else could possibly give the vipers the confidence to be running around down here?

As sprawling as Old City is, with a real conjure woman to clear the way and keep things secure, Jubal and his brood of vipers could potentially hide down here forever, draining the city above dry without having to fear sunlight or retribution.

It's the perfect set up.

Now do you understand why I say things are so fucked?

There's a long pause.

"Take off the hood."

"But Jubal—" Silas whines.

"I said get it the hell off him."

Silas' familiar meaty paws tear the cloth hood from my shoulders, almost taking my head off right along with it. Once my eyes stop rolling in their sockets, I take a look around and gauge the situation.

I immediately wish I had the hood back on.

I'm kneeling on top of an old, threadbare carpet so covered in dust and rubble that I'm unable to tell what color it is. The scent of smoke and mold hangs heavy in the air, stinging my nose and eyes and making them water. The smoke comes from the room's source of illumination: a series of iron barrels housing the fires I heard. I'm guessing they're for the hoodoo's benefit. It's not like the vipers need the fire for warmth or light after all.

The barrels are placed haphazardly about the room—a room I realize once served as a library. Tall shelves of wood bearing dusty, worm-eaten books rise up from behind Jubal and his crew, stretching back seemingly into infinity. But they don't. I know because an unending soundtrack of screams and moans is echoing from behind them. They could be cries of either agony or ecstasy. Most likely both considering what is doubtless going on back there.

One of Jubal's scant guard—a long-haired, goat-faced viper dressed in camo from head to toe—snatches a book off one of the shelves and tosses it into a burning barrel. The aged—*likely priceless*—volume gives up its ghost in a small geyser of orange sparks before joining the ashes of its brothers already piled high in the barrel.

Silas looms beside me, his own crew of S&M viper boys on his left flank. All of us face their master.

Jubal sits smoking a cigarette, perfectly at ease in the simple wooden chair serving as his throne. For a viper boss, his attire is relatively plain: a blue chambray shirt, dark denim jeans, and cowboy boots stained irrevocably with many a hard night's murdering. The only adornments Jubal wears that hint at the wealth he controls are a platinum, rodeo-style belt buckle and a black diamond ring. The latter rides his right pinky finger. But all this is really neither here nor there. What gives you pause where Jubal is concerned is his face.

Beneath the receding hairline of his wild, salt-n-pepper hair lays a topography of scars and creases earned in a hundred battles against the Yankees—battles that turned Jubal into a cold-blooded killer long before he ever became a viper. But worse still are his eyes. Unlike his lapdog Silas, there's no rage or hatred in the windows to Jubal's soul. Just emptiness. They are double zeroes—snake eyes in the truest sense. Those icicle blues let you know he can't be bought, sold, or reasoned with and that murder comes as easy to him as breathing did in his former life.

I look away lest Jubal enthrall me with those killer peepers. Jubal's conjure woman stands on his left, an elbow propped on his chair, making it look like we're all here solely for her benefit. Dressed in red silk and form-fitting black leather, she's an Asian fetishist's wet dream. Her dark eyes are large and full of secrets. The full lips resting between her freckled cheeks and delicate jaw are twisted into a perpetual smirk of condescension. Streaks of scarlet are dyed into her luxuriant dark hair, the bulk of which rests in a loose bun held in place at the back of her skull by two long pins. A strap of black leather snakes its way across her hip-length kimono, dividing and accentuating her small, firm breasts before terminating into a bag of hoodoo tricks that looks like it cost as much as my Harley. Despite her Asian heritage, she's almost as long and lean as Zora, the platform-heel go-go boots she wears admittedly helping in that regard.

Kneeling here potentially at death's door, my entire body throbbing with fear and pain, a piece of me that has to do with an entirely different kind of monster takes the time to drink in the sight of her and ponder what it would be like to see still more. Like as not, I'll never have the chance to know.

My mark stands on Jubal's right, leering at me. It's exactly where I expected to find him. Whitaker is still clad in his brown suit and topaz Bolo tie. He's as oily and silent as ever. Like any good lawyer, he knows when to speak and when to keep his mouth shut.

"You look like hell, Ash," Jubal says. "My boys do all that to you?"

I turn my gaze back to Jubal, or more precisely, his cigarette.

"Some of it. Bum one of those off you, Jubal?"

"Give him a cigarette."

Silas huffs beside me. "You got to be kidding me."

"Goddamnit, Silas. You make me repeat myself again, and I'm going to shove your ass topside so you can watch the sun rise. Hear me?"

Silas mumbles curses under his breath as he digs into his cargo pants for a cigarette. A second later, he unceremoniously shoves a cancer stick into my mouth.

I lean forward to show him my hands are still tied behind

my back. "I need a light, dipshit," I say from the corner of my mouth.

More curses, but a lit Zippo appears before my face. It's far enough away that I have to lean forward to stick the cigarette's end into the flame. It comes as no surprise when Silas' fist connects with my outstretched jaw. I see stars as laughter echoes in my ears.

Finally, the room stops spinning, and my eyes focus once again on the Zippo where Silas holds it just out of reach.

"Well, go ahead, fuck-face," Silas says. "Light up already." More laughter sounds from Silas' lieutenants, but that's not what causes the monster to growl deep inside me. Like me, it's simply had enough of Silas' juvenile stupidity for one night. Hell, for a lifetime.

"Do that again, Silas," I say, my voice granite, "and I'll kill you."

Silas cranes his head back over his steroid-swollen shoulder. "Hear that, fellas? Ash here's going to kill me."

This, apparently, is the funniest thing they've heard yet in this long night of gut-busting hilarity.

Silas leans in close as he moves the burning Zippo nearer to my face. "Go 'head, Ash. I won't hit you again. Scout's honor."

I give him an it's-your-funeral-look and lean toward the Zippo. The blow comes, bringing the guffaws of Silas and his gang along with it. But I roll with the punch, avoiding most of the force behind it so that my head stays clear enough for what I'm about to do. Before you can blink, I whip my head back around and drive it into Silas' nose, dislodging the cartilage housed there in a spray of blood and snot and sending it into his viper's brain—a brain every bit as vulnerable as that of a normal human. For a moment, I consider this may have been a mistake. Silas' gray matter can't be much larger than the size of a pea, after all. It's possible the cartilage could miss.

Silas goes rigid, and the laughter abruptly stops. He drops to his knees and falls face-first onto the filthy carpet, a stupefied expression plastered onto his face for all eternity. Fitting.

I shake my head, slinging Silas' blood and snot from my brow. With less difficulty than you'd think, I rise to my feet, watching Silas' former crew from the corner of my eye all the while. The vipers stand frozen in shock, as stupid and incompetent as their now double-dead leader ever was.

"Now, Jubal," I say, "who else do I have to kill to get a light around here?"

SEVENTEEN

"Fucking Silas." Jubal shakes his head as he eyes his former lieutenant's corpse. The firelight from the burning barrels creates a mosaic of light and shadow across the viper boss' weathered face. I keep my eyes trained on his nose so those viper eyes of his don't have a chance to enthrall me.

"He always was a dumb sonofabitch," Jubal continues. "Never got out of the piss and vinegar stage." He motions, and two of his enforcers cart the body away, making for the rear of the bookshelves directly behind Jubal, Whitaker, and the attractive hoodoo. "Reckon it's my fault for turning him when I knew he still had a lot of growing up to do."

Despite being deep in the Nooga's Old City and up to my eyeballs in viper shit, I grin. "Looking at it that way, you might say I did you a favor, Jubal."

For a long time, there's only the crackle of fire punctuated by the moans and screams issuing from beyond monolithic bookshelves. Then Jubal snorts laughter, and I feel some of the tension drain not only from me but also from the viper enforcers ringing the decaying underground library.

"As a matter of fact, Ash, you did." Jubal says, his throat full of gravel, his momentary lapse of seriousness already gone. "Silas had gotten too big for his britches of late. He'd been skimming from me for weeks. I was going to replace him. You've saved me half the time and trouble."

I nod. "Glad to be of help. Now what say you have one of your goons untie me so the two of us can get down to business?"

For a moment, I see the briefest flicker of hesitation in Jubal's eyes. It's not the result of fear. Just good sense. Jubal knows better than anyone what I'm capable of if left unchecked, my small demonstration with Silas the least of it. But whether it's his knowledge of the fact that I don't swing that way these days or the confidence brought on by having a hoodoo by his side, he gestures for one of Silas' former minions to let me loose.

The enforcer snaps to, and I give my freed arms a good stretch. I reach down and snatch the still burning Zippo from the ground and light up at long last. Sweet, delicious tobacco smoke fills my lungs along with nicotine, tar, and a hundred other things that will kill you slowly. I exhale twin streams of gray from my nostrils, feeling hopeful for the first time since I realized I was in the Old City.

Jubal shifts in his chair, blowing out his own cloud of smoke. "I figure you were tailing Whitaker to find me?"

"That's right."

"Well, find me you have." Jubal reaches out a hand. Whitaker produces my now rumpled photo of Suzanne Walker from his jacket and places it into his master's palm. The picture must have changed hands while I had the hood on.

Jubal lifts the photo. "Reason you're here have anything to do with the congressman's missing wife? If so, you're shit out of luck. I don't have her."

I take a moment and consider the fact Jubal could be lying. I mean, how did he even know Suzanne Walker was missing? Sure, he could've put two and two together easily enough. He knows the business I traffic in—he finds a photograph of the congressman's wife on me, it wouldn't be much of a leap in logic to realize she must be missing and that I'm looking for her.

Then again, he could just be playing dumb.

I decide to follow suit. "But you know who does. Have the congressman's wife, I mean."

Jubal shoulders rise and fall in a shrug. "To my admitted embarrassment, I don't. But even if I did, why would I tell you, Ash?" Jubal leans forward, resting his elbows on his knees and allowing the cigarette to hang in his loosely clasped hands. His gaze begins to level on my own, and my eyes find the dangling cigarette. "Point in fact," Jubal says, "favor with Silas or not, why shouldn't I just kill you right here and now?"

I rack my brain for a good answer but fail to come up with one even though my life depends on my doing so. I can talk fast with the best of them, but this is Jubal, and he won't fall for my usual line of bullshit. Actual negotiating has always been Zora's area, and right now, I feel the absence of my partner more than ever with Jubal's icy blues bearing down on me.

Amazingly, my salvation comes in the form of another hoodoo. Jubal's conjure woman places a hand of porcelain fingers with long, painted nails on his shoulder. "The viper who took this picture is operating in your territory without your consent and must be dealt with."

Irritation might have shown on a lesser spook, but Jubal's affect is as blank as ever. "Your point?"

"The hoodoo's familiar is looking for them anyway. Let him expend the time and energy doing so and then turn the guilty viper over to you." She raises those dark, secret-filled eyes to meet my own. "Unless, of course, you have a problem with that?"

I shrug. "No problem here. A dead viper is a dead viper. Nothing would make me happier than for all these sonofabitches to turn on one another."

Suddenly, I'm in the air, my toes dangling a foot above the ground, Jubal's cold, dead hand crushing my windpipe like a vise from Hell. He's crossed the distance between us in less than a heartbeat. I'd forgotten just how fast he can be. It may be the last mistake I ever make. My eyes focus on Jubal's fang-filled mouth. It's almost as bad as looking into his eyes would be.

"I always thought you were smarter than Silas, Ash, and yet here you are, disrespecting me in my own home." Jubal's scarred face is the picture of calm. "I won't have it. You hear?"

I grunt in acceptance before the black roses already blooming before my eyes can overtake me. Jubal drops me onto the floor in heap. I lie there, my hands grasping at my throat as I struggle to suck in the smoky air. There's a gust of wind, and then Jubal's back in his chair, lighting another cigarette. "Get him the fuck out of my sight."

Two arms like iron bars jam themselves beneath my own and lift me from the ground. Everything goes black as the hood is shoved unceremoniously back over my head. Something is crammed into my jacket pocket—likely the rumpled photograph of Suzanne Walker. My wrists are bound, quick and fierce, then I'm dragged away on my heels. I don't bother to put up a fight. There's nothing I can learn here, so the more distance I can place between Jubal and myself, the better.

As I'm pulled along, oxygen returns to my brain, allowing me to think more clearly. I curse inside my head, angry for having gone through all this trouble for nothing. I'd been sure Jubal could lead me to the viper holding Walker's wife. Granted, I'd planned on getting Whitaker to set up a meet with Jubal in a place far more agreeable than the bowels of the Old City, but the result would've been the same: a dead end, a day wasted. I'm still kicking myself sometime later when I hear the Asian hoodoo's voice. "Jubal wants me to take over from here. It's dawn after all."

Released, I drop onto my ass, the sound of my handlers' retreating footsteps echoing in my ears. There's a long moment pregnant with silence, then the hood is torn from my head for the second time. My eyes adjust to the sparse light of the electric bulbs strung along the rubble-littered tunnel I'm sitting in. I'm shocked to see the conjure woman squatting directly in front of me, her long, shapely legs on either side of my own. She's even more beautiful up close. She notices me noticing our closeness and rolls her eyes.

"This what you want?" She reaches between my legs and gives me a squeeze. I grunt and rock back, completely taken by surprise.

"A slave to your cock, every last one of you. But right now, I need you to pay attention. Are you listening?"

I stare at her lips, wet and glistening in the dim electric light as I enjoy the warm pressure of her hand through my jeans. She huffs, and her hand becomes a claw. Instantly, she has my full and complete attention.

"Jesus. Easy."

"Then mind what I say." She leans forward to whisper in my ear, the coolness of her dappled cheek brushing against mine, her hand never leaving me. This close, I catch mingling scents of leather, incense, and expensive perfume beneath the aroma of smoke enveloping her. Enveloping us both.

She says two words, the warm wetness of her breath tickling my ear. She speaks so softly I'm uncertain if I heard her say anything at all. Then the words come again, this time registering fully.

She leans back, and I feel both relief and regret as she releases her hold on me. She cocks an expertly manicured eyebrow. "Got it?"

I nod.

"Good. Exit's straight ahead." She rises to her feet and kicks me square in the jaw with the toe of her platform-heeled boot. The unexpected strike bowls me over onto my back. I lie there, staring up at the tunnel's crumbling ceiling, my chin a crystalline shard of pain.

The hoodoo leans over me and whispers one last parting sentiment into my ear. "Tell Zora we're even."

Then, like all the women in my life, she leaves me alone with my pain.

EIGHTEEN

Hours later, I hit the back of Earlene's, beat to hell from the night and the long walk home. I strip down to the mojo hand and take the world's longest, coldest shower, washing the stink of smoke and viper scum from the bruise that is my body. That done, I collapse onto my cot, soggy and dripping. I reach for my cell, intending to text Earlene, and curse when I realize what's left of my phone is lying in a gutter somewhere down-town—probably next to my Glock.

I walk into the bar, leaving a path of watery footprints in my wake, and buzz Earlene using the phone there. The line connects on the third ring.

"This is Hill. What's your deal?"

"Bear?"

"I just fucking said so, didn't I?"

"It's Ash."

"No shit."

"Your sister there?"

"Hold on."

Earlene's brother shouts her name, and I jerk the receiver away just in time to keep my eardrum from exploding. The next voice I hear is Earlene's.

"What do you want, Ash?"

"Hello to you, too, Earlene."

"Cut the shit, and quit wasting my time. If there's a point to this call, I'd sure like to hear it."

"I need you pick up my truck on your way in. It's parked out back of the Terminal."

"And just how in the hell am I supposed to do that, Ash,

seeing as I'll be driving my own vehicle?"

"Get Bear to ride along."

"Yeah, sure. He's writing. Who knows when he'll stick his gobber up and see daylight again? You're lucky he even answered the phone."

"Ask him."

The irritating sound of Earlene fumbling with the receiver. "Bear, Ash needs you to—"

Bear shouts, the sound of his voice a distant echo. "Go to hell, Ash."

More receiver fumbling. "Told you."

"Oh, well. Hey. What about that cosmetologist friend of yours? The bisexual hottie. You still seeing her?"

"Layla? It's been a while, but yeah. Every now and again."

"Good. Call her. Get her to help you get my truck here and hang out afterward. I have need of her skills, uh, other than those in the bedroom I mean. Having her will kill a couple of birds for me. Oh, and speaking of killing birds, I'm going to need a piece. And a burner cell."

"Regular or leaded on the piece?"

"Leaded."

"Consecrated don't come cheap."

"You know I'm good for it."

"The hell I do."

"Well, you know Zora is."

"You working with her on something? Word is, you two are on the outs."

"What? How the hell—?"

"Big city. Small town attitude. You know how chins wag around here, Ash."

"Yeah."

A long moment stretches by. "What the hell did you get into last night?"

"You don't want to know, Earlene. But I'll tell you what I can when you get here. We good on the piece and the burner then?"

Earlene hisses into the receiver. "Yeah, I suppose."

"Good deal. Earlene?"

"Yeah?"

"Tell Bear I said to go fuck himself."

"He loves you too, Ash."

I hang up the phone and head to my room in the back to get some shuteye. As it is, the best thing I can do for Suzanne Walker at the moment is rest up and let the monster heal me a bit.

I lie down on my cot. As tired as I am, I should be out before my head hits the pillow. But thirty minutes later, I'm still staring at the water-stained ceiling tiles. I can't get the night's events to stop running through my head. The white van tailing me from the Stone Lion. My run-in with Papa Lim's zombies behind the Terminal. Waking up at Sandy's only to almost lose my ass to Jubal in the Old City underground.

And what is up with Jubal having a hoodoo? And a fine looking one at that. The exotic scent of her is still in my nostrils. The vision of her in my mind's eye makes me ache with a pain that's sweet and even sharper than that of my bumps and bruises. Without even realizing what I'm doing, I reach down and take hold of my already stiffening sex as I think about her.

It appears she and Zora know each other. That's more than possible. Genuine hoodoos run in small circles. Even if conjure folk don't know each other personally, they've likely heard of one another. But this seems more than that. She said for me to tell Zora they're even, as though they have a history—and as though the conjure woman's suggestion to let me go had an ulterior motive, that of saving my bacon in payment of a debt she owes Zora.

Regardless, she obviously knows more than she's letting on to me or to Jubal. That can be the only reason for her whispered message to me in the Old City before she let me go.

What game are you playing at, darling?

I think about calling Zora, again, for the low-down on Jubal's two-headed doctor. But again, my pride refuses to let me get up and get to a phone.

"Maybe after I get some sleep," I tell the poster of Kasey Lansdale on my wall.

I close my eyes and concentrate on my memories of the Asian hoodoo. Her large eyes. Her delicate mouth. The porcelain hollow of her throat. I pleasure myself as I imagine her long, lean body beneath mine, her six-inch stilettos stabbing the air at impossible angles.

Deep inside me, the monster cackles and calls me a lust-struck fool. I find release, and it shuts up. But then sleep at last finds me, and I begin to dream of blood and death.

Earlene and her buddy pull in to the bar's parking lot just as the sun vanishes, and a chill bites the air. I drop the butt of my cigarette and grind it out beneath my heel. Earlene hops down from my pickup, her short, spiky hair brushing the top of the door frame as she exits.

I nod in greeting.

She returns the gesture. "Ash."

Her buddy hops down from Earlene's immaculately clean, Volunteer-orange Bronco, and I immediately realize this ain't the cute, petite cosmetologist I'd asked her to bring.

"What the fuck, Earlene? Where's Layla?"

Earlene grunts. "Couldn't make it."

"I'm afraid you're stuck with me, big boy." Earlene's pal's words sashay out of *his* mouth as a series of lisps. He's a short, dandy cuss in his late forties—his skin spray-tanned the color of Earlene's Bronco, his hair a salt-and-pepper construct mortared with enough gel to survive anything other than a direct hit by a nuclear warhead. He's dressed head to toe in lavender. The tails of a neckerchief of the same hue disappear into the thatch of graying chest hair exposed by his open shirt. A hard, plastic case cast in what's apparently his favorite color dangles from his left hand.

"Who are you supposed to be? Fucking Snagglepuss?"

He glides toward me, the picture of feminine grace despite the generous testicles revealed by purple pants so tight they could've been painted on. "Today's your lucky day, Mr. Owens." He places a well-manicured hand on my chest.

"Yeah?" I say, ignoring his hand. "Why's that?"

"Because the Doc is in."

"I need a makeup artist. Not a fucking MD house-call."

His hand rises to the hard line of my jaw.

"Your foundation is nice, but otherwise, you haven't given me much to work with here."

Sleep and the monster have healed the worst of my injuries, but my face is still bruised and swollen. "I'm having a rough day."

"Not to fear, Mr. Owens. They don't call me 'Doc' for nothing. This way, if you please."

He drops his hand from my face and struts into the bar like a model sashaying down a catwalk, the metal case swinging to and fro at the end of his arm.

"Well, ain't he the fucking Queen of Sheba?"

"Don't complain, Ash. Doc's good. Damn good. And it's going to take that by the looks of you."

"Everyone's a critic."

Earlene waltzes into the bar. I mumble the word *shit*, giving it extra vowels via a long stream of E's so that it comes out "Sheeeeeit" and follow after her.

Two hours later, the overpowering smells of Airwick and the Doc's cologne dancing the tango in my nostrils, the hottest thing I've ever seen peers back at me from the cracked mirror of the women's bathroom.

"Damn. I look *good*. You've outdone yourself, Doc."

Earlene's reflection shrugs, its broad shoulders rising and falling within the mirror. "I'd fuck you."

Doc places his hands on my shoulders, leaning over me from behind as he presses me into the barstool I'm sitting on. He stares into the mirror in awe of what he's done. "You are a vision, Mr. Owens. Quite possibly my masterpiece."

"Can't argue with you there."

I rise from the chair, stumbling at first in the ridiculously high heels I'm wearing. I peer at my reflection in the Dollar General-brand full-length mirror screwed into this side of the bathroom door.

The queen of all drag queens stares back me, blinking smoky, long-lashed eyes and puckering full, glistening lips painted the color of blood.

A slinky black dress clothes me from white-powdered shoulders to the fishnet-covered thigh. Strings of pearls drape my neck, and a faux diamond tiara rests in my auburn wig. Long black gloves and a matching purse complete my ensemble—well, that and the derringer Earlene hid for me in the latter. Considering I don't exactly have a waistband I can shove a Glock down, it will have to do.

Queen's weapon for a queen, I guess.

Speaking of queens, looking in the mirror, I decide I look like Audrey Hepburn in *Breakfast at Tiffany's*. Well, that would be stretching it a mite. But I am a dead ringer for Justin Bieber dolled up like a New York socialite, and that's even more girly.

"You even concealed my tats." I twist and turn, examining my reflection from all angles. "I barely recognize myself."

"Isn't that the entire point, Mr. Owens?" I look down to see Doc clinging to me like a second skin as he gazes longingly at my reflection. "You're beautiful."

"I'm flattered, Doc. But it ain't happening."

"Never?"

I grin. "Well, you could at least start by offering to buy a girl a drink."

NINETEEN

A lan Gold's. Those are the two words Jubal's Asian hoodoo whispered into my ear down in the Old City. Gold's is a discotheque smack in the middle of East Chattanooga. Though technically it's within Papa Lim's territory, like the Stone Lion, it serves as a sacred, neutral ground thanks to some ancient mojo inherent within the land. Zora once filled me in on the details, but that was an age ago, and while I may know a thing or two about hoodoo, I can't be expected to keep up with all that shit. That's what I rely on Zora for to begin with.

Anyway, Alan Gold's caters to all manner of norms, deviants, and spooks, including drug-dealing vipers. And it's vipers peddling bad mojo who're holed up with Suzanne Walker, wife of Congressman Jack Walker. So to Alan Gold's I go.

But my face and rep, bruised and battered as they are, are well known. Especially among Papa Lim's crew. So I can't exactly walk up in there, all smiles, batting my baby blues as I make inquiries about the congressman's wife. Not if I want to get anywhere.

That's why the Doc and me are rolling in Earlene's pristine orange Bronco rather than my mud-soaked pickup (*Also, it might throw off whoever the fuck was tailing me last night if they start feeling froggy again and go looking to jump*). I've enlisted the Doc as both my stylist and date for the evening. The makeup job and shemale, cocktail dress-wearing Hepburn getup he's disguised me in are damn fine pieces of work if I do say so myself and should more than hide my true identity. The cover story that he's come up with—that I'm an old *country mouse* friend newly out of the closet who he wishes to introduce into *proper society*—should be a good excuse to make rounds and ask questions too.

My hand leaves its two o'clock position on my truck's steering wheel to grab a pack of Basics from the glove box. "You know, Doc, you're pretty good at this."

"At what, Mr.—"

"Cut that shit. Call me Ash. You've seen me in my birthday suit for Chrissakes."

A wicked smile splits his face. "Indeed, I have."

I roll my eyes and light up. I remember my manners and offer the pack to Doc. He takes it, removing a cigarette and the lighter I'd stuffed inside the pack's clear outer wrapping. He lights up, moving with exaggerated poise and grace in even this small gesture.

"All right then, *Ash*. I'm pretty good at what?"

"The disguise. Coming up with a backstory for me."

"It was no bother. In a former life, I designed costumes for *Beach Blanket Babylon*. Even acted from time to time as an extra."

"You've lost me."

"*Beach Blanket Babylon*. It's a musical revue out in San Francisco. The longest to ever run in America. Jo Schuman Silver runs it now."

"The guy who put nipples on the Batman suit? That explains a lot."

Doc chuckles. "Wrong name. Wrong gender. *More or less.* But the show has hosted celebrities. Even royalty."

"No shit?" I say, genuinely impressed.

"No shit."

"Damn. How'd you end up here?"

A cloud of smoke leaves Doc's mouth, but no words follow for a long time. When they do, his face is dark, and his eyes are gazing off to somewhere—or more likely, *some when*—that only he can see.

"That's…a long story. One I'm not quite comfortable telling right now. But the reader's digest version is that I'm from here in the Nooga originally. And my hometown taught me how to create a believable fantasy as much as my time out West ever did."

"Sorry. You've lost me again."

Doc puffs. "What was that you called me when we first met? 'Fucking Snagglepuss' I believe?"

"Yeah." I expel twin streams of smoke through my nostrils as I take the off-ramp leading onto MLK. "About that. There's something you'll have to come to grips with if you and me are going to hang, Doc. The fact is, I'm an asshole."

Doc grins. "Do tell?"

"As a consequence, I blow a lot of shit. There's no malice behind it. In fact, it's when I've stopped talking and started ... well, taking a more *assertive* approach in my communications that one needs to worry that I may not, in fact, be all that sweet on them. But by then, it's usually too late for one of us, admittedly."

Doc ashes into the Bronco's tray. It's an understatement to say Earlene will be pissed to find we've been smoking in here. But it's the little things in life that make it all worthwhile, you know?

"So you're saying, Ash, in order for us to be friends, I have to put up with your bullshit even when you're in the wrong?"

My eyebrows rise in question. "Ain't that what pals are for?"

"So long as you realize that bullshit blows both ways, you uncouth piece of redneck trailer trash."

I feel an involuntary grin spread its way across my face. "Doc, you and me are going to get along just fine."

I take a left off MLK onto Georgia Avenue, passing business buildings as I head uphill and due north. "But anyways, you was saying how being from here taught you how to make believe or something?"

The Doc nods. "More or less. Being different in the Scotch Irish-descended South is hard even now. Back when I was growing up, it was impossible."

"Don't I know it."

"Oh, please, *Bo Duke*. What could you possibly—?"

The monster rages up from the pit of my stomach to shine in my eyes, making it impossible for the mojo hand on my hip—much less the makeup and faux eyelashes—to hide it. I stuff my demon back down before it can spread any farther, but the damage is done. Doc looks at me, the spray tan drained from his Botoxed face.

"I see." Doc recomposes himself. "But unlike you, I didn't have the benefit of your natural, country boy cool to mask who I am inside."

Doc throws a foot onto the dash. He uses the bend of his knee to prop up the elbow of his smoking arm. In an instant, his body language has gone from delicate and ethereal to loud and brash. "I had to make my own fucking 'cool' so I could get by around assholes like you."

I cock an eyebrow, recognizing the cadence of my own voice in Doc's words. "Doc, you're just full of surprises, ain't you?"

He deflates, his foot leaving the dash as the bones once again vanish from his wrists. "It's all an act, Ash. One I hated myself for perpetrating back then though I couldn't see an alternative at the time. It was only with maturity and a much-needed change in scenery that I was able to be who I really am."

Twin jets of smoke leave my nostrils. "Then you've got one up on me, Doc. People die when I reveal my true self."

I take a right onto McCallie, bypassing the lone tower that serves as the remains of Chattanooga's first church, then slide by stately Memorial Auditorium to ride between the brick and mortar buildings comprising the halls of UTC. The college's campus is mostly deserted, a large portion of the students who bustle through here during the day elsewhere at this hour, enjoying Chattanooga's night life, many of them probably gathered at mine and Doc's destination for the evening.

We drive by the large, decrepit homes constituting fraternity row before crossing the overpass that takes us by Warner Park and several blocks of small business buildings, the latter with iron bars encasing their windows.

In no time, the gravel of Alan Gold's overflow parking lot is crunching beneath the Bronco's tires.

We step out of the vehicle, and a shiver that has nothing to do with the night's chill makes its way down my spine. I look over at the hundred-plus acres of identical headstones staring back at us from the iron-gated veterans cemetery across the street. General Grant had over twelve thousand men buried there after he took the Orchard Knob region of the Nooga. Today, the cemetery holds three times that number, and its residents hail from every war America's fought beginning with the very first and ending with whatever cluster fucks we have going on at present.

Even a thick-headed spook like me can feel the necro-mojo radiating from the place like heat from an oven. It's some volatile shit that even Papa Lim won't touch directly even though it's smack dab middle in his territory.

Not that it would be hard for him, Zora, or any other hoodoo hereabouts. After all, opening the gates of Hell is no problem. It's shutting said gates afterward that's the real trick.

"You all right, Ash?"

"Huh?" I turn my head to gaze slack-jawed at the Doc.

"You kind of zoned out there for a minute."

I drop the remains of my cigarette and grind it out beneath my stiletto heel. "It's nothing. Let's roll."

I hobble a few steps through the gravel, nearly breaking my ankle six times within as many feet before I give up and launch the heels into the night. "How the fuck does anyone walk in those things?"

Doc shrugs. "You get used to it."

I sigh, hoping I can tolerate nothing but a pair of fishnet stockings protecting my feet from the ground. On the bright side, no matter how bad it proves, it has to be better than trying to walk in those shoes. *Je-sus.*

We cross the street, bypassing two men engaged in a heated argument. The first is a black man. His shoes are polished, and the creases of his khakis have been ironed to a knife's edge. The other is a white man who wears clothes that look like they came off a rack at Kmart circa 1990.

I see them size up Doc and me from the corners of their eyes even as they bicker. That and the way they move tell me these are two fools you don't want to mess with.

"Well, pardon the hell out of me, Mr. Collins," the black man says.

"Oh go fuck yourself, Leonard," the white man says, his voice full of East Texas twang.

Once they're behind us, I glance at Doc.

He shrugs. "Lovers' quarrel?"

A bald, tattooed bouncer straight out of the Village People greets us at the entrance of the conjoined brick buildings serving as Alan Gold's. The echo of heavy bass reverberates from the bar's interior.

We flash the bouncer our IDs (mine fake), pay cover, get our hands stamped, and walk inside. Here, the thumping music smacks me full in the face, walloping me along with the acrid-sweet smell of burning hemp. A line of men ranging from the bouncer's end of the spectrum to that of Ted Koppel's await their turn in the bathrooms of the short hall leading from the entrance to the club proper. Some sip beer and make out. Others merely lounge against the walls with the same feminine body language characteristic of Doc. The latter size us up on sight. But the looks they give me are nothing like of those of the East Texans we passed in the street. These men gaze at me with hunger in their eyes. The kind a veggie plate won't cure.

Doc takes me by the hand. "Sorry, boys. He's taken." I give my admirers an apologetic look as Doc leads me out of the hall into the club. Here, the din of music becomes deafening, and the pot-smoke smell all but suffocates me. The club's patrons are comprised of every race, age, gender, persuasion, life, and unlife imaginable. All of them crowd shoulder-to-shoulder on the small dance floor and the encircling, iron-railed promenade above, looking on as a crude drag show consisting of little more than pole dance routines ensues at the dance floor's center.

I touch Doc's arm and lean in close so he can hear me. "I'm getting a beer."

He looks me up and down, obviously sensing I'm a little off balance. "Want me to come with?"

I shake my head. "I'm a big boy. I just need a minute. This is your turf. Sniff around for vipers slinging mojo. But don't seem like you're sniffing around. I'll catch up."

He nods, and I step over to the perfect square of a bar on my right that divides the club, pining hard now for the lifelines of alcohol and nicotine to help me stay afloat among these waves. Granted, I've handled clubs a lot bigger and a lot louder in Atlanta and Nashville and a hell of a lot of other places. But in the end, I'm just country boy who needs open space and the ability to hear himself think.

The music blessedly diminishes to an almost tolerable level, and I raise a hand. "Bud."

The bartender—a grinning, moonfaced fellow with gelled hair and a single gold earring—ignores the others lining the bar to take my order. Being eye candy has its advantages. Once upon a time long ago, I felt ashamed for taking them. But then I grew up.

I light up as the grinning bartender sits the Bud down in front of me. "It's on the—"

"I've got it, Gregory."

The bartender's grin fades. His eyes become twin boiled eggs above his plump cheeks. He gives two quick nods that cause his double chin to quiver. I turn to see who's gotten his ass in such a pucker.

A tall, shirtless male who could've been chiseled from marble glides onto the seat beside me. Well, that's not exactly right. It's *gold* that's the stone in question here. Tall, sparkly, and handsome here is flecked with the stuff from his curly blond head to his bronze washboard of a waist. I see still more flecks swirling in his feline eyes and realize, while the Doc's beautification of me is only skin deep, my suitor's glamor runs to his gilded Faye bones. For all this, it's the luminous shade of green lining his bee-stung lips that has my attention. My beautiful, would-be suitor is a bad-mojo addict.

Midas eyes my drink. "Budweiser? I would've thought such a *lovely* as yourself would be inclined to imbibe something more … cosmopolitan."

I shrug and blow smoke in his general direction, playing hard-to-get. "Simple girl, simple tastes."

He grins, taking the bait. "I'm Raphael."

I take a sip of beer. "That's nice, Ralph."

He leans in, and the pleasant, earthy scent of him crosses through the smoke to find me. "What would be nice is if I could get to know you better."

I take a drag off my cigarette. "I said I'm a simple girl, Ralph, but I'm not *that kind* of a simple girl."

"Then exactly what kind of—?"

I whirl and press my index finger to his thick, jade lips, shushing him. I stroke his mouth, teasing him while making it clear what I want. "The kind who likes to party. That cosmopolitan enough for you?"

His lips encircle my finger and suck for a moment, making it clear what he wants in return.

"Are you carrying?" I ask.

He releases me and shakes his head. I feign displeasure, and he quickly adds, "But I know where we can score." Ralph stands, his hand extended. I take it, and he leads me through the gyrating bodies on the dance floor, the music cranking up to full blast once again.

We reach an exit overseen by another member of the Village People and step out into the night air. With a little luck, Ralph is about to lead me straight to Suzanne Walker's viper enablers. Bad-mojo peddlers are pretty territorial after all. If Jubal's hoodoo was shooting straight with me, then this could soon be a wrap with Suzanne Walker safe back home and her husband's money safer still in my wallet.

Ralph whirls and gently presses my back against the bar's brick exterior. He takes my face in my hands and leans in to kiss me. I readily comply, even entwining my tongue with his own. Never let it be said Ash Owens does anything half-assed. He tastes of deep earth and bad mojo, and whether it's the contact high or Ralph himself, my head starts to spin.

We separate a moment later, both of us snickering. He takes my hand once again and leads me around the building's corner. I'm shocked to come upon Doc standing by the bar's dumpster, a large figure the streetlights don't quite reach standing at his six.

"Doc, what are you—?"

"I'm sorry, Ash. They didn't leave me much choice."

Something eclipses my field of vision, turning the world black.

Like I said, Doc's just full of surprises.

TWENTY

When my face smacks cold concrete through the hood of cloth masking it, the first thought to run through my mind when the stars clear is, *It's fucking freezing in here.*

I'm pulled to my knees. The hood's jerked off my head (this is getting to be a bad habit). My wig goes along for the ride. The bite of blood and freezer burn hangs heavy in the frigid air. My eyes adjust to the room's cold, fluorescent light, and my breath appears before me in visible puffs.

I'm in a meat locker. Only it ain't sides of beef impaled on the steel hooks jutting from the ceiling.

The flayed corpses of men, women, and children encircle me like an upside-down forest of grotesque, red trees. Papa Lim stands before me in a space where the carcasses have been cleared away, his back turned, a bear in sunglasses, derby hat, and full-length mink coat.

He's flanked by two attractive female gangbangers packing heat, one a chocolate-skinned brunette, the other a pale, platinum blonde. The black girl on the bokor's right holds a jewelry box engraved with veves—symbols of voodoo.

The girls are bodyguards. Toys. But more importantly, they're zombies. I know this because, unlike Lim and myself, there are no telltale puffs of breath issuing from their mouths. Lim's kept them extremely well-fed so as to keep at bay the more severe side effects associated with his personal brand of spooks.

A living black boy just getting his whiskers stands before the trio, shirtless and shivering. Whether it's from the cold or just being in Papa Lim's presence, I don't know. Most likely, it's both.

Two more zombie gangbangers—these male and not so well-fed—stand on the boy's six, grins on their ashen faces.

Lim slips out of his fur coat and hands it to the white girl on his left. The shirtless ganglord is a mountain of tattooed muscle and gut. More veves here. Knives pierce hearts, and serpents writhe as sinews bunch and fat rolls. There's even a few brands.

Lim's not quite on par with Baby Shit in size, but he's pretty damn close. It's all the more impressive as Lim doesn't have any Faye blood in him in so far as I know. In fact, he's only human, speaking in the loosest of terms.

The bokor glances back at me over a branded shoulder the size and shade of a cannon ball. "Be with you in a minute, Ash." His massive head rotates on its axis. Halts. Reverses. "Or should I say, *Ashley.*"

I glance down and see my disguise of cocktail dress and fishnet hose is on its last leg. The purse and its derringer are gone, and I can imagine the streaks of makeup that must now be smeared across my face.

It's oddly satisfying to know my drag-queenization at the Doc's hands is ruined.

Fucking rat.

I don't know who I should be madder at: Doc for screwing me or Earlene for being so clueless as to spread my cheeks so he could.

Lim shakes me out of my reverie by plunging his right hand into the boy's solar plexus. The sight and sound of the boy screaming as Lim worms a bloody arm elbow-deep into the kid's torso are horrible beyond imagining. It's made all the worse by the bokor's soft chanting—as though Lim is singing him a lullaby to add insult to injury, mocking his death even as he delivers it.

Then it's over. Lim pulls out of the boy like a selfish lover, the youth's heart grasped in the bokor's blood-drenched hand. The boy's eyes find it, and for a moment, his shrieks intensify. But then his heart stops beating, and all sounds fade. The boy's eyes roll back in his head, and he falls. The zombies to his rear catch him and lower his lifeless body onto the gray concrete.

I halt the bile that had been making its way up my throat

and look up to see Lim gently laying the boy's disembodied heart into the jewelry box held in the black girl's outstretched hands. Lim continues to chant over the heart for a moment then halts and grins when the bloody organ flexes once, twice, and resumes a steady rhythm.

He gestures for his minion to close the box, and she obeys.

A moment later, the boy's eyes flutter open. The corpse rises into a sitting position under its own power and looks around the room, its gaze at last settling onto the open wound resting in its gore-drenched abdomen. The undead thing reaches inside itself. When it withdraws, its hand is glistening and red. The zombie stares at its blood-soaked knuckles, its expression a macabre parody of newborn curiosity.

Remember when I said it wouldn't do you any good to try and nail a zombie in the heart? *It's already been done.*

Lim gives a deep belly laugh and tears off the flayed limb of a nearby corpse dangling from a hook. He saunters over to the boy and kneels before him, all but shoving the small, severed arm into the zombie's face.

"Eat," Lim commands. "You belong to Papa Lim now. And Papa Lim takes care of his own. Eat."

The boy takes a reluctant first bite then begins to chow down, digging into the meat like a hog into slop. Papa Lim's massive gut trembles with laughter once again. He rises to his feet and pats the boy's face like a doting parent, leaving red palm prints on the boy's downy stubble.

A fifth zombie, another attractive black girl with twin afro-puffs on either side of her head, appears from among the forest of corpses carrying a damp, white towel. She helps Lim clean his arm of blood and then slides several rings of gold and diamond onto the sausages masquerading as the ganglord's fingers.

The white girl appears at the bokor's elbow, his mink coat held in her arms. With her help, Lim slips back into the garment, the numerous platinum chains he wears bouncing against his broad, tattoo-etched chest.

I'm seized from behind by hands that feel like rot over iron. More zombies from Lim's gang, their pants halfway down their asses. They drag me over to their master.

Lim turns in my direction, his shadow falling across me where I kneel like the veil of night itself. "Now, Ash. If you wanting to do some bad mojo behind that woman's back, why didn't you just come see your old homeboy, Papa Lim?" His sunglasses fall. Rise again. "You dressed up like a bitch 'cause you need a big dick in your skinny white ass, Papa Lim take care of that for you too."

I will my eyes to burn a hole through Lim's sunglassed face. "I been fucked by bigger and meaner than you, Lim."

He smiles, his grill flashing like that of an oncoming Mack truck. "True that, Ash. True that." Lim turns away, sauntering toward the rolling desk chair being brought into the clearing by one of his gangbangers. "Let him up."

The zombies haul me to my feet, and I shrug off their hands. Lim takes a seat before me, his makeshift throne crying out in protest as it takes on his weight. One of Lim's minions hands the necromancer his would-be scepter—a black cane with a diamond-studded-skull pommel. Another dead flunky places a cigar the size of a hog leg in Lim's mouth and lights it for him.

"Don't suppose you have one of those for me?"

"'Fraid not."

"Figures."

Lim leans his bulk forward over his cane, eliciting new groans from the chair. "Care to tell me what the fuck you doing running around East Chatt? I mean, since me and your handler have a truce and all—?"

I roll my neck, popping about six-hundred aching vertebrae, tired and irritable as the night is dark. "We really going to play this bullshit game, Lim? I can understand you bringing me here to test Zora—dribbling a little piss in her pool to remind her you're still out here, swimming around. But you know as well as I do Alan Gold's is neutral ground and that you ain't going to do a goddamn thing more to me than you already have. You got nothing to gain by it, and you stand to lose far too much."

I'm bluffing. Lim may or may not be as powerful as Zora, but he's definitely as smart. I'm counting on the latter to save my bacon here. Lim kills me, he knows she'll rain umpteen kinds of holy hell down on him and his crew for it. That kind of war is expensive and would end things for Lim in the Nooga one way or another.

Then again, Lim didn't get to be who and what he is by playing it safe, so I keep talking so he doesn't have time to be insulted by my bullshit.

"Besides, I get the impression Doc told you exactly what I was up to."

The brim of Lim's derby rises and falls in a nod. "Doc says you was looking for vipers peddling bad mojo."

"That'd be right. You know of any?"

Lim's chair screams as he settles back into it. He gestures with his cane, and the shriek of metal sliding against metal echoes throughout the meat locker. The flayed corpses encircling us jerk forward, bumping into one another with meaty thuds. They continue to move in assembly-line fashion, bypassing us on either side, new carcasses replacing the old. The last of these part, and two hooks adorned merely with twin skulls come rocketing out of the carrion toward me, locomoted along the overhead rails by two of Lim's zombies.

The impaled skulls come to an abrupt stop directly in front of me. I curse when I see the twin sets of fangs housed in their rictus grins.

Jets of smoke leave Lim's nostrils. "These two fools come up into Papa Lim's territory slinging bad mojo, he think, 'Oh hell, it's on.' Jubal done fucked up and give Papa Lim the excuse he been wanting to expand his operations.

"But my soldiers, they take these vipers, find out they ain't Jubal's. Ain't no one's. Don't know the players, the rules, or the game. They just fucking stupid."

Lim puffs his cigar. "Papa Lim say, fuck it. Vipers is vipers, Jubal's or not. Papa Lim can still use them as his excuse."

Lim adjusts his bulk, and the chair moans beneath him. "Vipers say, 'Don't kill us, Papa Lim. We got something for you: the wife of a congressman.'"

I keep my best poker face at Lim's mention of Suzanne Walker. Not that Doc hasn't already told the bokor exactly why I was at Alan Gold's, but there's no need for me to confirm it outright.

Damn it. If Earlene was stupid for bringing the Doc around, I'm dumber than shit for having let my tongue wag any more than was absolutely necessary.

Lim smokes and scratches the nappy scruff lining his jaw. "Papa Lim says, 'Okay, boys. Show Papa Lim what you got. He able to make something out of this, maybe he have mercy on you.' But we goes, and turns out they got shit. No congressman's wife. And no money or pull Papa Lim might have got by laying hands on her. Lim exhales a large puff of smoke that moves to encircle his head in a cloudy halo. "So they got no mercy from Papa Lim."

I repress the sigh of relief wanting to escape me.

Could the bokor be lying to me? Of course he could. But my instincts scream otherwise. So do those of the monster living inside me. While one set or the other might be fooled, both of them in tandem are the best fucking truth radar you're going to find.

Suzanne Walker's still out there somewhere. Alive, hopefully.

Lim pushes back the brim of his derby and scratches his head with his cigar hand. "So Papa Lim was back where he started: Use these two shits as an excuse to make war." Lim grins, his grill flashing. "But then he get a better idea. Instead of using the vipers to make war on Jubal, why not use them to make peace?

"Send Jubal the heads of these two, disrespectful dumb fucks as a gift. Say, 'Sure, Jubal. They're vipers in East Chatt. But Papa Lim knows they was disrespecting you by being here just as much as they was Papa Lim. Look, Papa Lim clean house for both of us. No muss. No fuss.'"

"Mighty big of you," I say.

Lim chuckles, his body heaving, his chair groaning. "Yeah. I'm all about bringing motherfuckers together and shit." Lim's body shoots into the air like an abruptly shifting tectonic plate. His chair rockets back into the dangling corpses, squealing like a kicked dog as it goes.

Before I know what's happening, Lim shoves his way between the dangling skulls. He winds up with his cane and lets fly. Pain fills my face, and blood fills my mouth as my nose repositions itself against my right cheek.

I drop.

Lim's shadow eclipses me.

"You can hide behind the bitch's skirts for now, Ash. But sooner or later, Papa Lim's coming to tear out your heart and eat it."

Cigar smoke wafts into my face, filling my broken nose and burning my lungs. "And on the day he does, it won't just be Papa Lim coming at you but the vipers and every other motherfucking enemy you and that cunt have made here in the Nooga."

Lim stands, his black silhouette forming into that of an Easter Island statue. Then he and his crew are gone, and I'm left alone among the slaughtered to contemplate just how long it will be before I join their ranks.

TWENTY-ONE

Earlene worms her fingers between my nose and the cheek it rests against. "On three. One—" I yell for Jesus, Mary, and Earnhardt as she snaps my face back into proper alignment. As it's morning, no one's around the bar who would give a damn.

"Fuck, Earlene."

"Oh, hush your cocksucker, Ash. You're fine." She hands me a damp cloth—one she's just used to clean the bar. "You're healing so fast it was either pop that thing back into place or let it grow out your ear."

She wipes her hands down the sides of the gray Vols T-shirt stretched across her blockish shoulders, finishing up on faded blue jeans riding similarly shaped hips.

I press the cloth to my face, tasting water and grit as I let it catch the new gush of blood spilling from my nose. "The kind of help you've been giving lately, I can do without."

"What the fuck were you thinking? Do you even really know Doc?"

Earlene nods. "He's real sorry, Ash. Said so when he brought back the Bronco." Earlene turns away and begins stocking the cooler beneath the bar with Longnecks. "Personally, I could've cared less what he did where your ass was concerned. I was just happy to have my ride back unscathed."

"He served me up to them on a fucking platter, Earlene."

Earlene halts her work and turns back to me. "Uh huh. What was he supposed to do? Fight off Papa Lim and his spooks all by his little self? All for you? Ash, you saw Doc. He ain't a force of nature like Zora or a brawler like you and me. He's a gentle sort. It wasn't me went asking him to tag along with you into the bullshit at Alan Gold's. You want to blame somebody for getting yourself screwed over back there, go look in a mirror."

I can literally feel the cartilage in my nose knitting itself back together as beats of time and silence march by. "I'm going to go take a shower."

Earlene returns to her work. "Yeah. You do that."

The water in the shower is cold and rust-tinged, but it does the trick of washing the night away. Afterward, I plop onto my cot, intending to just rest my eyes for a minute only to be awoken sometime much later by the sound of Earlene's insistent yells.

"I said, 'phone,' goddamnit."

It's Zora, I think as I rise from the cot. She's come around and wants to say she's sorry for shooing me out of her house the other day. And not a moment too soon as I'll be damned if I knew what I was going to do next.

I enter the bar, holding my towel closed with one hand. Earlene sits on the other side at a booth, going over her books. Without looking up, she pokes her thumb in the direction of the ancient, wall-mounted phone behind the bar. Its corded, beige receiver lies mouthpiece-up beside a clear, plastic container filled with limes. I pick up the receiver and put it to my ear.

"About goddamn time you called."

"Ashley?" I feel a frown work its way across my face as Senator Jones' nasal twang comes back at me through the receiver. "What are you talking about? I've been trying to reach you on your cell phone since yesterday."

"Yeah," I say, unable to help but grin as the image of my cell busting Silas in the nose flashes in my mind. "I'm going to have to get you a new number to ring. But you can leave messages for me here for the time being."

"Everything okay?"

"Just fine, Senator."

"No trouble then?"

"All proceeds according to plan," I lie. "I'll have it all taken care of in no time."

"Just how soon are we talking about, Ashley? I know how capable you are, but our mutual friend, well—" Jones gives me a chuckle I'm sure is aces at convincing his constituents that, beneath the suit, tie, and obscene fortune, he's just a good old boy like them. "We were both hoping to have had this wrapped up soon."

"Quality work takes quantity time, Senator."

"Yes, but—"

"When have I ever let you down, Bob?"

A sound like air leaking from a tire. "All right then, Ashley."

"Good deal. Be in touch."

I hang up the phone. "Fuck. I'm screwed."

Earlene huffs. "What else is new?"

"I've wasted a hell of a lot of time trying to run down two viper pushers only to have them turn up *finito* in East Chatt. If I want the senator's money, I need to turn up a lead on the congressman's wife. Fast."

Earlene stuffs more longnecks into the cooler. "I'd say tell Jones to go fuck himself, but you're right. You still owe me for the consecrated piece and ammo it took you all of one night to piss away."

I nod my head. "And I don't finish this job, word will get around. Then, before you know it, my phone stops ringing all together. And you know what that would mean."

"Yeah. You'd have to get a real fucking occupation. Oh, the horror."

The world letterboxes before my eyes. "I don't see you punching someone else's time clock."

"Yeah, but that's my luxury now, ain't it? I mean, I ain't living in the back of someone else's bar, you know?" Earlene stands straight and folds her beefy arms across her chest. She gives me a look she usually reserves for some asshole who has just yelled, "*Roll Tide.*" "You know what you've got to do."

I look at the beer-stained carpet and swear as I rub the back of my head. "Yeah, I reckon I do."

I pull up to the curb outside Zora's bookshop on Frazier Avenue and cut the Harley's engine. Once free of my brain bucket and goggles, I take out my cigarettes and light up.

I inhale a bounty of sweet carcinogens as I take in the coffee shops, yoga gyms, and restaurants that fill the two-story brick buildings rising up along either side of Chattanooga's North Shore—what I like to call *Hipster Row.*

White Collar MILFs and their LL Bean-clad children line the sidewalks. The ones on my side of the street give me a wide berth. They don't make eye contact, but they look at me all the same—both the moms and their coed daughters—every one of them coming to the conclusion that I'm bad news. I know because, even with the mojo hand on my hip, I can smell their fright.

And their excitement.

I close my eyes as I finish off my cigarette. The sound of children playing in the park behind Zora's building and the scent of the Tennessee River farther beyond reaches me on the breeze.

I ground out my cigarette beneath my boot heel and fish a Citgo-issue bouquet of roses from my saddlebags. They weren't the best quality of flowers to begin with, and the ride over hasn't done anything to improve their condition. They lie in my hand like a bundle of post-coital cocks, their petals dull and already beginning to shrivel. "Better than nothing."

I turn at last and face the brick and mortar building housing Zora's bookshop—Winder Binder. Well, Winder Binder ain't exactly a bookshop, per se. Imagine your favorite indie bookstore got a little too tipsy one night and, in a moment of under-the-influence indiscretion, made angry, passionate love to the local bad boy folk art gallery. Winder Binder is the bastard offspring that would result.

In other words, it's pretty cool.

I step through Winder Binder's glass-paned door, thankful for Zora's open invitation where I'm concerned. The tinkling of the antique bell above my head is accompanied by a bounty of familiar, welcoming sights, sounds, and smells. The creak of the birch hardwood floor beneath my boot. Row after row of bookshelves and their musty aroma. The abstract, asymmetrical depictions of Chattanooga hanging on the walls. The soft echo of alternative country-rock intermingling with the mechanical sounds of retro, wind-up toys. It's like the place is cohabited by Grandma Moses, J. Roddy Watson, and Dr. Seuss.

The shop's empty save for Geena and me. Zora's understudy stands behind the front counter, immersed in the latest fantasy by that Whedon-worshipping feminist she so adores. Geena's a pretty little bird of a girl with dark hair and an impressive honker that's pure Italy and pale, freckle-dappled skin that's sheer Ireland.

"Hey, kid."

The young coed looks up from her novel, exposing huge, crystal-blue eyes beneath a set of rockabilly horn rims that complement her female hipster ensemble. The pupils in those eyes are incredibly tight. It's like they're contracting, trying to form into something better suited to a cat's eyes. Their appearance is a genetic echo of whatever Faye ancestor became a branch along her family tree centuries ago. No doubt Geena's heritage is what gave her the knack—the mojo that made Zora take notice of her and take her on both as employee and apprentice.

Geena's gaze drops to the bouquet in my hand. "You shouldn't have, Ash."

"Next time, kid. Promise."

"Ha. Don't go to any trouble on my account. Not for those."

"Zora about?"

"She's upstairs—and expecting you. She said you could come on up."

I tense. "She what—?" I relax. "What am I saying? Of course she's expecting me. She's Zora, after all."

Geena nods in agreement.

I look down at her novel. "Ain't you a little old for Puss in Boots?"

Geena huffs and rolls her eyes. "You know very well there's a lot more to these books than that."

I shrug. "Maybe it's new paint. But it's still the same old barn. Not that that's a crime, or anything. Quite the opposite."

"Then what's your damage?"

"No damage. But you know me. Spreading cheer and winning hearts wherever I go. Anyway, you like this guy, you need to try Grossman's *Magician* novels. You'd dig them, kid."

"Don't call me kid."

"Sure, kid."

Geena snarls in frustration and then dives back into her book. I take that as my cue to exit and saunter off, losing myself among the rows of bookshelves, first those on the shop floor proper and then those in the back room beyond. The latter house Zora's more exotic tomes, the kind where the titles include words like grimoire and end in some *omicron* or other.

I plod up the creaking, wooden stairs that lead from the back room to the small apartment above the store. The latter is furnished with a desk, couch, and bed. It's the desk that Zora uses most—both for the shop's administrative needs and the moonlighting she and me tend to get up to.

I reach the purple door serving as the apartment's entrance and pause, taking in all the veves scrawled across its surface as a final defense. A defense against what, you ask? The truth is, I haven't a clue. Whatever super spook could make it this far into Zora's shop sans an invite would have to be unimaginably powerful, and I've yet to come across the like.

I knock. Zora's voice calls out to me from the door's other side. "Come on in, Ashley." She knows it's me. I'm surprised though I know I shouldn't be.

I push the door open and step inside what amounts to an attic room, complete with a wall angling into the ceiling at forty-five degrees. The twin bed and floral-patterned couch I've crashed on so many times are there, flanked by a couple windows and still more bookshelves. There latter are built in and house even more ancient, cryptic volumes than those in the back room below.

Zora sits at her desk, working on her Mac as she balances herself atop a gray exercise ball. She's dressed in form-fitting jeans and an indigo top with an intricate, tribal pattern, empire waist, and flowing sleeves. She twists to face me, hoods over her eyes, a smile on her lips. "For me?"

My breath catches in my throat. Not at Zora's teasing but just at seeing her. Her royal-blue eyes. Her mocha skin. Her aquiline nose. The scar by her bee-stung lips. Every time I look at Zora after having gone a week, a day, or even a minute without seeing her, it's—*well, shit*—it's like love at first sight, but only over and over again.

I know. That shit sounds stalker even to me. But it doesn't make it any less true. I mean, the power this woman has over me. And I ain't talking mojo neither. At least, not *that* kind of mojo. But it makes me uncomfortable. No one's had this effect on me since ... *since Sarah.*

The memory of Sarah—of what I did to my late wife—shakes me out of my reverie.

I look down at the pitiful flowers in my hand. "Stupid, huh?" I say and toss them into the small empty pail by the door.

"No, Ashley. You may be a lot of things, but you're never stupid. Although sometimes you come pretty close."

A moment pregnant with silence passes.

I summon every ounce of willpower available to me and look Zora in the eye. "I'm sorry about how I acted at your place. That shit was immature."

"Yes it was."

"I can't promise I won't act that way again."

"Wouldn't be you if you could."

"But I'll try."

"And you wouldn't be you, either, if you didn't."

"So are we—?" I jerk my head to gaze at the door leading into the apartment's half-bathroom as the flush of a toilet cuts off my words mid-sentence.

"Ashley, you need to prepare yourself."

I cut my eyes at Zora then look back onto the bathroom door. "Prepare myself? For what? Who the fuck's in there, Zora?" There's the sound of a running faucet, then the bathroom door opens to reveal Suzanne Walker. "You've got to be fucking kidding me."

TWENTY-TWO

Suzanne Walker scowls at me from the bathroom doorway of the apartment above Zora's bookshop. She's dressed in a gray sweatshirt and blue jeans. Despite her modest attire, she looks a hell of a lot closer to the blonde bombshell I sat behind that day at Neyland Stadium than the skin-and-bones mojo addict I saw in the photograph her congressman husband gave me when I agreed to find her for him. That likely means one thing.

"Unfucking believable, Zora. I've spent the last couple days running around Chattanooga, getting the shit beat out of me by what feels like just about every spook in the city, trying to find this chick, while you, my partner and supposedly best friend, have been sitting up here, playing hoodoo nursemaid to her the entire time."

Suzanne Walker folds her arms across her chest. "Who the hell is this loudmouth? He looks like a third Duke boy. *A slow one.*"

Zora scowls. "Like Ashley said, he and I are partners. But if he keeps acting a donkey, the best friend part is going to be up for discussion."

My cheeks go hot with fury. The monster inside me howls. "Why didn't you call me?"

Zora rises to her platform-heeled feet. "I gave my word that I wouldn't." Her hands drop to her hips. "Besides, I should ask you the same question. Anyone here should've reached out and touched someone, it was you, Ashley Owens. How was I to know you were looking for Suzanne? I might be a two-headed doc, but I ain't the freaking NSA."

"Yeah, but—?" My words are interrupted by the soft meow.

The black werecat from Zora's—this time in full feline form—slinks out from behind the exercise ball. She catches sight of me and hisses.

"The cat's here too?" I throw up my hands. "Of course."

Zora scratches the molly behind her ears. "Wanda is Suzanne's housekeeper, Ashley. And her friend."

Zora lowers her voice to a mumble. "Maybe her only one outside of us by the sound of things. Anyway, it was she who led me to Suzanne and helped me bring her back here where she'd be safe."

"Safe?" I ask. "From what? No, wait a minute. That's all right. On second thought, don't tell me. You want to keep secrets from me, Zora? Fine. I should thank you, after all, as my job here is done."

Zora's eyes laser in on me. "Job?"

The color drains from Mrs. Walker's face. "Jack hired you to find me, didn't he?" Her eyes drop to the cat. "You were right, Wanda."

I nod. "Yep. He's paying me to weed out both you and your journal. But a bird in hand is better than two in the bush, so if you will excuse me, I've a got a phone call to—"

Mrs. Walker barks a laugh. "Journal? Is that what Jack told you? That sonofabitch."

The congressman's wife leaves the bathroom to pace the apartment's blonde hardwood. The color returns to her face as a crimson born of barely controlled rage. Tears form at the corner of eyes, threatening to fall.

"It isn't any ordinary journal that Wanda has hidden for me in the Crossroads, Mr. Owens."

I snap my head in Zora's direction. "Crossroads?"

Zora nods and cuts her eyes back to the congressman's wife. I follow suit.

"If it's not a journal, then, Mrs. Walker, what exactly—?"

"Jack hasn't paid me any attention in years." Mrs. Walker continues, executing her tight boxstep. "But the moment I've got him by the short hairs, he sends one paid lackey after another chasing after me." Mrs. Walker halts in step. Her gaze moves up my body then back down. "He must really be getting desperate."

I shrug off the insult. "If it ain't a journal I'm looking for, Mrs. Walker, then what exactly would you call it?"

A snarl crosses Mrs. Walker's already enraged face. "Nothing less than the key to bringing my husband down, Mr. Owens. Him and everything he represents."

Mrs. Walker's chin begins to quiver. The tears that had been threatening to fall finally do. "For what he did—"

Somehow, Zora's there to catch the congressman's wife before she can collapse. Zora helps Mrs. Walker over to the bed and sits her down, letting her sob onto her shoulder. The werecat hops up into Mrs. Walker's lap and rubs its furry body against her as low, consoling purrs issue from its throat.

What a fucking mess.

I'm sure the congressman's wife is right. I knew Jack Walker for a sorry S-O-B the moment I caught scent of him. He's probably guilty of all sorts of things. When you've climbed as high in life as he has, you tend to have stepped on a lot of people in order to get there. But the question as far as I'm concerned is, *so what?*

How's bringing down a high-rolling politician with a Jesus fetish going to put money in Ashley Owens's pocket? The answer is, it won't. And that's really the bottom line here, now, ain't it?

I should head downstairs and call Jones right now and be done with this shit. I could be collecting my money in an hour, getting liquored up in two, and sexed up in three.

But I stand here like a damn fool, waiting on Zora to talk me out of this perfectly good-sense solution. And one good thing about Zora—the best of things, really—she never disappoints.

"Ashley," Zora says on cue, "we have to help this woman."

"And just why in hell do we have to do that? I took a job, Zora. For money. One that would appear to be close enough to completion for me to wipe my hands clean and get paid."

Zora's amethyst eyes lock onto mine. "When I found you, you was Jubal's boy, Ashley. Is that how it is with you and Jack Walker now? Or was it Senator Jones that hooked you two up? I bet it was. That sounds just about like ol' Senator Bob. So is that right, Ashley? You Jones' boy outright now?"

I surge forward, a literal growl in my throat. "I ain't nobody's boy, Zora." The werecat yowls and shoots out of Mrs. Walker's lap like an obsidian comet.

Zora lets go of Mrs. Walker and stands, my equal in height, her face inches from my own. "Then get your head out of your ass and stop acting like it. Money ain't shit to the Ashley Owens I call friend. Not when there's more important things on the line. And it don't get no more important than this, Ashley."

My body deflates, my anger leaving me on the thin stream of air pressing its way between my lips. "What, exactly is *this*, Zora? Jack Walker's a bad man, sure. I knew it the moment I laid eyes on him. But what politician ain't? What the hell's going on here?"

Zora waves me off. "You wouldn't believe what little I've been able to get out of Suzanne, Ashley, so I ain't going to waste either of our time trying to convince you.

"But I suspect what we find in Mrs. Walker's journal will do the trick. For you and everyone else."

I shake my head. "We've tried to bring down big players before, Zora. It never ends well. For anybody."

"Players are players, Ashley. But this one might be setting policy for the state someday soon or worse."

"You keep me in the dark, Zora, and then want to talk politics? No, I've had enough of this bullshit. I've got a phone call to make." I turn and head toward the door. It slams closed in front of me of its own accord.

Zora's mojo.

I turn, mad as hell, the monster inside me furious and ready to explode onto whatever and whomever it may, mojo hand or not. But when I turn around to see Zora, or rather, what's she's become, it's all I can do to keep from pissing myself.

"Ashley, I'm your friend, but I've appealed to your good nature for the last time. You need to listen to sense on your own right now."

Zora's purple irises have expanded to encompass the whites of her eyes. The shadows of her face have deepened, making the already hawkish angles of her countenance that much sharper. And she seems to have grown a few inches taller in the last thirty seconds. But beyond that, there ain't anything that's really different about her physically.

But there is something in the air around her—an invisible but palpable force that's causing the hairs on my arms and the back of my neck to stand on end. Something that has even the monster inside me cowering.

I've seen Zora gather her mojo a hundred times, but only once or twice has she ever wielded it against me, personally, in an offensive manner. And believe me, you do not want to be on the receiving end of a hoodoo's wrath—especially not one of Zora's power.

Not that she could spray me with fire conjured out of her ass or some other F/X movie bullshit.

But then again, here, in her own sanctuary, who knows?

I decide not to risk it.

And the truth is I love Zora, and I'm sick of being on the outs with her. She always knows what's best anyway.

I raise my hands in surrender. "Okay, okay. Easy, Zora. I give."

Zora relaxes, the white returning to her eyes, and the room seems to contract as whatever powers of conjuration had been pushing out against it leave.

"Like I said, Ashley: You may be a lot of things, but stupid isn't one of them."

I start to resume our argument, but Zora hugs me and kisses my cheek, and all thoughts of anger and dissent go up in the warm flame of her body.

We release each other, and I try not to reveal how empty it leaves me.

"We've got to go into the Crossroads and get that journal, Ashley."

"From what you say, the Crossroads is a big place. How are we supposed to—?"

The werecat yowls, her courage returned, as she appears out from under the bed to rub up against Mrs. Walker's shins.

Of course. Wanda the werekitty. She hid the journal in the Crossroads. She'll know where to go to find it.

"Okay, then," I say, my face a grimace. "Let the good times roll."

TWENTY-THREE

There are about a hundred different ways of accessing the Crossroads in Southeast Tennessee alone. But Wanda the werekitty, being the simple creature she apparently is, took the path of least resistance when she decided to hide Suzanne Walker's journal and entered at Powells Crossroads. I'm not kidding. That's literally the name of the place. It's one of many Podunk towns in Marion County, just on the other side of Suck Creek Mountain, and it's where the barriers between our reality and everything else are thinnest, at least in the Chattanooga area. The town probably got its name because its founders had some inclination as to the significance of where they'd decided to put down roots.

But I don't know, and I tend to only bother Zora about these things when necessary. Point is, getting into the true Crossroads from there shouldn't prove any trouble. Hell, we probably won't even need Zora to conjure us over. Like as not, we'll be able to head down a trail and simply wind up in one of the gaps in Creation.

I call up Earlene and imply what's shaking without saying it outright and say that we need her for a few hours. She tells me to go to hell and hangs up. A follow-up phone call from Zora does the trick. Like myself and so many others in the Nooga, Earlene owes Zora and then some.

By the time Earlene comes sauntering through the front of Winder Binder that evening, she's actually worked herself up into a good mood. At least for her, at any rate.

"Where's Geena?"

I look up from the Cherie Priest novel I found back among

the shelves. Not one of those steampunk yarns. This is one of her early works, and it's a doozy. "Zora sent Geena home for the evening. Asked me to help watch the front in her stead."

Earlene huffs. "Why the hell didn't you say Zora was the one asked you to call me?"

"I tried. Someone was too busy cussing a blue streak on the other end of the phone line."

Earlene shrugs the cement blocks she calls shoulders. "Yeah, well, I figured all helping you would do would be to cost me another piece or worse."

Zora appears from between the bookshelves, her tree-hugger top and platform heels exchanged for a form-fitting gray workout shirt, leather boots, and a very illegal sawed-off shotgun. "Speaking of guns, you packing consecrated, Earlene?"

Earlene winks, and a Glock I recognize and know to be blessed appears in her right hand as if by magic. "Never leave home without it."

Zora closes the distance to Earlene. "Good." Zora turns the sawed-off over in her hand and holds the grip out to Earlene. "Take this too. The shells and the shotgun itself have been prayed over. No spook wishing me and mine ill should be able to come up in here, but one can never be too careful."

Earlene takes the weapon and gives it a pump, ejecting a shell and loading another. Satisfied, she reloads the escapee in the back of the line. "So who is it you need me guarding while y'all go traipsing around the In Between?"

"A congressman's wife. Come on. She's upstairs. I'll introduce the two of you."

Ten minutes later, Zora reappears at the front of the shop carrying an oversize gym bag, the black werecat at her heels. Zora's free hand moves at high speed, and something comes flying through the air, heading straight for my head. "You're driving."

I snatch the keys she's thrown at me. "Your Thunderbird? Nice."

Zora shakes her head. "Uh uh. I'm leaving the Thunderbird for Earlene. We're taking her Bronco."

I slouch, defeated, and mumble under my breath like the

petulant child I am inside.

Minutes later, we're in Earlene's Bronco, passing her establishment in Red Bank to take a left onto Suck Creek Road for the Tennessee River Gorge. It's unseasonably warm this evening, and our windows are down to allow in the wind and the chirps of frogs and crickets. The river keeps pace on our left, reflecting a clear sky the same color as Zora's eyes. Tonight, the river's smell is damp and pure and holds no hint of industrial sludge.

Churches and tackle shops pass us on our right, playing a game of peek-a-boo from among the mountainside greenery.

Zora closes her eyes and smiles as she sticks her hand out the window to let it catch the breeze. Sitting here beside me, she appears every bit the Earth goddess, and it's as though all this is here solely for her enjoyment.

In other words, it's a wonderful night in the South, and it has the two of us feeling fine.

We're not the only ones either. Wanda the werekitty leaps up into the front seat between Zora and me to take advantage of the sights, sounds, and smells filling the Bronco's cabin. As the weather has us all so cheery, when I feel her tail brush repeatedly against my steering arm, I don't even make an issue of it.

By the time we're up and over Suck Creek Mountain, night has fallen. We ease into the outskirts of Powells Crossroads beneath country star shine, driving through dark, open fields interrupted only by the occasional illuminated house or barn. We hit the town proper and crawl by gas stations that have fallen to ruin in the decades that have passed since they last serviced a vehicle.

We come to a complete stop where Highway 27 crosses Alvin York and R.A. Griffith Roads to become 283—the crossroads for which I'm guessing the town was named—at least the paved version of it.

I pull the Bronco over to the curb and park it. Zora gets out of the car without a word, the werecat on her heels. I follow after, lighting up as I move to the Bronco's rear. Zora opens the vehicle's hatch and reaches for the oversize gym bag. My hand gets there ahead of hers. "I got it."

One corner of Zora's mouth cocks up in a grin, turning her scar into a scribbled line. "Well, I guess chivalry isn't dead after all."

I blow twin streams of smoke out my nostrils. "So what now?"

Zora turns and begins heading down Alvin York Road. "Now, we walk." The werecat trails after her.

I watch them go for a moment. "You ain't going to work a conjuration?"

"Don't need to," Zora says without looking back. "Not here."

I was right then. Here in Powells Crossroads, slipping over to the In Between should be as easy as, well, a walk down this road. Still, I wouldn't be me if I didn't find some reason to protest. "We just going to leave the Bronco here?"

"'Don't see anyone around who's going to take it, do you?"

I look up, realizing I don't. The Quick-E-Marts, mechanic shops, and Mom-and-Pop diners flanking 283 up ahead are completely deserted. Me, Zora, and the kitty could be the last living creatures on Earth.

"Early risers here in Powells, I guess," I mumble. But I figure the truth is that here, where the barriers between reality and everything else are thinnest, it don't pay much for normal folks to be out after dark.

I finish my cigarette and toss it aside. I head down the road after Zora and the werekitty, allowing my sensitive sniffer and the star shine above to guide me. Just as I catch up to them, the smell of the air around us changes, becoming cleaner and full of the scents of abundant flora and fauna. Then, as though with a flip of switch, twilight replaces the darkness around us. The pavement beneath our feet also vanishes, leaving behind a path of rock and dirt that divides a narrow field of high grass polka-dotted with blinking lightning bugs.

Wanda now stands before me on two legs, in her human form, thankfully clothed in a black dress with a frilly white collar that I'm sure was worn by any number of house servants in the late nineteenth century.

Zora's attire has also changed. Her workout shirt and jeans

have been replaced by a kaleidoscopic Haitian-style turban and frock. Beads adorned with crosses, ankhs, and other religious symbols dangle from her neck, matching the hoops hanging from her ears. She could be Marie Laveau herself.

The transformation of my own clothes is far less glamorous. In my dust-caked jeans, flannel shirt, and brogans, I look like a real hayseed. *Or a hipster.*

Even the gym bag has become a cloth knapsack tied to the end of a wooden stick.

I turn and look in the direction we came from. Dark forest now encroaches where the humble shops and restaurants of Powells Crossroads once stood. As I stare off into these unpopulated pines, cedars, and oaks, the frogs and crickets that had gone silent with night's fall once again return to their song. But I'm sure these ain't the same critters we heard on our way in over Suck Creek Mountain. Hell, I doubt the looming mountain in the East is the Suck Creek Mountain we know at all.

"Where to, now, Wanda?" Zora asks.

"In there. The journal's in there."

I face front to see Wanda pointing at three rectangles of orange light looming ahead of us in the distance. Faint guitar music accompanied by equally faint whoops and hollers drift down to us from the rectangles of light, pegging them as the door and windows of a juke joint silhouetted in shadow.

The place wasn't there before. That's how the Crossroads work. The reality of the In Between is a fickle thing, constantly shifting to meet one need or expectation or another. Such depends on all sorts of things, like who has what need and who's expecting what outcome. It makes having a guide all the more valuable when traveling the In Between.

I catch a lightning bug in my hand. "You sure that's the place?"

"Of course I'm sure," Wanda snaps.

I release the lightning bug, and it flies off to join its brothers.

As I turn away from Wanda to look back at the juke joint, the corners of my eyes reveal the werecat's true spook form to me: a bipedal feline over five-foot tall—one with black fur and multiple sets of thick, human teats. I look directly at Wanda again, and her dark skin and black dress return. Crossroads mojo at work.

I shudder to think what the In Between reveals where I'm concerned.

"I think it's time we broke out the hardware," I say.

Wanda scowls. "Carrying a gun up in there like to get you killed. *Or worse.*"

I grin and drop to a knee as I untie the knapsack. "Being up in there without a gun liable to have the same effect, I reckon."

I open the knapsack. The Glocks and Berettas Zora usually stocks it with are absent. Or rather, they've been changed into something else. By the Crossroads.

Along with Zora's hoodoo accoutrements, the knapsack now holds a derringer, a snub-nosed .38, a straight razor, and a pocket knife.

I stuff the knife and .38 into my jeans and hand Zora the derringer. I start to give Wanda the straight razor, but she holds up a halting hand.

"Got my own."

I catch the glint of metal in her other palm, and I realize she means this literally.

Where in the hell has she been keeping that all this time?

I shrug and close up the bag.

"We can leave the rest, here, in the grass," Zora says. "I wouldn't have time to work any real conjuration up in there should we get ourselves in a fix anyway."

"The Crossroads may have changed our weapons," I say. "But they're still consecrated, right?"

Zora nods, and I toss the knapsack and pole into the high grass growing alongside the path, scattering lightning bugs. "Then they'll do."

Without another word, the three of us head off down the path, the music and laughter sounding from inside the juke joint growing with our approach. As we close the distance, the shadows part to reveal the establishment's true form.

The place is little more than a shanty—one right out of the Depression-era South. The floorboards of its porch are rotting, several of them broken or missing altogether. Its rail and studs are literally tree limbs, the latter holding up an awning in as bad of need of repair as the floor it covers.

A blind, old Cherokee sits beneath said awning in a wooden rocking chair. He's positioned by the door. He wears a worn, silk top hat that's abuzz with lightning bugs. A once-red shirt, now faded pink, covers his torso, its buttons fastened up his neck to the last. Breeches held up by suspenders and mud-splattered boots complete his ensemble. His clothes are over a century out of fashion and fit right in with our own attire.

A jug of what my nose informs me is something similar to moonshine is gripped in his leathery, liver-spotted right hand. A Winchester rifle rests across his lap. A blue tick hound as old and blind as he is lies at his feet. The dog rips a loud, dry fart that stirs the lightning bugs crawling across its hide, sending them into the air.

"Buddy likes you," the old man says, obviously referring to the mutt. "You fine ladies may go ahead on in."

Zora nods. "Thank you, kindly."

I snort a laugh when Wanda gives an actual I'll-be-damned curtsy.

The two women give me cross looks and head inside.

I start to follow, and the old man's hand rockets up and seizes my wrist with a speed belying his age. And if I didn't know better, I'd say it wasn't a hand holding me but a steel vice.

"You, though," the old man says through teeth as jaundiced and rotting as his eyes, "Buddy doesn't like you at all."

Buddy the dog suddenly comes alive. Now on his feet, his ears flatten against the back of his head as a low growl issues from deep inside his throat.

TWENTY-FOUR

The monster inside me howls for me to go for the .38 stuffed in the back of my jeans and start picking off the lightning bugs crawling along the old Cherokee's top hat. Both those and the ones buzzing the old man's hound. What the hell is he thinking, anyway, laying hands on me? I mean, I didn't come to the Crossroads to be some ancient Cherokee's whipping boy. I've got the tell-all journal of a corrupt congressman's wife to find.

I reach for the gun, and both the old man and his dog *flicker*. I mean exactly what I said. One second, it's the old man and his mutt before me. The next, they're replaced by what I can only describe as two undulating swarms of lightning bugs. One man-shaped, the other canine in form. Then there's another flicker, and it's the Cherokee and his blue tick in front of me once again. The effect is similar to when I looked at Wanda the werecat from the corner of my eye but different too.

Whatever the hell kind of spooks the Cherokee and his dog are, I've never seen the like.

My hand closes over the butt of the revolver at the small of my back. I feel a cool, gentle hand slip over mine where it rests on the gun and turn to see Zora standing behind me.

"Please, Nunnehi," she says to the old man. "This one is my friend."

The old man and his dog snarl in unison. "He carries a dark spirit inside him."

Zora nods. "One his mojo holds in check."

A single eyebrow cocks above the old man's dead eyes. "His mojo?"

Zora grins. "I may have helped a little."

"It will consume him in the end," the Cherokee says. "Maybe you too."

Furrows form in Zora's brow. "I have more faith than that. In Ashley. And in myself."

"You care so for this skinwalker?" the Cherokee gazes past Zora's head, his cataract-sheathed eyes focusing on only the lightning bugs buzzing his head. "To keep him so close? To place at risk yourself and those you hold dear?"

"Ashley is my family too."

The Cherokee nods as if deciding something. "Very well." His hand releases my wrist, leaving hot needles of pain in its wake. In my fury, I had no idea the old bastard was gripping me so hard.

The old man's dog relents as well and drops back onto its belly. The blue tick is instantly asleep and snoring.

Zora's hand leaves mine. "Come on inside, Ashley." She disappears into the juke joint. I watch her go then look back at the old man. He's lost all interest in me. His cataract-sheathed gaze is locked onto the twilight sky above the forested horizon.

"You're wrong, old-timer," I say. "I've got a handle on the thing inside me now. Thanks to her."

The Cherokee stares out at the evening, his chest rising and falling with breaths that are ragged and filled with phlegm. Then, "Lie to me if you will, skinwalker. But do not lie to yourself."

"Yeah, well fuck you too." I spin on my heels and enter the bar before the old man can take insult at my words.

The view inside ain't much better than the one out on the porch. Dust and cobwebs blanket everything, and the smell in here is dry and dusty.

Ancient.

Not unlike the smell of the underground chamber in Hatra.

I shake the image of the monster's glowing yellow eyes from my head and focus on my surroundings.

In the corner on my left, four men shoot pool at a billiards table that's on its last leg. Literally. Three corners of it are propped up on wooden blocks. A dartboard hangs on a wall of wooden planks to my right between a set of mounted antlers and a black cast-iron heater. A haphazard trail of small, round tables and empty chairs pass the establishment's actual bar and its belly-uppers, making its way across an open space serving as a sawdust-covered dance floor.

Beyond that, there's a makeshift stage where a two-man blues band plays. The band's lead singer is also its lead guitarist. His sole backup is a fellow blowing on a French harp. Like most of the bar's pool players, barflies, and dancers, they're black. Also like most here, if I relax my gaze or look at them from the corners of my eyes, they *flicker*, their mud-stained overalls, prairie dresses, head scarves, and bowler hats blinking out of existence to make way for coats of fur, feather, scale, and chitin.

"My kind of crowd, unfortunately."

I bee-bop over to the bar and lay a coin down before a bartender so tall he'd fit right in with an NBA pro ball team. He eyes my offering warily.

"Don't worry," I say. "No silver dollars here. It's a tiny replica of the Batman's giant penny. One that hangs in his cave. I've had it since I was a kid. I don't love it or nothing, but it's special enough to get a drink in here, I reckon."

The bartender nods and turns away. Money in and of itself has no value in the Crossroads. It's all about the eye of the beholder here. That's what translates as currency.

I reach into my jeans for my cigarettes and come out with a pack of tobacco and rolling paper. It's been a while, but I manage.

Seconds later, my lungs full of smoke, a smudge-ringed tumbler of something that looks and smells a lot like whiskey but ain't sits on the bar in front of me.

Zora tells me it's never a good idea to eat or drink in the Crossroads—at least not without a hoodoo sniffing things out first. You never know if what you're ingesting might make you a permanent resident or worse.

The In Between is like that—always trying to make you its bitch.

But the way I see it, I've been the Crossroad's bitch ever since I got that nasty scar on my hip, so I might as well enjoy myself.

I down the un-whiskey in a single swallow that burns my chest and waters my eyes in the best of ways.

"I like a man who can hold his liquor."

I turn to see a short, plump white girl with orange hair and freckles ogling me. She might've actually passed for cute if she still had all her teeth in her bad-mojo stained mouth.

"Scoot on back to your boyfriend, darling," I blow smoke in her direction and turn away. "I'm afraid I ain't in the mood."

The floor leaves my feet, and my cigarette leaves my mouth. Then I'm across the room, the hard cast iron of the heater smashing into my back.

The band goes silent, so I have no trouble hearing the netherworldly shriek that rips through the bar. I look up, and the room solidifies enough for me to see the orange-haired snaggletooth gliding across the bar toward me on gnarled, jaundiced toes that barely touch the floor.

Her eyes have rolled up in her head, and the freckles on her face have become angry boils. Several of these pop as she approaches, allowing me to see the nests of bloody, wriggling maggots housed inside.

My heart sinks as I reach for the revolver only to find it missing from the back of my pants.

The next thing I know, a rainbow eclipses my field of vision. Gunfire sounds, and the banshee's shrill scream vanishes.

Zora's voice cuts the silence. "Anyone else?"

Silence. Not even the frogs and crickets outside make a sound.

"I didn't think so."

Zora whirls to face me, the smoking derringer held in her right hand. She holds her left out to me. "I swear, Ashley," she says through clenched teeth, "I can't take you anywhere."

I grip Zora's hand. Wiry muscles bunch beneath the multicolored fabric of her frock as she hauls me to my feet. I glance over her shoulder to see short, fat, and ugly writhing on the floor in pain, nowhere near as dead as I would like.

"Wanda's got the journal," Zora's chin tips in the direction of our werekitty friend where she stands by the door, holding something the size and shape of a book wrapped in parchment.

The journal in question, no doubt.

"That shot won't keep the banshee down long," Zora says.

"They ain't that easy to get rid of. We need to split. On the double."

"Don't have to ask me twice. What about Zatoichi and his pooch out front?"

"His charge is to keep unwanted things out, not worry about what goes on inside. But doubtless he'll be happy to see our backsides."

"All right then. Let's decamp said asses on out of here."

We hit the door at a jog and are sprinting outright by the time we trade floorboard for earth.

"I warned you, hoodoo woman," the Cherokee yells. "The skinwalker will be the death of you."

I glance back long enough to salute him with my middle finger. It proves a stupid maneuver, as is customary in my case. My foot snags a root, and I'm only able to keep my feet because Zora's strong hand is there to catch me.

God, I love that woman.

We run on, chased only by the Cherokee's laughter.

In no time, we're back on reality's side of the Crossroads—gym bag in hand—dressed in our modern digs and loaded up in the Bronco. An hour and several failed attempts at reaching Earlene and Zora's Aunt Jackie by mobile after that, we're pulling up to the curb outside Winder Binder, the midnight sky above our heads thanks to time speeding along out here while we were in the Crossroads. You never know whether it will be daylight or dark when you come out of the In Between. Time follows no rules inside the Crossroads.

We exit the Bronco. The sound of its doors banging closed echoes up and down the empty street.

I light up and step around the vehicle to stand beside Zora and Wanda on the sidewalk, the latter once again returned to her feline form.

"I'm going to try Jackie by land line," Zora says. "Apparently, the Crossroads mojo is going take a while to dry out of my cell phone."

"Rookie mistake to have carried it over with you," I say. "You know modern tech doesn't translate well in the going and coming."

Zora shrugs. "What can I say? It's been a while since I journeyed into the In Between. I'm rusty."

"Nobody's perfect. You got any beers upstairs?"

Zora passes Suzanne Walker's journal—its former covering of parchment now a manila envelope—from her right hand to her left. "I might have a tallboy or two for you."

"Out-fricking—" A mingling of familiar smells bypass the odor of cigarette smoke to fill my nose: soap and deodorant that should be unscented but ain't. Not to my nose. Not when I've just returned from the supernatural battery-charger that is the Crossroads, mojo hand on my hip or not.

Headlights flash into existence across the street accompanied by the roar of an engine.

"Get down." I lose the cigarette and yank Zora to the curb, covering her body with my own.

Sounds erupt into being. The squeal of tires. The *pop-pop-pop* of a semiautomatic. Cement splintering as chips of the stuff hit my face. The yowl of a cat. *Wanda's yowl.*

I yank Zora's Glock from the back of her pants and surge upward. I laser in on the back left tire of the escaping white van I know all too well and curse at the dry click that sounds when my finger closes around the trigger.

Apparently, Zora's cell ain't the only thing the Crossroads mojo still has yet to leave. The stupid pistol still thinks it's a one-shot derringer. One that's already spent its round.

I whirl to see Zora kneeling in a pool of blood, Wanda's naked human body cradled in her lap and deader than hell.

"Earlene," I shout. "Fuck."

I leap to my feet and hit the door leading into Winder Binder shoulder-first. It gives way with little protest, having already been compromised, and if crossing the threshold causes any hoodoo fireworks on my insides, I fail to notice them.

I sprint through the bookshelves and up the stairs to Zora's apartment, Earlene's name a howl in my throat. One that goes unanswered.

My heart sinks at the sight of the purple door at the top of the stairs standing wide open. I pick up speed and enter Zora's apartment.

"Earlene!" At first, I don't see her. I'm too distracted by the blood-splatter on the wall behind Zora's twin bed. Then I see a single Doc Martin poking out from the bed's other side. I move then with Crossroads-charged speed and strength, slinging both bed and box-spring across the room so I can get to Earlene unimpeded. She's still and covered in blood. I collapse beside her, my hands going to her shoulders.

I don't know what to do, so I continue calling her name, using it as a plea.

I almost swallow my tongue when she whispers a single word, her voice so low I likely wouldn't have heard it without the sensory-enhancing mojo I soaked in up the Crossroads.

"Ambulance."

Zora's voice reaches us from downstairs. "Ashley? Is—?"

"Earlene's alive, Zora," I yell. "Call an ambulance."

It's only later, with the sound of approaching sirens in my ears, that my mind clears enough to realize Suzanne Walker is nowhere in sight.

TWENTY-FIVE

"It's getting harder and harder to cover your shit up, Owens." Police Detective Marcus Vincent's large index finger punctuates his sentence right into my chest.

I knock his hand away on reflex and lean in so my face is only inches from his own. "That's Earlene in there, Marcus. You want to do this, fine. But not here. And not now."

Marcus retreats a few steps more out of respect for Earlene than fear of me.

Marcus is a good damn cop. A good damn normal, too, for that matter.

We met up years back when he was just a beat cop here in the Nooga. There was some deep hoodoo going in town back then, and he and me both wound up smack in the middle of it, guns blazing.

He handled himself well, and we came out on top that time. Marcus won the commendation that set him on the path to becoming a homicide detective, and Zora and me landed a powerful friend on the force.

Marcus has gained a lot of gray hairs on his chin since then, but if you were to put a patch over his eye, he could still pass for a Sammy L version of Nick Fury.

Marcus turns away from me, his gaze falling across the off-white walls, tile floor, and fluorescent lights of the Erlanger Hospital hallway. His hand goes to the back of his shaved head the way it always does when he's feeling trapped in a nightmare he can't wake up from.

"I'm serious, Ash. It ain't like back when Jones was in office. The mayor we got now, sure, he don't want this kind of spook shit made public, but his is a zero tolerance kind of attitude if you know what I'm saying."

"I don't much give a rat's ass about your current administration one way or another, right now, Marcus. I just need to know if you can keep this on the down low until Zora and me can find these motherfuckers and give them the business."

His body deflates as the air leaves it in a huff. "I'll see about getting a couple guards outside Earlene's room."

"'Already got that covered, Marcus.'"

As if on cue, the biggest, meanest biker you've ever seen rounds the corner at the end of the hallway, filling it with seven feet of solid muscle and gut. He lumbers up the hallway toward us, tattoo-covered arms better suited to a gorilla swinging at his sides, threatening to knock down the walls.

"Ash," he calls. His voice is like the sound of concrete blocks grating against each other.

"Baby Shit," I answer, "You used a glamor after all. Good deal."

He reaches me, and we bump fists.

"I thought about it, and you were right. It's better this way. A disguise should make any tasty Christians happen to be about less inclined to piss themselves at the sight of me." Baby Shit winks. "Besides, maybe it'll fool whoever tried to do Earlene, and they'll make another go of it."

Looking at the hungry grin on Baby Shit's glamored face, I almost pity any sonofabitch foolish enough to try.

Almost.

I feel Marcus' hand on my arm. "Can I talk to you for a second?" he whispers. "In private."

I shrug and roll my eyes at Baby Shit.

His grin widens as Marcus pulls me aside.

"Are you fucking kidding me, Ash?" Marcus whispers. "Baby Shit is precisely who I don't want around civilians."

I glance over Marcus' shoulder and see Baby Shit licking his chops at the sight of a passing female nurse with curly brown hair and a behind so big and gorgeous that it hangs around a second or two after she goes before *pop-pop-popping* on down the hall.

I can't tell whether Baby Shit wants to lay her down or gobble her up. Most likely, it's both.

"He'll be fine, Marcus. Trust me."

Marcus recoils as if I'd slapped him. "Trust you? Ash, do you remember what happened the last time you asked me to—"

"Marcus." On Zora's lips, the detective's name is a song. She appears before us as if out of thin air and wraps Marcus in her arms. I watch, jealous as hell, as her touch drives the anger and frustration right out of him.

For a time, Marcus was a genuine competitor for Zora's affections. At least he was in my mind. I never truly got to find out back in the day, thank goodness, because either Zora was seeing someone while Marcus was flying single or vice-versa.

Marcus is a dedicated husband and father now, so it's a moot point. But old, envy-green habits die hard.

"Come on in, Marcus," Zora says. "Earlene's awake for the moment. She'll want to see you."

The two of them exit the hallway for the ICU, leaving Baby Shit and me on our own.

We shoot the shit, mostly talking trash about what we're going to do to the bastards who shot up Earlene once we get our hands on them.

Baby Shit has launched into a fantasy that involves ripping out eyeballs and sticking his tree limb of a cock into places no penis should ever be when Marcus and Zora rejoin us.

"All right," Marcus says. "Baby Shit can stay. But the first hint that he isn't acting strictly in the interest of guarding Earlene, his ass is out of here."

Baby Shit shrugs. "Sure, Marcus. Whatever makes you feel better."

Marcus wants to protest. I can see it in his face. But the truth is, Baby Shit is the proverbial four-hundred-pound gorilla who can sit wherever he wants. And if he wants to guard Earlene, he guards Earlene. Heaven and Earth would fall into ruin and pass away before anything and anyone moved him from his post or found a way to get by him.

And that's exactly the kind of protection Earlene needs right now.

To his credit, Marcus knows that too.

"I'm still going to see about getting a guard at the other end of the hall. One to keep an eye on you, Baby Shit."

Baby Shit's shoulders rise and fall once more. "Like I said, Marcus ..."

Marcus shakes his head. "I'll be in touch, Zora." Then he's gone.

"How's she doing?" Baby Shit asks.

"About the same as when we called you," Zora says. "In and out but stable. I've prayed over her. Done what I could for now. You ever get ahold of Bear?"

Baby Shit shakes his glamored head. "There's a note at Earlene's house says he's gone hunting. Could mean squirrel. Could mean pussy. He'll be out of pocket for days, regardless."

Zora's face darkens. "Earlene says they killed Suzanne, Ashley. Double tap to the head, just like they tried with her. I should've known better." Her voice trails off, barely a whisper. "I should've protected them. Wanda ..."

"Well, I'll be damned," Baby Shit says. "Who could've ever guessed the plate in Earlene's head would prove her salvation twice?"

I shake my head. "Shit, Zora. They were lying in wait for us too. Or at least for Wanda. This was a hit. One orchestrated by pros."

My gut sinks into my feet as a horrible thought occurs to me. "What about Sonny and Aunt Jackie? Are they—"

"Already on their way out of state to my cousin's. You're right. I have to assume the worst. If we're dealing with professionals, they might have done their homework and know where I live as well as where I work." Zora studies me for a moment. "You and I have a lot to talk about, Ashley."

I feel my cheeks go hot. I know what Zora's thinking. And she's right.

It's my fault the congressman's wife is dead and that Earlene is lying up in here, shot to hell.

I led those fucks in the white van right to them.

To Zora's credit, she doesn't cut my head off, much less lecture me.

My body deflates in a huff. "Yeah, we've definitely got some jawing to do. But we should get some sleep first or else we ain't going to be much good for nothing."

Zora nods. "I'm admittedly exhausted. Are you good here, Ronnie?"

"You guys go get some shut eye. I got this."

Zora and me bid Baby Shit goodbye and leave the hospital. We enter the parking garage and retrieve the oversized purse housing Suzanne Walker's journal from Zora's T-bird.

But instead of taking Zora's car, I find a chromed-out Lincoln SUV with tinted windows that's more or less out of camera shot and hotwire it. Zora fails to protest.

Like me, she may hate having to steal a vehicle belonging to someone visiting family here in the hospital, but our lives are literally on the line. If we're being followed, from here on out, running and gunning in our own rides ain't the wisest of options.

Besides, judging by the way the Lincoln is tricked out, its driver can afford to take the hit.

We leave the garage, and I drive around town in circles, glancing back all the while in the rearview mirror for a tail but finding none.

A half hour later, Zora speaks. "I think we're good, Ashley. But I need get inside my shop unseen."

"What the hell for? If we're trying to lose these guys, we need to stay away from familiar stomping grounds."

"I hear you. But I took a look at Suzanne's journal while you were in with Earlene. It's coded."

"Coded? What? Why?"

"Suzanne Walker may have been a lot of things, but she wasn't no dummy. She must have realized that if her husband ever found out what she was writing, it wouldn't go well for her."

"You think there's a connection then? Between Congressman Walker and our assassins?"

Seconds march by in the silence. "I don't know for sure if there's a connection or not," Zora says at last. "But I sure as hell aim to find out."

TWENTY-SIX

I aim to find some things out too. That's why—after we use the first level of Old City to enter Winder Binder from below and nab the books and supplies Zora needs—I stop by a service station pay phone and place a call to my employer.

I watch the first of the sun's rays appear over the Appalachian Mountains in the east, the smell of gasoline and asphalt in my nose as, on the other end of the line, the phone rings once. Twice. "This is Senator Jones."

Six o'clock in the morning, and Jones sounds fresh as a daisy. He was probably in bed by nine last night, up and jogging by four this morning, and dressed and going over today's schedule by five. He's one of *those* people. I don't know what you'd call them. They ain't spooks per se, but they certainly ain't normal either.

"I don't like it when folks jerk me around, Bob."

"Ashley," he says. His voice is pure good humor. No hint of surprise or anger. None at the fact that I'm calling him at the crack of dawn. And none at the fact that I'm still alive to do so. Maybe Zora's suspicions about Congressman Walker are wrong. "I was hoping that you'd—"

"The River City Club. Be there at four this afternoon. Bring your boyfriend."

I hang up. Ballsy of me considering Bob's congressman pal is writing my checks at present. Or at least Jones is writing them on his behalf. But considering the night I've had, my people skills are working even better than usual.

I rejoin Zora in the white Impala we boosted after ditching the Lincoln somewhere the cops would be sure to find it. We drive south of town to the adjoining burg of Lookout Valley and park in the lot of a twenty-four-hour Walmart located across the street from a cheap motel. We go inside, pick up a couple of burner phones, and hoof it next door. We sign in under false names, paying cash so as not to leave an easy trail for anyone who might be looking for us.

Our motel room reeks of smoke. It's also ugly, all puttied sheet rock, yellowed blinds, and crawling paisleys.

I let Zora shower first. When it's my turn, I twist the shower knob on to scalding and leave it there, allowing the water to burn the night away. But, just like the scar on my hip, a portion of it refuses to be washed aside. Blood and death are stubborn bastards that way.

When I'm finished showering, I wrap a towel around my waist and open a window so I can sit on the toilet lid and smoke while I let my mojo hand dry out.

Smoking in here is for Zora's benefit. Granted, it probably wouldn't make a difference considering how the bedroom smells like an ashtray, but never let it be said Ashley Owens can't be a gentleman when he has to.

I finish my cigarette and exit the bathroom. Zora has managed to hang the paisley comforters over the blinds, giving us added darkness. The hoodoo herself lies atop the remaining covers on one of the twin beds, dressed only in panties and an oversize Batman T-shirt, an arm draped over her forehead.

I watch her for a moment as her chest rises and falls in time with her soft, girlish snores, admiring her long, muscular legs where they leave her T-shirt to run on forever.

It speaks to how tired I am that I don't go over and try a creep move.

Because, make no mistake, I am a creep.

Instead, I tuck her in, repositioning those lovely buttercream legs of hers beneath the covers before pulling them up to her chin.

Zora hardly stirs.

I kiss her cheek and then run a final recon of the door, making sure not to disturb the brick dust Zora has poured across the threshold.

I lie down on the twin bed next to her and watch my best friend in the world doze, until sleep and the nightmares it heralds come for me.

But tonight, there are no bad dreams. For the first time since Hatra, my sleep is peaceful. Sometime during the day, I wake up and realize why. Despite being only semiconscious, I realize Zora has left her bed for mine. Somehow, she's managed to dress me in my boxers and get me under the covers. But all that's neither here nor there.

What does hold my attention, such as it is, is Zora lying asleep within the crook of my arm, her cheek resting against my chest. I can feel the warmth of her. The pressure of her body against mine. The sweet, earthy scent of her overpowering all other smells.

Judging by the needles pricking my arm, she's been like this for some time.

But I don't care.

If this is a dream, it's not one I ever want to wake up from. I drift back to sleep, only partially aware of the grin spread across my face.

When I do wake up in full that afternoon, I'm disappointed to discover Zora has left me. She's moved the room's small TV from its chest of drawers so that she may use the latter as a study table. She sits there, disappointingly dressed in full, poring over her books and the late Suzanne Walker's journal. The TV itself rests on the floor. Zora has it on and tuned in to a local afternoon talk show.

There's no mention of last night's fiasco, much less the untimely deaths of Suzanne Walker and her changeling housekeeper, Wanda. I give a mental curse at this. On one hand, I'm glad Marcus is keeping things quiet. But on the other, we told him what was up, more or less. Marcus is a good cop and would've pulled every string he had in order to get the city's entire police force on the trail of that white van. No mention of it or anything else in regard to last night lets me know their search has come up null and void so far.

"'Afternoon," Zora says without bothering to turn around.

"'Afternoon." I toss the covers aside and sit up in bed,

half-yawning, half-groaning as I stretch my arms toward the ceiling. "How's Earlene?"

"Ronnie said she was awake but weak," Zora says. "The prayers and medicine are working."

"Sonny and Aunt Jackie?"

"Right as rain."

I nod though Zora can't see me with her back turned. I go to my jeans where they lie draped across a chair and fish my cigarettes from a pocket. "How goes the code breaking?"

"It's really more translating than code breaking," Zora says, still not looking up. "And I'm almost done. It's not quite what I'd expected. A lot of it Suzanne had already told me, but I still have several pages left to go. Anyway, you want to make your meeting with Jones and Walker, you better get going."

"You be all right here by your lonesome?"

At last, Zora looks up at me, aggravation that's only partially feigned apparent in her eyes. "It's not me who needs looking after. If Walker's behind his wife's death, it could be risky business for you walking up in there alone."

I wave my hand. "I'm a big boy. I'll be fine. Besides, no matter Walker's involvement, if any, he and Jones still don't have the journal. They'll want to know any intel I may or may not have where it's concerned. Walking out of there after they've had a chance to feel me out might be a different story, admittedly."

Zora nods. "Here." I wince as she rips a page out of the late Mrs. Walker's journal. "Take this with you. I've already translated it. Make up a bullshit story about how you came by it. Tell them you're still on the trail of the journal it came from. That should secure you a safe exit."

I take the journal page from her hand. I scan it and pick out a few words in Latin. Still more in Greek. Most, though, are written in languages I don't even begin to recognize.

"They'll have me followed after I leave of course. If you're right about them."

Zora grins. "Like you said, Ashley, you're a big boy."

Her subtext that I won't make the same mistake twice goes unsaid.

I bring it out in the open anyway. "Yeah, fool me once. Zora,

I'd seen that white van before last night."

"I thought as much."

"It tailed me while I was chasing down leads on Walker's wife before I swallowed my pride and called you. Whoever was riding in it busted me up outside the Terminal before I could get a look at them. When they left me alive, I sort of put them out of my head, figuring whoever they were after, I wasn't it, or maybe kicking the crap out of me was enough for them. I have my share of enemies around town, after all.

"Don't we both?"

"Anyway, to tell you the truth, I didn't think much about it after it happened. And that's my bad because obviously, it wasn't me they were after. I was just their dog, running down their prey for them."

My eyes go hot, but no tears fall. I learned to shove them back down a long time ago after all.

"I should've known better. Acted smarter."

Zora gets up from the table and hugs me to her. I return her embrace, nothing other than love and gratitude on my mind.

"Earlene isn't on you, Ashley. Not Suzanne or Wanda either. Only the fools who pulled the trigger are to blame." Zora's voice turns hard. "Them and those who gave the order."

We release each other, our hug reduced to a mere holding of hands.

"One thing we know now," Zora says. "It ain't spooks we're dealing with."

"How's that? I've known many a spook killer just as comfortable with a gun as he was his claws."

Zora shakes her head. "True enough. But no spook short of the Dark Man himself could've gotten through the conjuration I had around Winder Binder."

I feel a snarl cross my face. "And it would've taken someone damn good to get the best of Earlene in a fire fight. Someone *professional*, just like we've been saying."

We look into each other's eyes, our mutual affection replaced by shared indignation, the unspoken truth passing between us that we're going to make the sonofabitches who shot our friend pay.

TWENTY-SEVEN

"Where's Walker?"

I snag a chair and whirl it around so that its back is to my abs when I sit down beside Jones at his usual table inside the River City Club. The white-haired senator is dressed in a dark-blue suit with a maroon, red-state tie.

Captain America formal wear.

The smile that never leaves Jones' face widens. "I'm afraid Congressman Walker is indisposed at present."

I sit in silence, giving Jones rope. He's too smart to take it. He simply sits there, smiling like the idiot he most certainly is not.

Vernon the waiter appears at my elbow and takes my drink order before vanishing once more.

"Me and mine got ambushed last night, Senator. By someone who wasn't no spook."

"I assume you're referring to the people who killed Congressman Walker's wife and her Negro housekeeper?"

I reach across the table and seize Jones' tie, pulling his face in close to my own. "You fucking bastard."

The few people inside the bar clear out, Vernon included, none of them so much as looking in our direction as they go.

"Now, now, Ashley." Jones' hand gently touches my own. "I had nothing to do with that. Or what happened to your friend, Earlene."

"Yeah? What about your boy, Walker?"

"Insofar as I know, Jack only learned of last night's events after I called to give him the unfortunate news of his wife's passing."

"After you—" Of course. Jones was the Nooga's mayor for some years. It would figure he has powerful friends on the force same as me.

I release Jones, and he falls back into his seat.

"Well, who the fuck did have something to do with it then?"

Jones adjusts his tie. Runs a hand through his thick gray mane. Intertwines his fingers. Smiles.

"Who knows what thugs Suzanne became involved with after absconding?"

"Uh huh." I take out my cigarettes and light up, pretty damn certain Senator Jones is lying his ass off. To his credit, if he is, he's able to hide it from the monster inside me.

But I don't know.

It could be that, when it comes to politicians of Jones' ilk, telling lies comes as natural as breathing air.

I inhale smoke and blow it out through my nostrils in twin streams. "With the congressman's wife dead, I reckon it's time for us to settle accounts then, Bob."

"There's still the question of the late Mrs. Walker's journal."

I fish the journal page from my pocket and toss it onto the table in front of Jones.

"I'm still looking for the rest of it."

Jones picks up the page and studies it. "It's coded—written in foreign languages."

"No shit, Sherlock."

"So you don't know what it says?"

"Again with the brilliant deductions. I'll hunt the thing down for you, Bob, but making out what it says inside is on you and Walker."

I fail to add that I'd bet my ass whatever's in the late Mrs. Walker's journal has everything to do with why she and Wanda were gunned down in cold blood.

There's no way in hell Jones would confirm my suspicions anyway.

Jones folds up the paper and places it inside his jacket.

"Very well. You are still on the clock then."

"Out-freaking-standing." I grind out my cigarette and head for the door.

"Oh, one more thing, Ashley."

I halt in step, my spine a ramrod.

"My sources also informed me that last night's … *hiccups* happened outside your friend Zora's bookshop. I'd just like to reinforce the fact that discretion in this matter is key," Jones says. "There's no need to go getting her involved. She sees the world differently than people like you and I know it to be. She might not understand our need to ensure that, first and foremost, nothing occurs that might prove a disruption for Congressman Walker's gubernatorial campaign. Are we clear?"

I grit my teeth. "As clear as crystal, Bob."

I almost knock the door off its hinges as I make my exit.

I don't even reach the bottom of the stone steps leading to the street before my burner is ringing.

I press the Talk button. A voice full of bass that's pure Midwest comes on the line. "How's your bull dyke friend, Owens?"

"Who the hell is this?"

"A man who has let you live twice now."

Mr. White Van.

"You boys must be high tech to have gotten this number. Especially considering I haven't used this phone to make any calls. You're government then. In the employ of the good senator. I think I'll go back inside and rip out his throat."

I hang up and turn around. Two stairs up, the burner rings again.

"Got something to add before I kill your boss, G-man?"

"Nice T-shirt."

I look down and see little red fairy lights flittering on my chest. Laser sights.

"Third time's a charm, Owens."

"If you wanted me dead, we wouldn't be talking." I hang up. The burner rings again before I can get it inside my pocket.

"We've kept surveillance on Jones' mobile," Mr. White Van says. "Once you were in range of the senator, we were able to triangulate your burner."

He could be lying. I have no way of knowing for certain.

"Rest assured, Owens, we're operating outside of Jones'

authority," he says as though he's able to read my thoughts. "Our benefactors might frown upon you killing him, but that would be the limit of their concern."

"What do you want?" I ask.

"To talk."

"Then find a gay bestie. I got other things to do with my time."

"Your troll friend may be tough, Owens, but I doubt even he would survive it if the entire hospital were to blow up. The bull dyke, as touch and go as she is, certainly wouldn't."

I stand in silence, the burner pressed to my ear.

"Face it, Owens. If we don't sit down to chat, the terrorists win. Think about it. Your pals. All those people ..." He mimics the sound of an explosion.

Deep inside me, the monster growls. But up here on the surface, I sigh in defeat.

Zora would know what to do. What to say. Unfortunately, she ain't here.

"Meet me in the food court of Hamilton Place Mall," I say. "An hour from now."

He laughs. "Surround yourself with a thousand people if you like, Owens. It still won't stop my men and me from killing you if we want to."

Not *us*, but *my men and me*. He is military then.

An officer whose arrogance is getting in the way of good judgment and discipline.

I've seen it happen before.

"We'll see about that."

"Okay, then," he says, the laugh gone from his voice. "We'll do it your way. But be sure you leave your conjure woman friend behind or else there's going to be more collateral damage. Understand?"

"Roger that."

"Good. And Owens—"

"Yeah."

"Bring the journal."

"Journal?" I ask. "What journal?"

A moment of silence. "For your sake, Owens, I hope you're joking."

He hangs up, and the red fairies disappear from my T-shirt.

An hour later, I'm on the northern edge of town, seated at the food court within Hamilton Place Mall, mobs of teenagers, families, and their screaming babies all around me. The noise they make is a din in my ears and every bit as overpowering as the stink of what must be thirty deep-fryers in bad need of cleaning going full-tilt.

I hate fucking Hamilton Place. I made the mistake of coming out here once during the holidays to buy Sonny a Christmas gift. Even on the Harley, I was stuck in traffic for over two hours. It was shoulder to shoulder once I got inside too.

And all this I braved only to discover they'd sold out of the toy I'd come looking for.

I promised myself then and there I'd never set foot here again.

The mall is Hell on Earth. At least for a wide open space-loving country boy like me.

But today, Hell might just work in my favor. I'm hoping that, despite his boasts to the contrary, the crowds will make Mr. White Van and the black ops squad I'm guessing he's in charge of a little less inclined to end me.

A man in a black windbreaker and a Braves baseball cap takes a seat across from me. The cap is pulled down, so I can't see his eyes, only the square, clean-shaven jaw attached to the bottom of his face. That and the white cord trailing down from his ear into his windbreaker.

"Where's the journal?" A deep voice that screams Kansas. Oklahoma, maybe?

"Tell me who hired you," I say, "and it's yours."

Captain Ball Cap looks up so that I can see the dark eyes bookending his aristocratic nose.

He's almost as handsome as me in a Jon Hamm, clean-cut sort of way. If you're into that sort of overbearing, alpha-male shit.

"The journal, Mr. Owens. Now."

"Was it Walker?"

Captain Ball Cap leans forward. His right hand slips into the pocket of his windbreaker, doubtless wrapping itself around a pistol. "I'm going to ask you one more time, Mr. Owens. If don't hear the answer I desire, my men will execute someone, sitting right here, in this food court, at random, in such a way no one even realizes they're dead."

My gaze darts across the food court. Several men who weren't here before now sit at tables. One reads a newspaper. Another, a Kindle. A third, a mobile device. Any one of them could be assassin or victim.

I lock eyes with Captain Ball Cap and lean back in my chair. "Fine by me, friend. I couldn't give a shit."

Captain Ball Cap's spine becomes as ramrod as the Beretta Tomcat Zora has tucked into a fast food sack pokes into the base of his spine.

"This lady, on the other hand ..."

Captain Ball Cap glances from the corner of his eye at the attractive East Indian woman in a sari holding a gun on him. "Hello, lover." It's with Zora's voice that she whispers. "The first person we see slump over like they're taking a nap, you'll be taking one yourself."

Captain Ball Cap faces me once again. "I told you not to bring the conjure woman."

"Yeah, you did," I say. "But afterward, I had a long conversation with myself, and we both decided we didn't want to wind up dead. Now I'll ask *you* one more time, friend: Who hired you?"

Captain Ball Cap's perfect, masculine chin moves left then right. "I won't talk. If I die, Glory awaits. But if my men execute you and your witch, Mr. Owens, the only thing either of you have to look forward to is Hell's fiery embrace."

"He telling the truth?" the lovely Indian woman Zora has glamored herself into asks.

"About us going to Hell?" I say. "Yeah, I figure that's where I'm—"

"Ashley."

"Yeah, I reckon he won't squeal," I say. "Better give it to him, Zora."

Captain Ball Cap tenses, readying himself for the shot to come. But instead of a bullet, Zora hits him with a large manila envelope.

Captain Ball Cap's eyes dart from the envelope where it lies on the table back to me, his face full of confusion.

"Go ahead. Take the thing. I'll be damned if Zora or me could make heads or tails of it."

Captain Ball Cap picks up the envelope, studies it. "Suzanne Walker's journal—it's inside?"

I nod. "Yep. It's all yours. Just like you wanted. All we ask in return is your cap."

The bill of Captain Ball Cap's hat perks up as the brow beneath it furrows. "My cap?"

"Give us your cap," I say. "You take the journal. We go our separate ways."

Captain Ball Cap straightens in his seat once again as Zora presses the gun into the small of his back. "Now."

"Fine," he yanks the cap off his head and tosses it onto the table, revealing quite the bald spot. No thick-maned Jon Hamm after all.

"Much obliged."

I snatch up the cap and pitch it to Zora. We stand up.

"In case you and your boys get any bright ideas about keeping us from leaving here on our feet," Zora says as she holds up the cap, "just remember: I've got this."

"Why the hell should I care?"

I grip either side of the food court table and lean in so that my face is only inches away from the captain's. "You ever seen what a hoodoo woman can do with someone's personal possession?" I ask. "Something they've owned? Touched? Something that carries follicles of their hair? Their sweat?"

Captain Bald Spot swallows hard, and I know our bluff has worked.

Sure, Zora could use the cap to work out a conjuration and fix the Captain. But that kind of thing takes time and prayer. Case in point, the stockpiled glamor she's wearing now took a week to prepare.

Besides, Zora doesn't like using dark mojo on a normal. Even a bastard like the captain.

Thankfully for us, he doesn't seem to realize any of this.

"This is definitely the late Suzanne Walker's journal?"

Zora nods.

"Then get out of my sight."

We don't wait around to be asked twice.

TWENTY-EIGHT

Zora and me steal a navy blue Altima out of the mall parking lot and head to East Brainerd to lose ourselves among miles of never-ending suburbs. It'd be damn hard for anyone to follow us here among the prefab homes and well-manicured lawns without us spotting them. That is, unless of course Captain Bald Spot has a satellite or some shit. And, if that's the case, we're pretty much fucked regardless. Hoodoo or not, there's no way Zora and me could compete with those kinds of resources.

Between neighborhoods, we pit-stop at a gas station to piss and grab some road food. We also use a pay phone to check in on everybody. Satisfied all's well, we load back up and cross into Georgia by way of Old Ringgold Road while munching on snacks and sipping cold drinks. A granola bar and Diet Coke for Zora. Beef jerky and a Budweiser for me.

"How long you figure until they realize you gave them a glamored Gideon's Bible?" I ask.

Zora grins with a mouth better suited to a Bollywood starlet. "A day or two. Maybe more. It depends if they have anyone on payroll versed in the occult." Zora shrugs. "But I got the impression they don't look favorably upon such." She sighs. "Then again, 'know thy enemy.' But sooner or later, they will come."

I nod. "They're trained military, Zora. Too much for us to handle on our own."

Zora nods. "You don't know the half of it yet."

"Yeah, about that …"

"There will be time enough to talk about such later, Ashley. Right now, we need a plan. Some back up."

"Well, I'm fresh out of ideas and willing souls in that regard."

We ride in silence.

Somewhere around the Tennessee border, she reaches into her overnight bag and retrieves a pack of wet wipes. She opens them and begins washing the glamor from her face.

"We have to go home, Ashley."

"You know we can't, Zora."

"I'm not talking about Chattanooga."

Realization dawns on me. "South Pittsburg? Oh, hell no."

"We need his help, Ashley, and you know it."

I don't have to ask who it is Zora means.

Elijah.

He was once my best friend. And Zora's lover.

It's the latter part that ruined the former.

Well, that and the fact that Elijah's an asshole.

But, I guess if I'm being honest, it takes one to know one, I reckon.

"Elijah ain't going to help us, Zora. He's washed his hands of this world and everything in it. Including you and me."

Zora's mouth goes tight. She knows what I'm saying is true, but she doesn't want to hear it.

Refuses to, apparently.

"You're wrong, Ashley. Elijah will help us. He still—" I can see Zora wanting to say the words, *loves us,* but she catches herself at the last second. "He still cares."

A wiser man would trend gently at this point. Unfortunately, it's only me here. "Oh, bullshit, Zora. The only thing Elijah cares about these days is that big bully in the sky the two of you are so fond—"

I hear the slap more than feel it.

"That's for blasphemy," Zora says. Whether she's talking about God or Elijah, I don't know.

I doubt she does either.

They say you never love anyone again the way you do your first, and Zora and Elijah were like wild horses running against the wind of the world.

So I can't blame Zora for still harboring feelings where he's concerned.

Hell. For the longest time, I loved the sonofabitch too.

We travel in silence along the most convoluted route possible, taking I-59 back into Georgia, heading over the backside of Lookout Mountain to pop up again in Tennessee. Somewhere along the way, night falls, causing us to reach South Pittsburg under a blanket of darkness.

We take our exit and pass a Tennessee-orange welcome sign that lists the many state championships the local high school has won.

I tried sports for a while. It didn't take.

I found I liked lying in the backseat of a car with the quarterback's girlfriend a hell of a lot better than I did standing out on the field with him, getting my head bashed in.

Elijah, on the other hand, now there was a baller.

At least until he wasn't.

He won *Mr. Football* so many times I think the TSSAA retired the award after he left.

Zora had skills too. She turned down a volleyball scholarship to Middle Tennessee State to go live and work in New Orleans. I guess the things she wanted to study at the time weren't in any college text book.

But Zora eventually earned her degree anyway just so in case Winder Binder ever went belly up, she'd have options.

Funny, that.

You can prepare for life's contingencies all you want, but the bitch will still shift like a freaking tectonic plate and swallow you up in the crack left behind.

That's pretty much our situation, right here and now, truth be told.

Zora and me ride into South Pittsburg proper on Highway 72, passing government subsidized housing and a Fred's Supermarket that was a Red Food Store when I was a boy.

I can't see the Tennessee River running behind the latter, but I can smell it, no monster mojo required.

The water has a different stink to it here. Less bite. I guess the sludge and shit the Nooga pumps down here has had time to dilute along the way.

72 becomes Main Street, and gas stations, shops, and

restaurants appear in the windshield along with bricked-in sidewalks and antique, street corner clocks. The vehicles we pass are either Fords or Chevys. Nine out of ten of them are oversized pickups, and eight out of those nine have gun racks in the rear window.

South Pittsburg could be Andy Griffith's Mayberry from this angle.

We hang a right, and the façade disappears. Every picturesque, white-picket-fenced house on either side of the block is bookended by two more obviously running crack or meth or both.

The latter are all junk, chain link, and black signs with *Private Property: Keep Out* written in neon orange. Every one of them has a starving pit bull or Rottweiler chained up. To a tree if the home's just short of condemned. The rusted hulk of a vehicle set up on blocks if the house is all in.

The dogs' heads turn to watch us drive by, hunger in their beady eyes.

We reach the modest, white building that is Elijah's church, and I'm half-relieved to see there ain't any vehicles parked along the street.

"Wonder where they all are?" I say.

It ain't Sunday or even Wednesday, but that don't matter none when it comes to Elijah and his congregation.

They hold prayer meeting each and every night.

I pull up to the front of the church and park the car. "Maybe there's a singing somewhere?" Zora says.

I huff. "You know why Elijah and his flock don't believe in premarital sex, don't you?"

Zora gives me a blank stare.

"It leads to singing and dancing."

Zora frowns, shakes her head, and gets out of the car.

I follow.

We climb up the church's concrete steps and find a note tacked to the building's double doors. Someone has used a black sharpie to write, *Brush Arbor Service Tonite*, misspelling *tonight*.

"Come on," Zora says. "They're at the shrine."

Minutes later, we're crossing the Tennessee River by way

of the Shelby Rhinehart Bridge, heading into my old stomping grounds—the rural community of New Hope. We bypass field after field of cattle before hanging a left onto a paved road flanked by trees on either side that was only dirt and gravel when I was growing up.

Several twists and turns later, we crest a hill, and the trees open up to reveal a series of burning torches staked into the ground. They surround a latticework of vines, branches, and shrubs serving as a shelter for Elijah and his flock. They've erected the brush arbor before the shrine's charred remains, using the stone slab benches radiating from it like church pews.

I don't know why they bothered. Not a single member of the congregation is sitting down. In the light created by the torches and our headlight beams, I can see every one of them, young and old, black and white, poor and poorer, cavorting as they shout in tongues, their arms raised in exaltation, a jar of strychnine held in each right hand, a venomous snake in each left.

It's like an upper rung of Hell, and it makes me sad.

And a little bit afraid.

Like so many who grew up here, I lost my virginity at this shrine. Back when it was beautiful and whole. The place had a strong, positive mojo about it. It's probably why the Catholics in the area, few as they are, built the shrine out here in the first place.

I like to think the shenanigans that so many of us young lovers got up to around here only added to that.

But whatever agape love the shrine harbored left when it burned down.

If God's still around, he's strictly Old Testament these days.

Elijah and his bunch wouldn't have it any other way.

We park the Altima on the green beyond the arbor among the vehicles belonging to Elijah's flock. Their leader's horse and buggy are also here. The former, a muscular giant even for a draft horse, stands hitched to a hickory at the tree line, munching grass.

Zora and me get out of the car and approach the arbor. The air is cool and full of the scent of torch smoke.

We reach the last of the stone benches and come to a halt, neither Zora nor myself wishing to tread among all the snakes gathered beneath the arbor to crawl underfoot. The scraping sounds they make as they slither across the ground en masse join with the nonsensical shouts of the congregation, the noise of rattling, serpentine tails punctuating endless calls of "Amen."

It's early autumn. Snakes shouldn't even be out yet, much less slithering around like it's the height of summer.

To say I'm a little fazed would be an understatement.

But I shouldn't be.

This is Elijah, after all. Signs and wonders are par for the course.

Speaking of tall, dark, and born again, he stands at the head of the congregation before the ruins of the shrine, a monolith in his own right.

Elijah is six-foot-going-on-seven with shoulders half as wide set above a narrow waist. He's dressed in dark-blue Dickies and a shirt of the same hue buttoned down to his wrists and up to his Adam's apple so that the only skin showing is the ebony of his hands and face. And even with absurdly long dreads and beard covering much of that face, it's plain to see it's a handsome one.

A little white girl lies on one of the stone benches before Elijah, bawling, her arms and legs bound with silver chains.

Ceremonial chains.

"Please," the girl pleads between sobs, "I'll do anything you want, just don't hurt me."

Elijah looks down at her, bored. "Reveal yourself." His voice is like thunder dipped in honey.

The little girl's crying ceases. Her face becomes a snarling abomination as she vipers out. She spews a litany of curses from between her fangs up at Elijah.

Moving slow but with purpose, Elijah reaches down and curls his long, thick fingers around a large timber rattlesnake. He lifts the rattler before him, praying aloud as his hands move down the length of the snake's body.

It's as though the rattler was a blade he was unsheathing.

As it turns out, that's exactly the case.

When Elijah finishes, the snake lies rigid and straight in his hands, its silent, still rattle forming what could the pointed tip of a snake sword.

The viper's curses continue, rising above the whoops and hollers of the congregation.

Elijah leans down and places the snake's rattle just to the left of the viper's breastbone.

"And Jesus said: 'Behold, I have given you authority over all the power of the enemy, and you can walk among snakes and scorpions. And crush them.'"

Elijah sinks the snake's rattle into the viper's chest. Her curses cease, and the already loud shouts of the congregation rise to become wails of ecstasy.

Seconds later, there's nothing left on the stone slab but dust and ashes.

There may be crack houses and meth dens in South Pittsburg, but there sure as hell ain't no spooks, vipers or otherwise.

Not with Elijah around.

Elijah lowers his rattlesnake sword to the ground. The moment it touches the grass, it slithers away, having returned to its usual serpentine self.

Elijah looks up, his gaze locking onto Zora and me. It's the first acknowledgement of our presence he's given.

He steps around the stone bench—or rather, the altar—and walks toward us. The members of his flock reach out their hands to touch him as he passes among them, desiring to make contact with the divine.

By contrast, the snakes crawling across the ground open and close their ranks in succession to accommodate Elijah's footfalls, somehow aware that one of God's chosen walks among them.

Elijah reaches us and halts, the fabric of his shirt going taut to reveal muscles chiseled out of granite as he folds his long arms across his beard and chest.

"Hello, Zora," he says in greeting. "God said you'd be here."

TWENTY-NINE

I befriended Elijah the day he saved my life. We were just kids in junior high, but I was more or less the same little shit then that I am now.

Case in point, at the time, I was selling beer and weed to my fellow thirteen-year-olds behind the school bleachers by leave of the high school cartel: three pimple-faced white kids with behavioral problems who thought fashion began and ended with Slayer T-shirts.

One day, they discovered I'd been holding out on them and decided to take me down into the locker rooms beneath the high school gymnasium to have a chat about it.

I was face down in a pool of my own blood, my pants down around my ankles, when Elijah blew in like a whirlwind and saved me from what was about to happen.

Elijah wasn't no Jesus freak then. In fact, like me, he was quite the opposite.

But he was formidable. Even then.

And, despite being no older than me, he sent those punks packing. All three of them.

From that day forward, we were partners in crime. Literally. If there was trouble in Marion County, Elijah and me were smack in the middle of it and more than likely the cause.

It was fucking great. There wasn't a joint we didn't smoke, a poker game we didn't play, or a cheerleader we didn't enjoy.

It's why folks just couldn't understand what Zora saw in trash like us—why she'd take us on as friends and eventually even much more where Elijah was concerned, to my own chagrin.

Not that Zora was a saint. Far from it.

But she sang in church, did well in school, and was a prodigy on the volleyball court. Everyone knew Zora had big things ahead of her and that Elijah and me would only drag her down.

They proved right in the end on account of me at least.

I think half the reason Zora went off to New Orleans was out of guilt for what she and me did that night up on Colburn Town Mountain. Some part of her thought she was being unfaithful to Elijah and needed to serve penance. Never mind that he'd already broken things off with her and then some.

In any case, full disclosure: I'd be lying if I said that my satisfaction that night wasn't about more than just unrequited love.

I was as good a liar as they come. Even back then. But the time I'd spent being able to smile and pretend that everything was okay between the three of us, after Elijah swooped in and stole the only girl I'd ever loved in life up to that point, had come to an end.

We all three should've dealt with it then, but life intervened. Zora went to New Orleans, I enlisted with Uncle Sam, and Elijah went to jail.

Somewhere along the line, Elijah found God.

No. That ain't right.

God found Elijah.

Chose him to take the deepest of Nazarite vows, according to Zora. That means his days of booze, bad women, and haircuts are behind him. As a consequence, Elijah is the most powerful conjure man to come along since Moses.

No, scratch that.

He's Moses, Samson, and Solomon all rolled into one.

That ain't no understatement neither.

I've seen Elijah do some crazy fucking conjuration. No prayer. No preparation. Full-tilt, holy-rolling shit. Tonight being the least of it.

Elijah is why I believe in God.

And as far as I can tell where the uncaused bastard in the sky is concerned, it's par for the course for Him to take on an asshole like Elijah for His prophet.

Standing here, looking up at the judgmental smirk on Elijah's handsome, bearded face, all these repressed thoughts and feelings come flooding to the surface.

Ironically, they've got nothing to do with the monster inside me. Not the one I picked up in Iraq, anyway. It's actually silent for a change.

But I can feel the beast down there. Watching Elijah with wary, hooded eyes, its claws wrapped around cage bars comprised of mojo and thought as it sizes him up the way a cobra would a mongoose.

The sensation is akin to how it regards Zora.

It ain't fear it's feeling exactly. I think that fear might be impossible for the monster.

But the emotion is probably the closest it can muster in the way of respect. And that's saying something.

"So God told you we'd be here, huh?" I ask. "Well, Elijah, since you two are so fucking chummy, you tell that cosmic psychopath I have a bone or two to—"

"Ashley," Zora gently squeezes my wrist.

I yank away. "Fuck this. I don't know why I came along. It was stupid."

"I agree," Elijah says. "You are cursed and not welcome here." Elijah nods in the direction of the shrine. "Lost beyond saving just like the viper girl. You should prostrate yourself upon the altar before the Lord and allow me to—"

I ball my hands into fists, readying to hit him. Zora strikes first. Probably having about the same success I would have.

She swings her open palm at Elijah's face, and he catches her hand in his. She counters with her other hand, but the result is the same.

He stands there, holding her.

Touching her.

"There's still hope for you though, Zee." Elijah's voice is tender and pleading.

Zora scowls at him, her chest heaving. She's furious.

And damn it. Maybe a little excited too.

"Renounce the evil one, Zora," Elijah says. "Give up your witchcraft. Let God save your soul."

Zora jerks free of Elijah's grasp.

"I'm no witch," Zora says. "I practice conjuration. Same as you, if we're being honest. And my soul doesn't need saving. Especially not from the likes of *your* God. Come on, Ashley. You were right. We'll get no help here."

Zora turns and walks away.

"Mighty Christian of you." I give Elijah the bird and follow after Zora. We're halfway to the car when Elijah calls to us.

"Lamb's blood."

Zora and me whirl to face him, both of us ready to lash out.

"Excuse me?" she says.

"Lamb's blood. God said that too." Elijah shrugs. "I don't know what it means."

"Fucking lamb's blood." I shake my head. "Like I said, *psychopath.*"

Zora and Elijah stare at each for a long time. Finally, she turns without a word and gets into the Altima.

I climb into the driver's side and start the engine.

We pull away in silence. In no time, Elijah, the shrine, and New Hope are nothing but retreating images in our rearview mirror.

We drive for miles in silence until I can't take it anymore.

"So what do we do?"

I wedge a tallboy between my thighs and pop open the tab with my right hand as I steer with my left. When I take a drink, the Bud is lukewarm and full of the tang of aluminum.

But beer is beer.

Zora sighs, acquiescing that she's going to have to do more than brood about Elijah.

"If we can't get reinforcements, then we need insurance."

"Sorry," I say. "Don't follow you."

"Suzanne's journal is nothing, Ashley."

It's all I can do stop myself from spewing beer across the dashboard. "Nothing? What do you mean, nothing?"

Zora shakes her head. "Sorry. Let me rephrase that. The journal is Suzanne's written account of what all this is about and could serve as her posthumous testimony I guess."

I swig beer. Wedge the tallboy between my legs. Wipe my chin with the back of my wrist. "Well, that don't sound like nothing to me. But whatever the journal says inside, it's clear Congressman Walker wants it supressed. And even if the journal was to come to light, I can see him and Jones getting it dismissed as the ramblings of a deranged drug addict."

"Right," Zora says. "The journal hardly serves as proof of what she talks about within its pages. Not in and of itself."

"What are you getting at, Zora?"

Zora turns and looks at me. "The journal's last pages are directions, Ashley."

"Directions? To what?"

"To the proof we need. Head back toward Chattanooga by way of Lookout Mountain."

"Where we going, Zora?"

Zora returns her attention to the road. "Forest Hills."

I chuckle. "Of course."

I turn on the radio and tune it to KZ106, hoping to lose myself in classic rock and beer for the rest of the ride. It doesn't work out so well.

I think of the Walkers. If I've seen one dude like ol' Congressman Jack, I've seen a hundred. Shit-birds who've played the puritan for so long they've fooled everyone. Even themselves.

I also think of the congressman's wife and daughter, Suzanne and Jocelyn, and how, despite the less-than-tender moment I had with the former back at Winder Binder, I empathize with her. Or, at least I did.

There's nothing worse in the entire world than losing a child.

I know and then some.

Like Suzanne, I tried to dull the pain with drugs. And sex. And bar fights. And just about everything else you can imagine.

Still do.

But like the monster inside me—the monster that killed my baby girl and caused my hurt to begin with—the pain's always there, eating me away from the inside out.

For the sake of my sanity, my thoughts move on, at last coming to Walker's son, Christian. He has to be off at some Ivy League college by now.

Does he still carry the wound of his twin sister's passing? And how will it be for him when he finds out his mother's checked out on him too?

The Tiftonia exit appears on our right, and I'm spared having to ponder these questions any further.

We take the off-ramp and stop off at an Ace Hardware where we pick up a lantern and a couple of shovels. We trade the Altima for a silver Passat sitting in the parking lot and rim Lookout Mountain before heading on into the South Chattanooga borough of St. Elmo.

Less than a mile in, we hang a left and park the car across the street from the Forest Hills Cemetery. It's damn near midnight, so the gate is closed. But Zora and me have no problem hopping the fence even with our equipment.

I begin to sweat the moment my feet touch the ground despite the nip in the air. Forest Hills is Chattanooga's oldest cemetery. It's also huge. To say the place is a mojo oven would be an understatement.

Zora switches on her flashlight. "Come on."

We navigate the oaks, hickories, statues, and headstones polka-dotting the landscape until we find the grave Zora wants.

To no surprise of mine, it turns out to be that of Congressman Walker's daughter, Jocelyn. The headstone is in great shape, but a large bouquet of flowers at least two weeks dead lies at the base of it.

I sweep the dead flowers aside to discover the ground beneath has been disturbed. A patch of dirt lies among the grass like a manhole cover.

"Who in the hell did Suzanne Walker get to bury something here?"

Zora shrugs. "The vipers who supplied her with bad mojo, according to her journal."

"We going to have to dig her daughter plum up?"

"Let's hope not." Zora says a quick prayer and plunges her

shovel into the earth covering Jocelyn Walker's corpse.

I set the lantern down and pick up a shovel to join her in her work.

Three feet of dirt later, we uncover a rectangular, black container I recognize as a dry box.

"What's in it?" I ask.

"Best case scenario," Zora says, "an end to this whole sorry mess."

THIRTY

W e drive back across the mountain and grab some food to go from a Waffle House before checking ourselves into a cheap motel, the kind favored by cheating spouses and meth addicts.

Zora and me eat our lukewarm bacon and eggs in silence, both of us very aware of the dirt-encrusted dry box we exhumed from Jocelyn Walker's grave resting on the floor on the far side of the room.

We finish our meal and take much longer than needed to clean up after ourselves, the two of us reluctant to do what needs doing despite our anxiousness to have an end to things.

When at last we can't put it off any longer, I go over and pick up the dry box and set it on the dresser holding up the room's small, box TV. I undo the dry box's clasps and lift its lid.

An unassuming smartphone lies within the dry box's foam interior. I reach for it, and Zora's hand comes to rest on my arm.

"Let me, Ashley."

I nod and step back.

Eons seem to pass in the seconds it takes for Zora to pick up the phone. Once she has it in hand, she scrolls through its apps until she comes across what it is she's looking for. She gives a final press of her thumb and stands the phone up against the TV before retreating to my side.

The two of us watch as a tiny comet chases its tail on the smartphone's dark screen.

Then a video begins to play.

A stone escarpment with a few tiny, stubborn pines growing along its expanse fills the bottom of the smartphone's screen, accompanied by the sound of high wind. On screen, above the precipice—but in reality, far below it—a wide river flows, winding its way through a forest of green trees that meets a sprawling cityscape along the horizon.

It's the city in the background that tells me where the person who filmed this is standing.

Stone Mountain, Georgia.

I've stopped off there a time or two with Zora and Sonny during trips to Atlanta, eaten cotton candy, and ridden the skyway car that takes you up top to have a look around.

The video blurs as whoever is filming makes a nausea-inducing one-hundred-and-eighty-degree turn to reveal the stony, unlevel mountain top and the six hooded figures in white robes standing atop it.

All but one holds a lit torch in hand.

They encircle a modest altar of stacked stone. A brush pile rests upon the altar. A young girl who is unmistakably Jocelyn Walker lies atop of the brush. She's bound from shoulder to toe in a ceremonial white sack—a burial shroud. Her cries are audible even through the gag in her mouth and the whistle of wind.

A seventh figure—an elderly man in a turban and a midnight-blue robe with a bejeweled breastplate—stands before the altar, swinging a smoking thurible by its chains with one hand as he flings water from an aspergillum held in the other. He seems to be praying as he sprinkles the congressman's daughter, but his words are swallowed up by both Jocelyn's cries and the howling wind.

The video shudders for a moment as whoever is filming shifts his grip on the smartphone. When the picture stills again, the man in the turban has stepped aside to make way for one of the figures in white—the one without a torch.

Zora and me don't have to wait long to see who it is.

The robed figure's hands come up and push back his hood.

"No fucking way," I say, still not wanting to believe my eyes.

Jocelyn's sobs rise as her father lays his hands upon the length of her swaddled, writhing body. The man in the turban does the same to the congressman, both of them bowing their heads as they pray.

I swallow hard as they finish giving thanks all but knowing what's about to happen. It's the last thing on Earth I want to see, but I can't tear my eyes away.

Congressman Walker reaches into his robe. When his hand reappears, it holds a long, curving dagger.

The wind falls silent so that only the gag in Jocelyn's mouth muffles her screams.

Moving in businesslike fashion, Congressman Walker places his free hand atop his daughter's forehead and pushes it back so that he has no problem drawing a messy red line across her throat with the knife.

Jocelyn's cries cease, and her body stills. The wind returns stronger than ever to tug at the figures' robes and the flames of their torches.

Walker steps back, and those gathered advance and touch their torches to the brush pile. Seconds later, a flaming pyre burns atop the stone altar.

The robed figures lift up their hands in seeming exaltation, and the video ends.

For a long time, Zora and me don't say anything. We just stare at the smartphone.

Then, "He killed her, Zora," I whisper. "He killed his own daughter. In ritual sacrifice. Like she was a fucking goat."

I sink onto the foot of the motel room's bed. My face and the palms of my hands find one another. I shudder with revulsion and rage and sadness as hot tears sting my eyes.

The mattress sags farther in as Zora sits beside me and places an arm across my shoulders, hugging me to her.

"When Suzanne found this," she whispers, "she couldn't believe it. It was a shock, realizing the man she'd shared a bed with all these years was someone she didn't know. Couldn't know. Someone capable of not only doing what he did but covering it up. Making it all appear like an accident had occurred and getting everyone to believe it. Even her. There's a word for people like that, Ashley."

My face leaves my hands. Hot tears leak from my eyes to run down my cheeks. A growl rises in my throat.

"Monster."

Silence. Then, "Suzanne didn't know who to trust," Zora continues. "Certainly not those within their circle of friends. Any one of them could've been beneath those hoods."

I wipe away my tears with the back of my wrist, my anger preventing me from the embarrassment I'd normally feel at crying in front of someone.

"So she turned to Wanda," I say. "The housekeeper. The spook. Someone considered far too lowly by Walker's ilk to ever be a part of that ... that fucking cabal or whatever."

Zora's hands leave my shoulders, and I sit up.

"That's true," Zora says. "But Suzanne and Wanda were friends too. Over the years, they'd come to love and respect each other in their own way."

"Sounds like a fucking Beecher Stowe book."

Zora shrugs and looks at me with sad, tired eyes. "Life is strange. And more often than not, it doesn't give a shit about what's PC."

I stare at the smartphone resting against the TV for a long time. "What are we going to do?"

Zora sighs. "Like you said, Ashley, this is too big for us alone. We've got to go to Marcus."

I shake my head. "Uh uh. No way. My rep would be ruined. Working alongside the police is one thing, but turning rat outright? I'd never see another job again. You either."

Zora huffs and throws up her hands, letting me know she's somewhere I've never seen her before: at her wit's end.

"I don't know what else to do, Ashley," Zora says. "We've got trained military on our asses. Probably under the order of Washington power players who murder their own children in ritual sacrifice. We can't go home or anywhere else. We've got no backup, and the bad guys could be coming after us again any time now. So if you have a better suggestion than going to the police, I'd like to hear it."

She's got me there. I always count on Zora to be the lady with a plan. But squealing to the authorities—even on the likes of Walker—stands in opposition to every single strand of southern DNA I possess.

But since I have no better ideas, I stall.

"Tell you what, Zora. It's the fucking wee hours before dawn. I don't know about you, but I'm bone-tired, and I imagine Marcus is home snuggled up against that plump Latina wife of his. Let's allow him that and get an hour or two of shut-eye ourselves. If we don't get inspired between now and morning, we'll go on in to police headquarters just like you said."

"Ashley, we should go right—"

"Please, Zora? Let me sleep on it. Just a little bit."

Air presses its way between Zora's lips.

"Fine. But come first light, you and I are on the road, headed downtown."

"Fair enough."

Zora returns the smartphone to the dry box and places it beneath the bed. She just as quickly takes it back out and stores it in the motel room's closet. This is all perfectly fine with me. I don't care for the idea of such evil—or even its recorded facsimile—lurking under the bed where I'll be sleeping.

Zora goes into the bathroom to wash her face and dress for bed, giving me a chance to smoke a cigarette outside. When I return, she's already turned in, the top of her Batman T-shirt peeking out from above the covers.

I disrobe and crawl into bed beside her, keeping to my own side with no thoughts of doing otherwise running through my head.

To say I'm not in the mood would be an understatement.

I switch off the lamp on my side of the bed and stare through the darkness at the ceiling. The light petering in from between window blinds paints it in cold, ghostly hues of blue.

Zora slips her hand into mine, and I close my eyes.

Soon, I'm asleep. But unlike my last shared slumber with Zora, this one is far from peaceful.

I dream of Stone Mountain and hooded, robed figures holding burning torches. I dream of a young girl lying atop a stone altar. At first, she is the viper-child from the shrine, bound in silver-plated chains. Then she is Jocelyn Walker, all sewn up in a burial shroud. And then she is my own daughter, Anna.

When at last it's time for her sacrifice, it's not Congressman

Walker who wields the dagger that slices open her throat. In fact, it's no dagger that ends my child at all but a claw.

One attached to the end of my own arm.

THIRTY-ONE

For once, I'm up and dressed before Zora. I let her sleep until the sun is in full view above Lookout Mountain, then I sit on the bed beside her and give her a gentle nudge.

Her eyes pop open. I feel her body tense and then relax beneath my hand.

"I used your burner to call Baby Shit," I say. "Earlene seems to be doing better."

"So?" she asks, her voice husky from the night.

"You're right, Zora," I say. "That bastard killed his own kid. Maybe his wife too. He deserves to burn. Jones, too, if he was part of it."

Zora's eyes close and open in time with her sigh of relief.

"Let me freshen up and get dressed. I'll just be a few minutes."

Zora disappears into the bathroom, and I make a call on her burner to Marcus, having dispensed with my own prepaid phone after the little escapade with Captain Bald Spot and crew outside the River City Club.

The detective is already at work as I knew he would be.

I tell him to expect us, but I don't bother going into detail as to why. I don't have to. Marcus knows me well enough to realize that if I'm calling him directly, serious, drop-everything-else business is afoot.

I hang up with Marcus, and the burner rings in my hand. Zora comes out of the bathroom, looking a little disheveled in her jeans, long-sleeve T, and pulled-back hair, but still more beautiful and sexy than most runway models on their best day.

I hand her the phone, and she answers it.

"Hi, baby," Zora says. "You're up early."

"That my Sonny?" I ask. "Tell her Uncle Ash says hello."

Zora retreats into the bathroom with the phone pressed between shoulder and ear. When she reappears, she's put the phone away so that she can hold her overnight bag in both hands.

She tosses the bag to me and grabs the dry box from the closet.

"Let's roll."

I nod and head out the door, Zora on my heels.

We climb into the silver Passat and toss our burdens onto Zora's floorboard, where she can get to them on the quick if need be.

We forego Lookout Mountain in favor of the interstate, ready to be done with this horrible business as fast as possible. Traffic's heavy on I-24 from the early morning rush-hour spillover but moving well enough.

We come around Moccasin Bend and, looking out at the reflection of sun and sky dancing on the Tennessee River where it runs alongside the interstate, I actually start to feel good about what we're doing: bringing this asshole to justice.

The sensation lasts until I spot an all-too-familiar white van in the driver-side mirror, moving at high speed as it closes ranks behind us.

I reach for my seatbelt and join Zora in being strapped in. "Hang on."

I stomp the accelerator. The engine roars, and the Passat leaps ahead just as the van passes the last of the vehicles separating us.

"Gun," Zora shouts.

I glance into the rearview mirror just in time to see an orange flash erupt from the muzzle of an automatic rifle sticking out of the van's passenger window.

I swerve across two lanes of traffic, almost colliding with another midsized sedan and then a pickup as the echo of machine-gun fire rips through the air along with the sound of the Passat's rear windshield imploding.

Shards of glass pepper the back of my neck. They sting, but

at least they ain't bullets. I've been shot before and know the difference, so I keep my hands on the wheel and my foot on the accelerator.

Zora screams, and I spare a glance to see if she's okay. She's twisted around in her seat, the Glock at the end of her arm spitting lead at the van behind us.

She's not hurt. She's angry.

In the rearview, I see the machine-gunner withdraw under her onslaught. But I pucker down below at the sight of Zora's bullets striking our pursuers' windshield only to bounce off.

"Bulletproof. Goddamn—"

"Ashley!"

I glance left just in time to see a second van, this one black, eclipse the view through my driver-side window. It slams into us, and the Passat veers right, the friction of the steering wheel burning my hands as it spins out of control.

I snag the wheel just before the black van can bounce against us a second time. I'm ready for it this time and keep the car under better control.

Bees buzz my ear, and I realize the white van's machine-gunner is back in position and firing.

I catch a bit of luck, and the black van has to slow in order to keep from ramming the vehicle ahead of it. I make the most of the opportunity and whip the Passat into the emergency lane to speed ahead.

The white van follows.

The defunct US Pipe plant flashes by on our right, followed by green signs heralding the impending highway split and the exits leading to downtown.

I veer left, leaving I-24 for 27 North. The city of Chattanooga appears on our right. The black van on our left. This time, it doesn't try to sideswipe us. Instead, its side door slides open, revealing two men in Kevlar vests and ski masks with automatic rifles aimed and ready.

I start to play the only card I have left: giving the black van a taste of its own medicine by trying a sideswipe of my own.

But the man standing only yards ahead in the middle of the highway changes all that.

"Oh, Lord, no." Zora's voice is a whisper.

I jerk the wheel right. The Passat misses the pedestrian to bounce off a guardrail and die. The impact ensures some chiropractor or another's fortune but leaves Zora and me alive.

I glance in the rearview mirror and see the black van overtake the man standing in the road. Only it ain't the man that gives but the van. The vehicle comes to a dead stop as its front end collapses around him, enfolding him in a coffin of plastic and metal.

Other cars ram into the back of the wreck to suffer the same fate, causing a full-blown pileup across the width of the highway. Whether or not the white van gets caught up in it, I have no way of knowing thanks to the crumpled mass of vehicles blocking my view.

At last, the carnage stops. For a moment, nothing moves. Then, what's left of the black van shudders.

Then explodes.

A lone figure limps out of the dust cloud left in the aftermath, dragging its foot behind it like some ghoul. Could be a man. Could be a woman. It's hard to tell. What clothes it wears are nothing but shreds. Its body is little more than hamburger and bone, its face a bloody, noseless rictus with a single good eye. The other dangles from its socket on the end of a partially shredded optic nerve.

If it's in pain, it gives no indication. It staggers toward us on legs that shouldn't be able to move.

"Go, Ashley," Zora says. "Go."

I turn the key. The engine whines and whines.

"It's no good."

We look at each other a second longer before both of us race to see who will get out of their seatbelt first. Zora wins and snatches the bag and dry box from the floorboard as she hops out of the car.

She tosses the bag over the hood of the Passat, and I snatch it from the air, already out of the car and moving at a jog.

I glance over my shoulder to see the meat thing has dropped onto all fours to scramble after us, its limbs bent at impossible angles so that it moves like a jittering spider.

A very fast jittering spider.

One crawling in our direction.

We pick up our pace. "What the hell is that, Zora?" I ask between pants. "A zombie?"

"No," Zora says. "An angel."

"Angel?"

"Of death. One that's possessed a human so it can interact with the natural world. No more questions, Ashley. We've got to make it the few blocks to Saints Peter and Paul Basilica. It's our only chance."

We hop the guard rail and race down the green running alongside the off-ramp leading to MLK. We get there and run out into the street, heedless of traffic. The oncoming cars slam on their brakes in order to avoid us. Honking horns and angry shouts follow in our wake.

Then the screams of the dying.

I look back to see the angel ripping the head off a bicycle cop as the latter's partner unloads his weapon to almost no effect.

I pick up speed as we cross Broad Street for Market, passing between several midsized business buildings.

But my body betrays me.

The bag begins to feel like a lead weight in my arms. A knife enters my side, and razors fill my lungs as we reach the open brick structure adjacent to Miller Plaza. I start to slow, but Zora shoves me forward with her free hand.

"Move your ass, Owens. We're almost there."

We sprint uphill, weaving through the cars of multiple parking lots and then running up East Eighth Street to duck between two government buildings comprised of sandstone and brick.

I look back to see the angel of death closing in fast, every bit as gruesome as its namesake.

I face forward and see the huge brick church that is Saints Peter and Paul Basilica ahead on our right.

I sure as hell hope Zora knows what she's doing.

Zora reaches the church ahead of me. She bounds up the stone steps out front to find its double doors locked.

I get there and remedy the problem with a swift kick of my

boot, and we rush inside. In spite of everything, I notice the change in temperature and air pressure as we enter. The way sound travels differently in the vast expanse of the sanctuary.

Under different circumstances, I'd be impressed with the basilica's statues, vaulted ceiling, and stained-glass windows. As it is, I just want to get to whatever trick Zora believes this place has up its sleeve.

"What now?" I ask.

"The sacrament." Zora sprints up the blood-red carpet lying between the pews, and I follow after her. She reaches the central alter and veers left, bypassing a statue of the Virgin Mary for an alcove housing a smaller altar.

A small vessel draped in gilded cloth with a locked, golden band sits on top of the altar between twin candles.

Zora sets the dry box next to the altar and withdraws her Glock from the back of her jeans. She shoots the lock off the vessel's golden band, the sound of her fire echoing throughout the sanctuary. She unceremoniously tears away the gilded band and cloth left behind, revealing a clear case housing wafers and a bottle of wine.

A loud boom sounds at the opposite end of the sanctuary, and Zora and me turn to see the church's doors implode.

The angel of death comes galloping into the sanctuary at impossible speed. It plows through the church's pews as though they were tissue paper as it makes a beeline for us.

Zora opens the case and retrieves the wine bottle.

She yanks out its cork and splashes it contents in my face before doing the same to herself.

"Zora, what the—"

Then the angel of death is upon me. It halts directly in front of me, its face mere inches from my own. I hold my breath and stand perfectly still, clenching up as it studies me with its one good eye. Sniffs at me with the bloody slits left in the wake of its nose. I don't see what it can hope to glean. Its own smell—the tang of blood and raw meat—is overwhelming.

Something flies by the right side of my face, and the angel's head jerks in Zora's direction as it snatches the recorked bottle of wine that she's hurled.

I dare a glance over my shoulder. Zora stands at my six, her Glock gripped in both hands and leveled onto the angel.

"'Yea, he had power over the angel,'" she says, "'And prevailed.'"

She pulls the Glock's trigger, and the bottle of wine explodes, showering both the angel and me in wine and shattered glass. Neither really bother me. But when the wine hits the angel, it's as though it were acid.

The angel's skin sizzles and then bursts into flame.

A netherworldly shriek from everywhere and nowhere fills sanctuary, and the stained-glass windows running along either side of the building explode.

Then the flaming carcass falls backward onto the floor to lie there and burn.

Something else happens too. I can't explain it other than to say there's the sense of something passing on—of something enormous moving from this world into the Crossroads and beyond.

"It's over," Zora says, confirming my suspicions. "It's gone."

She drops her gun, and I drop her bag as the two of us collapse into each other's arms.

THIRTY-TWO

Zora and me decide not to wait around on Marcus and his fellow boys in blue. The last thing either of us want to do right now is answer questions. And while Zora has vanquished the angel of death who was after us, it don't mean that another one or something even worse couldn't follow along behind it.

It's unlikely, sure. Assuming the angel didn't cross over on its own, the complexity of conjuration required to call forth one of the Host would've been staggering, even for a congregation of hoodoos working together after having had months to prepare ahead of time.

To call over a second being of such supernatural girth on the same day would be damn near impossible.

Again, I ain't saying it couldn't happen. It's just highly unlikely.

But we have to expect the worst at this stage. If something else nasty does come along, it's best Zora is somewhere where she has the tools to put up a fight. That being the case, we decide to head across the river to Winder Binder.

I mean, shit, we've got nothing to lose at this point.

We wash our faces with wet wipes from Zora's bag before stealing an olive-green Subaru.

We hang a left onto Georgia Avenue and drive across Veterans Bridge to Chattanooga's North Shore. Ambulances and police cruisers zoom by us along the way, moving in the opposite direction, their sirens blaring.

We park the Subaru in the lot adjacent to the riverfront green behind the shop. Not long afterward, we're inside Winder Binder, lounging on a couch nestled beneath a shelf of antique toys and sipping coffee.

Neither one of us could bear going upstairs with all the innocent blood still staining the walls and floor.

"How did you know?" I ask.

Zora looks at me from above the rim of her oversize coffee cup.

"Know what?"

"How to get rid of it? The angel of death, I mean."

"Oh, him." Zora folds her legs beneath her in an exaggeratedly feminine way. "Elijah."

I halt in the act of bringing my coffee cup up to my lips. "Elijah? What? That lamb's blood shit?"

She nods. "In ancient Egypt, the angel of death passed over the homes of the Israelites who'd wiped lamb's blood along their doorframes."

"Yeah, I went to Sunday School a time or two, Zora. I know the story. Still don't follow you."

Zora sips her coffee. "Christ resides in the blessed sacrament. The bread is his body, and the wine is his blood."

I stare at Zora, keenly aware of both the stupid look on my face and my inability to do anything about it.

"Christ is the lamb of God, Ashley." Zora's coffee cup tilts up, then down. "So, *lamb's blood.*"

"Ah," I say, still not exactly sure what she means. But I'm tired of trying to figure it out, so I take another sip of coffee. As the cup touches my lips, I feel my cheeks rise in an involuntary smile.

"What are you grinning about?" Zora swallows coffee, her own grin wrinkling her scar.

"I almost shit my britches back there in that church."

Zora spews coffee back into her cup, and we begin to laugh hysterically, releasing the agony of what we just went through and that of the last few days in general.

The shop's phone rings.

"That could be Aunt Jackie." Zora's words come between guffaws. She lies on the couch on her side, cradling her stomach, laughing hard enough to bring tears to her eyes.

The phone continues to ring. I decide to come to Zora's rescue.

"Don't worry," I say, my own guffaws quieting, "I've got it."

I walk toward the counter up front, certain the phone will stop ringing just as I get there.

It doesn't.

I lift the cordless out of its dock. "Yeah?"

A familiar, Midwestern-accented voice comes on the line. "Owens. Tell me you've got the phone with the video."

"Captain Bald Spot."

He coughs. "The name's Major Copeland."

"Baldy, then."

"I don't have time for your attitude, Owens." More coughing. "I need that phone."

"What phone?"

Zora appears at my elbow, her eyes wide and questioning. I nod to her.

"It appears my employers have grown impatient, Owens," Baldy says between coughs. "They're looking to shore up all loose ends. None of us are safe now."

More coughing comes over the line.

"You don't sound so good, Baldy," I say. "Did you take a beating in that wreck? Are there others from your squad who survived?"

He ignores my questions. "That angel of death out on the highway was after both of us."

"So it is just you left then?"

"Owens, the phone—"

"I told you, Baldy, I don't know what you're talking about."

He coughs. Clears his throat. "I'd say it's time that we dispensed with pretense, wouldn't you? You have the journal, and the conjure woman has had ample time to decode what it says. You *do* indeed know about the smartphone and its video. The question is, do you have it or don't you?"

"Sorry, Baldy," I say, "Again, I don't know what you're—"

"Ask your lady friend how things are down in Lafayette."

I place my hand over the receiver. "He said to how ask you how things are in Lafayette?"

The color drains from Zora's face. "He knows where Sonny is, Ashley." Her jaw squares. Her chest swells. "Bluff that sonofabitch. Remind him of his ball cap and what I can do with it."

I remove my hand from the receiver.

"Still there, pretty boy?" he says.

"I'm here. Do you have what I need?"

"I do. I also have your ball cap, lest you forget. Touch one hair on my family's head, and it will be the last thing you ever do."

"I have no desire for things to come that." Baldy erupts into a coughing fit. Regains control of himself. "Believe it or not, I'm a godly man, Owens. Harming more innocent civilians is the last thing I wish to do."

More coughing.

"You should really see a doc about that cough, Baldy."

The major's coughs quiet at last. "Just give me the phone, and we can all go our separate ways. For real this time."

"There's that *we* again. Is there anyone else left in your squad or not, Baldy?" I press my luck. "Answer the question. And don't lie. We have your cap. We'll know."

A long pause interrupted only by Baldy's coughing.

Then, "I'm on my own. But that doesn't mean I can't make a call and have an operative in Lafayette at a moment's notice if I have to."

"Fair enough," I say. "I'll make sure you don't have to."

"Meet me on the Walnut Street Bridge," he says, a cough building his throat. "Thirty minutes." He coughs. Clears his throat. "Come alone this time. I see your friend—or any or other woman around—I walk and make a beeline for Lafayette."

The phone line goes dead.

Half an hour later, I'm on the Walnut Street walking bridge, smoking a cigarette as I stride out across the Tennessee River to a point halfway between downtown and the North Shore.

Ed Johnson's ghost hangs from a noose attached to the blue girders above, his long-ago death-by-lynching here on the bridge allowing him to apparate over the water. His tarred, feathered feet dangle above a smiling family of four who are oblivious to his presence. Thankfully, the adults and their two-point-three kids make up the bulk of the folks on the bridge today. I guess the ruckus downtown has all but stalled the Nooga's tourism biz for the moment.

I nod to the haunt and blow smoke in greeting.

"Ed."

The haunt's only response is to slowly rotate at the end of his rope so he may watch me pass.

It's odd to see the dead black man dangling out here at the height of day. But apparently, even a haunt will come out of the shadows if there's a big enough train wreck to watch.

I suspect Ed's in for a doozy.

Major Copeland stands a few yards ahead at the railing on the bridge's west side, pressing a handkerchief to his mouth as his body shakes with fits of coughing. He's still clad in the same windbreaker I saw him in the last time we met, but he's found a new cover to hide that bald spot of his, one that pegs him as a Bama fan. But the cap does little to hide the dark rings under his eyes or the unhealthy, pale shade of his skin.

I join him at the rail and flick the remaining nub of my cigarette into the river.

"You look like shit, Baldy," I say.

He ignores my jab. "Give me the phone, Owens."

"In a minute," I say. "I've got a few questions first."

He coughs. "Really? You're going to draw this out?"

I shrug. "We like to take our time here down South, Baldy. But I can see you ain't feeling so hot, so I'll get right to the point. You've said your employers would have little concern over Senator Jones' death. Can I assume you're not working for him, then?"

Baldy coughs. Shakes his head. "The truth is, I don't know."

"Are you lying? Don't forget, Zora still has your ball cap. She doesn't like to conjure dark mojo on a normal, but I reckon she will if you give her enough cause."

He coughs. "I'm not lying, Owens."

"What about Congressman Jack Walker?"

"Not directly, no."

"Now just what the fuck is that supposed to mean?"

Baldy coughs. Wretches. Presses the handkerchief gripped

in his hand to his face. When it comes away, it's red with blood.

"It's not something a heathen cur like you would understand."

"Try me."

The sweaty expanse of his brow furrows as his eyes laser in on me. "I serve the Lord. He who is most high. As does Congressman Walker."

"I'm sure the local pastor would be glad to hear that, Baldy. But what I'm asking is, who signs your checks? I'm guessing 'The Lord thy God' ain't what's written on the signature line."

The bill of his cap moves right then left as he shakes his head.

"I answer that, and bringing my employers the phone becomes a moot point."

"Oh yeah?"

Copeland nods. "I'd be as good as … as good as …" He tries to finish his sentence, but the coughs wracking his body won't let him.

The major drops to his knees. Blood spews from his mouth to cover both bridge and rail.

His body jerks, and another fount spills from his mouth down the front of his windbreaker.

I lean down so that my face is close to his.

"Nobody hurts my family."

He looks up at me with eyes full of rage and understanding even as he coughs up still more blood.

"That's right," I say. "Zora may not be much on conjuring dark mojo on normals, but I sure as hell don't give a fuck when it comes to assholes like you, *Major*. I'm actually surprised you've lasted this long."

Copeland convulses and falls forward onto his hands as blood pours from his mouth.

I squat and lean farther in, grinning every bit as much as the monster inside me as I whisper into his ear.

"Now, I ain't no conjure man or nothing. But I been around Zora long enough to pick up a thing or two."

Copeland's body jerks, and blood gushes out over the bridge in red waves.

"It was small task to grab a dash of that and a sprinkle of this when her back was turned. And the shit a conjure woman carries around with her? Hellfire, man. When mixed properly, I reckon it makes anthrax look like child's play."

Copeland's body convulses. I glance back to see that the seat of his pants is soaked and that watery, red rivulets are leaking from the cuffs of his trousers.

"Yeah, highway wreck or not," I say, "you and your men were fucked the moment you opened that envelope we gave you, Baldy. It was a gamble you wouldn't do it in open public, but I figured it for a good one." I sigh. "Zora never would've dreamed up such a thing much less done it. But then, she ain't no monster. That's my department."

Somehow, someway, Copeland finds the strength to turn his head in my general direction. "God will have vengeance," he says, his chin dripping with blood.

I smile as his convulsions resume.

"Well, I reckon you'll be seeing the Almighty any second now. When you do, tell Him Ashley Owens sent you and that I'll be making good use of that video."

I stay by Copeland's side until his convulsions cease and his body stills. When at last I rise to my feet, the ghost of Ed Johnson is standing on the other side of the major's corpse. The noose now hangs limply from the haunt's neck to dangle alongside his tarred and feathered body.

His eyes hold accusation in spite of their emptiness.

Or maybe that's just me reading into things.

Either way, it's not like this is going to cause me to lose anymore sleep at night than I already do.

I turn away from the haunt and retrace my steps, thinking about the cigarette I'm going to have the moment I get off this fucking bridge.

THIRTY-THREE

"Hello, Bob."

The faux antique clock on the wall reads three thirty in the afternoon when Zora and me take a seat at the senator's table in the River City Club. He's dressed in a black suit and red tie. Zora looks like a cover model despite being dressed in a modest white blouse and skirt. I'm rocking my usual attire of T-shirt, jeans, and shit-kickers and looking damn good doing it in spite of how I'm feeling on the inside.

Senator Jones swallows the pill of Zora with a disdainful glance. "I must say, Ashley, I'm disappointed to see Ms. Banks with you. No offense, Ms. Banks."

Zora glances around the RCC, her upper lip curling as though she smelled something rotten. Her gaze lands on Senator Jones and then falls to her oversize purse. She reaches inside her bag and brings out her smartphone so that she may lose herself within it. "By contrast, you do nothing but offend me, Senator."

Jones frowns. "Ashley, may I assume you've had us brave the present commotion downtown because you have good news to report?"

"Well," I say, "I guess that all depends on your way of looking at things, Bob."

Jones fingers pyramid. "Do you or do you not have what Congressman Walker has authorized me to pay you to find?"

"Again, that depends, Bob," I say.

"On what, precisely?"

"On whether or not you have my money?"

"Really, Ashley, haven't you and I—"

"You may deposit it into my usual account."

Jones stares at me.

"Go ahead," I say. "I'll wait."

Senator Jones eyes me a second longer. Sighs. Retrieves his mobile from his jacket. His fingers work at its keypad.

"I'm sending it now."

He finishes and returns the phone to his coat.

"So, now may we—"

I raise a halting finger into the air.

"Ah-ah-ah. Patience, Bob."

We sit in silence.

Then, "It's in." Zora turns her smartphone around so that I can lay eyes on the confirmation text.

"Outstanding," I say. "Give him the goods, Zora."

Suzanne Walker's journal appears on the table. Jones' jacketed arm reaches out, and the journal disappears.

"The journal, you bought and paid for," I say. "The phone, I'll toss in for free."

"Phone?" Jones asks. Neither I nor the monster inside me can tell if he's lying. Either the senator sincerely doesn't know what I'm talking about, or he's one damn good politician.

Zora tosses the black smartphone out onto the table. It lies there like a giant dead cockroach.

At last, Jones reaches out. "What's this?"

My own hand slams down over the phone before his can get there.

"How much did you know when you hired me, Bob?" I ask. "Was it you who took the video that's on this phone?"

Jones looks at me, revealing nothing.

"Did you get a thrill out of watching Walker murder his own daughter?"

Finally, a rise. At least what passes for one where Jones is concerned. His eyes go left. Right. Find no one. Even Vernon the bartender is conveniently absent from his station.

"I suggest you lower your voice, Ashley. If you continue to hurl accusations like that, someone might walk in and get the wrong—"

"Oh go fuck yourself, Bob. Zora and me have a friend in the hospital thanks to you and your filicide of a gubernatorial candidate. So how about you cut the bullshit and show a little common fucking courtesy and shoot straight with us?"

Jones shakes his head. "Ashley, I'm afraid I don't know what you're talking—"

"The two of you used me as your bird dog, didn't you?" I say. "You let me rustle the bushes. Waited until both Suzanne Walker and what she had on the congressman came flying out. Then, bang."

"Ashley, I'm afraid you've got it all—"

"Call me Ashley again, and I'll fucking kill you." The words come out as a growl. I see my reflection in the senator's wide eyes. Watch as my own irises flash yellow before fading back to their normal shade of blue. "Only my family calls me Ashley, and you ain't family. You ain't nothing."

Zora's hand comes to rest on my arm, and I relax. I nod to her, letting her know I've got a grip on myself.

Jones straightens in his seat. Buttons his coat.

"I have what I came for. You've been paid. I believe our business here is concluded."

"Not quite, Bob," I say. "I want to know what all this is about. Why did Walker kill his own daughter on top of Stone Mountain? What did he hope to gain? Who was he sacrificing her to?"

Senator Jones stares at me. "I told you—" He starts to say "Ashley." Catches himself. "I don't know what you're talking about."

"Well, that's a crying shame." I scoop up the phone and begin to rise to my feet.

I get about halfway there before Senator Jones raises a halting hand. "All right. All right. I'll tell you what I know."

I return to my chair. "I'm listening."

"May I please have the phone first?" Jones asks.

"Certainly." I slide the phone across the table to him.

Jones picks it up and examines it. "You have not copied or shared the video contained herein?"

I raise my right hand and place my left over my heart. "Scout's honor, Bob."

He sighs and places the phone inside his coat.

"I said I'd tell you what I know," Jones says, "but it isn't much."

"Keep talking."

Jones takes several moments to compose his thoughts. Then, "There are powerful people in Washington. Maybe elsewhere too. Places like London. Moscow. Rome. No one knows who they really are, but they call themselves the Fellowship. Walker is one of them. And of special importance from what I can—"

Jones' eyes roll back into his head. He falls forward, his head bouncing off the table as he collapses onto the floor.

Zora is at his side before I can move.

"He's not breathing, Ashley. There's no pulse."

Zora's smartphone rings where it lies on the table.

I pick it up and press the talk button.

A male voice born and bred of the Deep South comes onto the line. "'And the anger of the Lord burned against Uzzah, and God struck him down there for his irreverence.'"

"Who is this?"

Zora looks up at me, her eyes questioning.

"In about thirty seconds," the caller says, "an electromagnetic pulse will bombard the establishment in which you are now standing, erasing the contents of the phone you handed over to the late Senator Jones."

I huff. "Do what you like. I told the senator the truth. I didn't share the video, but my partner sure as hell did."

Zora comes to stand beside me, and I tilt the phone so that we can both hear.

"Check YouTube," Zora says. "Twitter. Reddit. And likely about a thousand other places online by now. Viral won't be the word."

A good-natured chuckle. "Ah. Ms. Banks. We put an end to your feeble attempt at a coup d'état almost quickly as you uploaded it. No one will be seeing what transpired atop Stone Mountain. And even if they were to find, translate, and read the late Mrs. Walker's journal, well, who knows what kind of deviant thoughts and notions can possess someone deep in the thrall of drug addiction?"

Zora and me trade glances, knowing the caller is right. If we brought the authorities the coded gibberish in Suzanne Walker's journal, best case scenario, they'd laugh at us. Even Marcus.

"But the question, my dears," the caller continues, "is if people did indeed learn of the goings on atop Stone Mountain, would they even care? The world has become a vile, evil place after all. But change is in the wind. Mind you and yours don't get swept up in it."

A pause. Then, "Enjoy your money, Mr. Owens."

The phone beeps and dies as the lights inside the River City Club extinguish.

Two months later, I stand in a forest beneath the light of a full moon, my breath issuing before me in visible puffs as I look out over Jack Walker's estate. An unending train of limousines circles through the driveway of the manor house, dropping off the elite of both Nashville and Washington in succession. They've all turned out for Walker's victory party. Doubtless, they've come to congratulate the Governor-elect on his landslide win and offer their support for what the press has already dubbed the inevitable presidential campaign to come.

Me, on the other hand?

I'm here for much different reasons.

Not least among them a little girl and her momma.

Now, I know I shouldn't be here.

Zora and Earlene both warned me not to go off half-cocked and do anything stupid when we sat in the bar, watching Walker cry crocodile tears for his murdered wife even as he dedicated his victory to her memory.

I played it cool and assured them I wouldn't.

But this ain't the first time I've lied to my friends. And if I'm being honest, I know it likely won't be the last.

What can I say?

I'm a monster.

It's a skill set I'm about to put to good use.

The thing inside me waits in silence, patient as Job even with the full moon above. Even after all this time caged up by Zora's mojo hand.

I guess maybe it doesn't want to act up and give me reason

for pause now that dinner is about to be served on a fucking platter.

Either way, it needn't worry.

There ain't nobody going to leave Walker's house alive.

Not tonight.

I unzip my pants far enough to reveal the mojo hand that holds my creature at bay. The trick's red flannel appears dark blue in the moonlight. The ugly scar stretching out from beneath it ghostly white.

I tear the mojo hand from its leather cord and fling it into the woods.

Then I throw back my head and roar, blood on my mind and bad mojo in my heart.

.

ABOUT THE AUTHOR

Shane Berryhill is a novelist, screenwriter, and comic book writer. His work has been praised by Publishers Weekly, NPR, NBC, Today.com, Wired Magazine, and others. He's been a guest and speaker at events ranging from the National Council of English Teachers Conference to San Diego Comic Con. Discover more of his work at http://www.crossroadpress. com.

Curious about other Crossroad Press books?
Stop by our site:
http://store.crossroadpress.com
We offer quality writing
in digital, audio, and print formats.

Enter the code FIRSTBOOK
to get 20% off your first order from our store!
Stop by today!